Sherlock Holmes at the Breakfast Table

Sherlock Holmes at the Breakfast Table

L.F.E. Coombs

ROBERT HALE · LONDON

First published in Great Britain 2012

ISBN 978-0-7090-9593-4

Robert Hale Limited
Clerkenwell House
Clerkenwell Green
London EC1R 0HT

www.halebooks.com

2 4 6 8 10 9 7 5 3 1

Typeset in 10/13½pt New Century Schoolbook
by Derek Doyle & Associates, Shaw Heath
Printed in Great Britain by the MPG Books Group,
Bodmin and King's Lynn

Acknowledgement

To my family for both support and inspiration and particularly to Andrew for advice on the storylines.

To Meg and David Boswell for conserves and inspiration.

To Richard Walden, as both agent and editor, who skilfully steered the book to a successful conclusion.

Contents

The Railway Van That Vanished

In which bullion on its way to Russia is borrowed.

Part One

I was standing with my friend and companion Sherlock Holmes at the sitting-room window of 221B Baker Street. We were surveying the vehicles and pedestrians passing back and forth below. My wife had gone to stay with one of her cousins who lived in Surrey, so for a few days I was back in the familiar surroundings of the great detective's household.

'Here we are,' said Holmes, 'looking down at a microcosm of our city of five million or more people. Below there are statesmen and dustmen, bankers, servant girls and errand boys, all bustling about their various businesses and tasks. And to think that only a mile or two from where we stand some unfortunate women have been found horribly mutilated. I am somewhat surprised not to have been requested to help with the investigation by the official police.'

One particular pedestrian attracted my attention. It was a stout man in a frock-coat and check trousers. I drew Holmes' attention to the man. 'Possibly that is the client who telegraphed to say he had important business to discuss and would be with us at ten?'

'You mean the stout man in the frock-coat and check trousers with a newspaper under one arm?'

'Yes, that's the one. He is early and no doubt is waiting until the exact time of the meeting. It gives us a few minutes to determine who and what he is.'

Holmes observed him for a minute and then said, 'The vivid check trousers suggest someone interested in the turf. The paper under his arm is no doubt the *Racing Times*. His hat is set at a slight angle to the perpendicular which suggests he is a man of the world, as they say. The silver-topped ebony cane could be a swordstick with which to defend him against the more unsavoury persons to be found around a racecourse. Don't you agree, Watson?'

'A very comprehensive set of observations,' said I.

A minute later the page boy ushered in the object of our scrutiny. 'Good morning, Mr Jones,' said Holmes. 'I received your telegram and have awaited your arrival. Please take this chair.'

Holmes always endeavoured to place a client in the light from the window in order to observe their mannerisms and dress.

'Did you have a good journey up from Surrey? The sand on your boots leads me to believe that is where you live.'

'No, Mr Holmes. I have only come from Highgate and walked part of the way across the Heath.'

'Well, never mind. I anticipate your visit concerns racing. So many of my clients get into difficulties with trainers and, regrettably, bookmakers.'

'Mr Holmes, I assure you that horse racing, let alone betting, is something I will have nothing to do with. It's a fool's game. I have come about—'

Holmes interrupted him, saying, 'Then you've come about an affair of the heart?'

'Sir, you are very much mistaken indeed.'

I observed that Holmes' keen eye had noticed how the client kept glancing at the tantalus on the table.

'Before we continue, may I offer a stimulating drink? Brandy, perhaps?'

'Certainly not, Mr Holmes. I do not approve of strong drink.'

'A cigarette then.'

'I do not smoke, thank you. Obviously you have noticed the discolouration of my fingers. It's a varnish stain that comes from my cabinet-making hobby.'

'My apologies, Mr Jones.'

'Mr Holmes, I have not come about myself. I am here on behalf of the Southern Counties Insurance Company. I am a claims investigator. My profession is not given on my card in order to avoid alerting people to why I may want to speak to them.'

After the terms had been agreed under which a very serious attempt to defraud the insurance company would be investigated and our visitor had left, Holmes threw himself into his old chair.

'I have to admit, Watson, that appearances can sometimes, indeed, be deceptive.'

Nothing more was said about the visitor. A little later Mrs Hudson, the housekeeper, entered holding a telegram.

'I say, listen to this, Watson. It's from the Bank of England. The governor wishes to consult me on a very important and confidential matter and will I come at once? The Bank of England! Well, well. Of course, I should wish you to come with me.'

We passed through the lofty and magnificent rooms of the Bank of England. Our guide threw open the door to the governor's office and announced, 'Mr Sherlock Holmes and Doctor Watson, sir.'

The features and voice of the man in whose hands rested the security of the nation's finances reflected his anxiety. He motioned us to sit down.

'Gentlemen, I am more than pleased that you have agreed to help. We, that is the bank, have lost a vast amount of bullion. The railway van or wagon in which it was being conveyed to Newcastle to go on board the SS *Dog Star* was removed from the train somewhere between here and the port. The two railway companies involved cannot explain how such a large wagon could vanish. When the train reached its destination it was apparently in its place behind the engine. However, it was not the same as the one which left here. There was no inner steel container and the roof, through which the container is loaded, was intact.'

We listened intently to the strange events. 'You mention the fact that the van left here? Where exactly is here. Surely there is no railway line into the bank?' asked Holmes.

The governor replied, 'We take the bullion boxes – under guard, I assure you – to the goods depot under Smithfield Market. There they are loaded into the special van.'

'Admittedly the circumstances are very strange. I have had to deal with many cases in which something has disappeared although never one involving something as large as a railway van.'

'You will appreciate that this matter is extremely confidential. Were knowledge of the loss to reach the City, or even more so the foreign markets, the consequences could affect the country's international reputation financially. The Home Secretary has been informed and I understand he has given instructions that you will have the fullest support from the police. We are relying on you, Mr Holmes.'

'Have you a list of the names of all persons who might possibly know about the special van, the loading arrangements, and particularly the railway officials responsible for its security?'

'I anticipated such a request, Mr Holmes. Here is the list. It is not very long and as you see only two railway officials are listed: they are superintendents respectively of the Great Northern and the North Eastern railways.'

A visitor awaited our return to Baker Street. I was not surprised to find it was Inspector Lestrade, who immediately said, 'You've been to the bank, no doubt. I have been ordered by the commissioner himself, who is under great pressure from the Home Secretary, to give you every possible assistance. I am armed with the necessary documents for opening all doors and the loosening of all tongues.'

'I am most delighted to have your support,' responded Holmes. 'The governor has given some of the facts of this very unusual case. I might even say a singular case.'

'I admit, Mr Holmes, that I am at a loss to know where to start.'

'Well, as Alice said, it is best to start at the beginning. I am sure you will agree that that is at Smithfield. I cannot see much would be gained by examining the counterfeit railway wagon at Newcastle?'

Lestrade said, 'I agree.'

Below Smithfield we met the railway official responsible for seeing that the special van was attached to a goods train. He explained that it was kept hidden behind a screen of tarpaulins until the time came for it to be attached to other wagons. A Great Northern locomotive came from the sidings at Finsbury Park and took the train along the partly underground 'Widened' lines, past Farringdon Street and King's Cross stations on the Metropolitan, up round the Hotel Curve and on through the tunnels north of King's Cross mainline station. At Finsbury Park the wagons were shunted with other wagons to form a longer train with the bullion van coupled next to the locomotive. During the shunting operations an official of the railway was charged with ensuring that it was in its correct place in the northbound night goods; even though he was not aware of its valuable contents.

Holmes then said, 'Apart from the fact that the van's exterior was no different from that of any other of the same class, were there any identification markings that might distinguish it from others?'

The official thought for a moment and then replied, 'Well, you see, most wagons are marked with chalk to indicate their destination. In this case we apply an additional mark to make sure we do not lose the van when it is being shunted around at Finsbury Park.'

'Therefore, that means that anyone wanting to keep an eye on the van with intent to rob it might also know about the special chalk mark.'

'Yes, Mr Holmes, that is so.'

'You say that after leaving London the train was only intended to stop at Little Newark, Grantham and York.'

'Yes, the train only made those three scheduled stops. The first in the loop which ends just before Little Newark station to let other trains precede it, then at Grantham to change engines and again when it was handed over to the North Eastern railway at York. At Grantham and York the change of engines takes place in full view of a number of people. There is no way in which the van could have been detached and replaced with another without someone noticing.'

'So what you are saying is that Little Newark would appear to be the only place where the vans could have been changed over.'

'I am certain of it, Mr Holmes.'

Accompanied by Mr Devereux, the superintendent of the Great Northern railway, we stood on the platform at Little Newark station. By means of a drawing, he explained the purpose of the different tracks and the signals.

'As you see, the road bridges that cross over the railway and the sharp curve in the line prevented the signalman or anyone else on the station seeing the train as it stood in the loop.'

I could not resist interposing, 'I understand that this arrangement is one with which the Board of Trade is not very happy. Legislation is about to be enforced that will require that all points connecting running lines must be within 200 yards and within direct sight of the signalman—'

Holmes interrupted me. 'Yes, yes, very technical, Watson. I anticipate that your recent interest in railway-operating minutiae will prove most helpful. Knowledge of such pending legislation does not alter the fact that the signalman or others on the station would not be able to see any suspicious activities.'

The official led us down the platform ramp and under the road bridge until we stood alongside the line on which the train had waited for about thirty minutes. Holmes searched the ground alongside the track where the locomotive had stood.

'Lestrade, look at this! A large round object has left an imprint in the mud. It may have been formed by a small barrel.'

He looked closely. 'Yes, I'm sure you are right, Mr Holmes. I see that there are many footprints. I suppose you will be able to deduce the number of people that have been here and their occupations?'

'Well, not really. They are all muddled together as if a party of men had been moving about.'

Holmes continued his investigation. All he found of possible interest was a pair of leather gloves. 'I shall take these gloves with me for further examination. They may or may not be of importance. I see from the plan that the loop line extends into a siding.'

The official then explained the purpose of the different lines and the points. 'Yes, as you see, the points are kept in their present position to a train coming along the loop line so that should it overrun the signal it will run onto the siding and not into the path of a train on the main line.'

Again, I was anxious to air my interest in railways. 'The signals and the points are all connected together so that the signalman cannot move the points if either of the signals has been cleared; that is "pulled off". Am I correct, Mr Devereux?'

'Indeed you are, Doctor Watson. How refreshing to find someone who is not on the railway having such an accurate understanding of such matters. Newspaper reporters and writers of books take dreadful liberties when describing the way a railway is operated.'

I was most encouraged by the comment. In the past I had frequently been criticized for my lack of knowledge on the subject.

Soon there was the sound of a train approaching. We stepped back as the locomotive and its train of wagons came up to the signal and stopped. The superintendent explained, 'This one will wait here until two passenger trains have passed and then it will be let out onto the down mainline. I must have a word with the driver.'

'Please wait a moment,' said Holmes. 'There's something I need to test.'

He moved alongside the engine until he was at the footsteps leading up to the footplate. He then turned and came back to where we waited.

'As I expected, Superintendent, the enginemen are having something to eat. They were not aware of my presence.'

'Most likely, Mr Holmes. They know that they will not be able to go further until the two passenger trains have passed, so they often take the opportunity to refresh themselves.'

'Gentlemen, I suggest we examine the siding,' said Holmes.

We walked along the track.

'You say this line leads, as I can see, between some warehouses,' observed Holmes. 'Now what are these round platforms with rails laid upon them, Mr Devereux?'

'They are called turnplates or turntables. You see, if a wagon is moved onto one it can then be turned through an angle so that the rails are aligned with one of the sidings set at right angles to it. A wagon can then be pushed into one of the warehouses.'

'Let me see your plan. Now if the engine that night were to just take the bullion van and move it over one of these plates then the van could have been turned and pushed into one of the warehouses. This is rather like those puzzles you find in children's books where an engine and some wagons have to be shuffled to achieve a certain order.'

'Indeed, Mr Holmes. However, there is a flaw in your argument. The turnplates are not intended to bear the weight of a large engine.'

'Therefore the shuffling puzzle to be solved is how did the van, in effect, get in front of the engine?'

Holmes walked past the second turnplate and gazed at the track.

After a moment's thought he exclaimed, 'I think I've solved it. You see these cinders between the rails? Surely, they could only have come from underneath a locomotive. The gang must have moved the engine over the plate and hoped it would bear the weight. Watson, you will recall the Failed Bridge case where we found that engineers usually make things much stronger than they need be. It is possible that the designer of these turnplates specified that they be used only for wagons; otherwise the continuous use by locomotives would eventually weaken them. The gang took a chance and won. And I assume that an identical van was kept out of sight in the warehouse as part of their plan. When the bullion van had been moved off the turnplate, the other van was manhandled on to it, turned, and then shunted back by the engine onto the goods train.'

'That is a good explanation. I expect that our engineers will find on closer examination that the plates have been strained,' replied the official.

In one of the warehouses, we found the missing van.

Its wooden doors had been forced open to expose the steel door of the inner container. There were numerous marks and dents around the edges of the container door where an attempt had been made to break in. We made a careful scrutiny on the roadside of the warehouse. The tracks in the mud of the road revealed that a large cart had come along and been drawn up against the back door to the loading bay.

'Mr Holmes, these ruts must have been made by a heavy wagon. Don't you agree?' said Lestrade.

'Certainly. You will also observe the size of these two sets of horseshoe impressions. They could only have been made by shire horses. And that leads me to the conclusion that the robbers may have intended to transfer the bullion onto the cart. Knowing the weight of the gold bars, I expect that they would have had to make more than one journey to where they intended to hide it. There are also these impressions of the boots of the robbers. Ah, what have we here! These have been made by the boots of a boy or a small man. They are about size six.'

'Lestrade, I think we had better leave things as they are and await the return of the robbers. More than likely they have gone to find special cutting tools. Why they did not think of it before I cannot imagine. Unless, of course, their informants within the railway or the bank failed, either deliberately or by mischance, to tell them about the inner strong door. Another possibility is that something has gone wrong with their plans and they have been forced to leave the bullion here. In the meantime they will be thinking up a new scheme.'

'I agree, Mr Holmes. Let us leave everything as it is. We don't want them to know we are on to them. The local police will now be requested to keep a watch on the warehouse from a distance. I must telegraph the bank officials to let them know where their bullion is. I expect they will not be too pleased to find we are using it as bait.'

'A very valuable lure indeed. Now before we leave for London, I should like to talk to the signalman. Is that possible?' asked Holmes. The railway superintendent agreed to his request.

We walked along the down platform and up the stairs into the signal box. The visit to Little Newark was proving most interesting. I had always wanted to see inside a signal box. The signalman explained the various levers and instruments. Holmes took a particular interest in two devices on a shelf which were making a ticking sound. 'What is the purpose of these?' he asked.

The signalman explained that they were the Morse sounders of the railway telegraph system. 'It tells us what's going on. This one's for the down line and t'other for the up.'

'When you say "going on" what do you mean?' said Holmes.

'Well, at the moment the down telegraph line is telling me that the next express from the south is running ten minutes late. It helps us to know if we have time to put a goods train out on to the main line in front of it.'

'I see. So anyone who understands the Morse code and was listening to one of these might learn much about the movement of the trains. Is that correct?'

'No, not really, Mr Holmes,' answered Superintendent Devereux. 'You see, there is a special way of making the messages up. I don't think anyone outside the railway could make head nor tail of them.'

Away from the signal box, Holmes questioned the railway superintendent about the telegraph. 'You say the train carrying the bullion could be identified by someone listening to the telegraph apparatus in the signal box?'

'Correct, although, as I explained, only a few people knew of the contents of the missing van and the signalman was not one of them. And, of course, the train's identification number was not a special one. However, this does suggest that someone may have listened covertly to the telegraph messages concerning the progress of particular trains. Provided, that is, they could read the Morse code. Somehow they had discovered that on that night one of them would include the bullion van.'

'As we know, the timetable requires the train to wait here for at least thirty minutes, a fact relied upon by the thieves. Could it be further delayed for any reason?'

'That does happen frequently, Mr Holmes,' replied Devereux. 'You see, north of here is a point where the Midland Railway crosses ours on the level. Their signalman has control of the crossing and naturally favours his trains. Hence there are frequent delays to ours. The gang knew that not only would the bullion train be held for some time to allow other trains to get ahead, there was a reasonable chance it would be further delayed.'

'That explains a lot, except we still have to consider the two men on the engine.'

'They were questioned extensively,' responded the superintendent. 'Both have exemplary records with the company and there has never been anything warranting a reprimand. I feel sorry for both. They persisted in saying they did not fall asleep. However, both mentioned that they found it strange when the signal cleared for them to proceed when they had only been in the loop for a few minutes. They assumed the trains they usually waited for had been delayed and they were given the opportunity to get ahead. The driver said that when he looked at the station clock, as they passed it, he was surprised to see it showed they had been held for over thirty minutes. He distinctly remembers comparing the time with his watch. Another thing, both found on starting the train that they had not eaten all of their snap. The lids of the snap boxes had not been shut. The usual stop in the loop gave plenty of time in which to eat and drink.'

Holmes listened intently to the railway official's report. 'Thank you. You have provided some very important clues to what happened that night,' said he.

Holmes turned to Lestrade, saying, 'I shall now attempt to reconstruct the events of that night. The villains were alerted by someone who overheard the telegraph and could understand its messages. They had been lying in wait, possibly for a number of days, away from the railway so as not to attract the attention of anyone. Once the train had stopped in the loop they approached the engine and somehow rendered the driver and fireman unconscious. They must have had a driver with them in order to move the van. As we saw, the map of the station indicated clearly that the bridges and the sharp curve of the line would have made it very difficult for the signalman, for example, to see what was going on. However, this does not account for the lack of action from the guard in his van at the back of the train.'

'Guards have been known to "nod off", as it were,' explained the superintendent, 'when their train is held for some time in a siding. He would also have been some distance back, and on past the two overbridges.'

'Thank you for your help, Mr Devereux. Now, Lestrade, I expect you will want to stay with the local police. Please keep me informed of events.'

Back in the comfort of Baker Street and away from the rain and mud and the harsh environment of the railway, Holmes examined the gloves he had found. The application of some chemicals enabled him to determine that they had been in contact with rubber.

'Is it possible, Watson, that a rubber tube was passed into the locomotive cab and that a somnambulating gas came from a pressurized cylinder? You will recall the impression in the mud of such an object. And, of course, I was able to get right up to the steps of the engine's cab without being seen or heard.'

'Gas is a possibility,' I replied. 'Although I know little about unusual gases. Particularly one whose effect can be judged with such precision. The villains only had about half an hour in which to keep the enginemen unconscious. Had they administered too strong a dose then the men might have died. And then the signalman would have been alerted to something wrong when the train failed to move after he had cleared the signal for it.'

'That would not matter, Watson. You see the whole scheme depended on the exchange of vans. Whatever happened to the train afterwards was of no consequence to them. After all, they anticipated that the theft would not be discovered until the substituted van was opened at Newcastle.'

'Yes, I can understand that. Yet I am not so sure about the use of a gas. As you saw, the cab of a locomotive is open to the elements so that the gas would have been dispersed.'

'Of course, you are right. However, Watson, there is a possible alternative. Someone may have added a substance to their meal. An opiate, for example, whose quantity could be just sufficient to render the men unconscious for about twenty minutes. If they had left their metal snap containers unattended at any time, anyone could have administered the opiate. The robbers relied very much on the enginemen's habit of eating while waiting at Little Newark. You recall that the lids of the food containers had not been closed. The impression of a cylindrical object and the discarded gloves were more than likely false clues.'

'Yes, I agree with that conclusion. Although those who planned this audacious robbery must have relied very much on the train keeping to the timetable. Had it been delayed somewhere else on its journey the enginemen could have eaten their meal earlier than the villains had anticipated. They then could have been overcome soon after restarting with possible disastrous results.'

'Indeed, Watson, a dreadful possibility. Apart from that there is the mystery of the villains' lack of knowledge over the manner in which the steel container was secured. You know, that brings me to the conclusion that no one in the bank was an informer to the gang. Otherwise they would have known how to open the container very quickly. Furthermore, they anticipated that the container door would have been secured by a combination lock. One of their number may have been a professional safe breaker. In the end his skill was of no use to them.'

I pondered on these facts and then said, 'Another thing that exercises me is why consign the bullion van to a train that was more than likely to make a long stop at Little Newark? Surely it was inviting trouble?'

'A very good question. I shall telegraph the governor of the bank immediately and put the question to him.'

The reply to the telegram indicated that the bank was not overly concerned about the train stopping at any point along its journey because they were confident that few knew about the special van and no one knew about the very secret method of securing the door to the container. The method used was one that did not rely on conventional locks and was put in place by an official of the bank with no other persons present.

Part Two

Two days after the successful location of the bullion, when Holmes and I were having breakfast, I thought, this is the moment when a telegram usually arrives. Indeed it was so.

'This telegram from Lestrade,' said Holmes, 'reports that two men on horseback approached the warehouse. It was too dark to make out their faces. One was tall, the other short. Watson, you recall the footprints we examined at the back of the warehouse, one set of which was that of a small man or boy?'

'Yes, I remember you remarked on them.'

'Lestrade goes on to say that they just looked at the van and, as we agreed, he did not arrest them. Oh! This is most interesting. After they had ridden off he examined their footprints and decided that one of them had mounted on the wrong side. I must say, the inspector is becoming more and more observant with each new case.'

'By the way, why should someone want to mount on the offside?'

'There are a number of possible reasons. However, for the time being, I am unable to relate any of them to the case. No doubt Lestrade and the local police will find and arrest the whole gang. While we await the turn of events, there are other matters to be attended to. For one, I have to complete my notes on the diluted milk case. Oh, and these most flattering letters arrived from the Home Secretary and the governor of the Bank of England. I am informed that I am to receive a substantial reward that will relieve me of any concerns over my finances for at least ten years.'

'Perhaps a complete change of interests might be of benefit. I happen to have two tickets for the D'Oyly Carte Opera. I am sure you would enjoy the evening. I find Gilbert's libretti most entertaining and amusing.'

'I need time in which to think about your kind offer, although I must confess I am led to believe from some reports that the music may not be to my taste.'

A week later we sat in the dress circle. I could not fail to notice that now and then Holmes' long fingers were tapping his knee in time to the music. Suddenly, during one of the less noisy scenes, he exclaimed, 'I've got it!' Those around us shushed.

In the hansom on the way back from the theatre, I mentioned my friend's outburst.

'I apologize, Watson. I could not help it because the Japanese nature of the performance reminded me that, in the east, horses are mounted, so I believe, from what we term the offside. It means, of course, that one of the persons at Little Newark may have been an Oriental.'

'That adds to the mystery, Holmes. Why should someone from the Orient be in the middle of England and involved with a bullion robbery?'

'Indeed, why?'

'Did the bank give any indication of how the bullion was to be loaded aboard the ship at Newcastle without attracting attention?'

'None. Mind you, I was aware that the governor was reluctant to say very much about the transfer of so much gold to St Petersburg.'

Another morning passed and no word from Lestrade. However, late in the afternoon two telegrams arrived. One read: 'Cannot make much progress. Your help would be much appreciated. Can you come to LN? Signed Lestrade.' The other, from the commissioner of police, read: 'The Home Secretary and the Foreign Secretary request that Mr Holmes takes up the case again. Lestrade informed.'

'As you see, Lestrade's quarry has gone to ground somewhere, so we have to pick up the trail again.'

The next morning, as we stepped onto the platform at Little Newark, we were met by Lestrade.

'I'm very glad to see you, gentlemen. I've had two or three messages from London urging me to find the villains. Apparently for some reason they must be caught as quickly as possible.'

'Like you, Lestrade, I've not been made party to all the facts in this case. I can only assume that the person or persons we have to find must hold some important secret. Therefore, they must be caught before they can cause further trouble. However, although we may not know all about the purpose of the task it is still, after all, just another straightforward search for one or two robbers.'

'I wish it were as straightforward, Mr Holmes,' said Lestrade. 'We've searched around the station and the warehouses for more clues but found nothing. By the way, the van was on its way to Newcastle yesterday. However, we have had a report from the police at Nottingham concerning a body found alongside the railway. It has been difficult to determine from the injuries whether it is a case of foul play or an accident. More importantly, further investigation has disclosed that at one time he was an engine driver who had been dismissed because of drinking spirits when on duty. More than likely he was the rogue driver that night. It is likely that, as he had access to the engine shed in London, he was the one who put the opiate in the enginemen's snap.'

Holmes nodded agreement and then asked to be left on his own to make another search for clues. I sat with Lestrade on a platform bench. The ticking of one of the telegraph instruments in the signal box prompted me to say, 'You know, Lestrade, there may still be some clues in the signal box. Shall we have a look?'

I doubted that my ulterior motive for being in the signal box escaped Lestrade's attention. I confess that I was more interested in the way in which the signalman operated the many levers and in the sounds of the variously toned bells than in looking for clues.

During my time in the signal box, Holmes was searching the warehouse carefully, paying particular attention to the bits of paper and other rubbish that had accumulated in one corner. It did not appear that the local police detectives had examined them. That would not have surprised him because very few detectives in the official police were given any training in what to look for at the scene of a crime.

Holmes rejoined us. He was holding out a small piece of crumpled paper. 'This was missed by the local detectives. It could be of importance because, as you see, these characters appear to be Chinese.' Turning the paper over, he showed us where someone had written in pencil what appeared to be an address. Only part of each line remained.

'I can make out "BKADUGANSKWR LONDON WES". Note how badly formed the capital letters are. It is as if they had been written by a very young child,' said I.

Lestrade tried to guess what the missing letters were. 'Obviously somewhere or someone in London. The WES suggests the West End.'

'Perhaps I may have more time than you in which to ponder the address,' said Holmes. 'I shall take it with me. The letters "KADU" may be of particular importance.'

We made a further examination of the ruts and marks in the road at the back of the warehouse, which had been made at the time of the attempted robbery. Most had been obliterated by rain. We decided that there was little to be gained by trying to find out from where the cart had come, or in which direction the two men, seen later on horseback, had gone.

'Gentlemen, my instinct is that we should return to London. We are wasting our time here,' said Holmes.

'Your instinct is usually most reliable, Mr Holmes,' responded Lestrade.

The October gale gusted along Baker Street, rattling windows and throwing the fallen leaves into every corner. In the warmth of number 221B, we discussed the case of, as it is now called, 'The Van That Vanished'.

'By the way, Holmes, did you learn anything from your friends at the School of Oriental Studies about the Chinese characters on that piece of paper?'

'I learnt one important fact. They are Japanese not Chinese. Although the Japanese characters are related to Chinese there are, apparently, subtle differences.'

'Ah, then the small man at Little Newark was Japanese?'

'More than likely.'

'Then, as you might say, Holmes, we have a singular coincidence for I read in this morning's papers that relationships between Russia and Japan continue to be a source of tension. The extension of the railway through Siberia and on to Vladivostok is seen as a threat to Japanese interests. The Russian government is increasing its gold reserves and is calling in the large loans made to other countries. You know, it could be that the bullion with which we are involved is part of the movement of gold among the countries of Europe.'

'Watson, you have indeed filled in a big hole in our facts. Yes, it is more than likely the small man was Japanese and that he was an emissary overseeing an attempt to prevent the gold reaching Russia.'

'Another question that needs answering concerns what the gang would have done with the bullion had they taken it?'

'It is possible there was no intention of disposing of the gold. All they needed to do was to keep it hidden somewhere for as long as possible. The important thing was to delay its journey to Russia. They anticipated that the van would eventually be discovered. Therefore, we might assume that it was not they who attempted to open the van and remove the bullion. They employed robbers who in the end attempted to cheat them by making off with it. Now what we have to do is unravel the strange string of letters on this torn-off piece of paper.'

I spelt out the letters 'BKADUGANSKWR' as Holmes wrote them spaced out on a sheet of foolscap. A number of different arrangements were tried.

'Could this be a code?' I suggested.

'I think not. "LONDON" suggests that it is, as we first thought, an address. There is also the possibility that DUGAN is someone's name. It could be an Irish name and that might indicate that, after all, we are involved with a Fenian plot to steal gold. Except, of course, we have the Japanese characters and the small man.'

'What if the writer of the note had only a rudimentary knowledge of English and wrote down what he heard? For example "KADUGAN" can be pronounced as Cadogan.'

'My dear fellow, brilliant. The "SKWR" then is "SQUARE". Now we have Cadogan Square. And all we need now is the number, which was most likely on the missing part. Unfortunately, all we are left with is the letter B.'

'Well, that could be part of the number. As with your address here in Baker Street, the B is part of the number.'

The street directory revealed a 38B Cadogan Square W. There were no other numbers with an appended B.

At that moment Mrs Hudson ushered in two gentlemen. The

larger of the two was Holmes' brother Mycroft, who introduced the other.

'Sherlock, this is Sir Charles Seebroke.'

Holmes gave a slight bow and said, 'I have had the honour to meet the Foreign Secretary on a previous occasion. Please sit down, gentlemen. I surmise that this visit to Baker Street predicates a matter concerning the attempted bullion robbery. I have responded to your instructions that were passed on to me by the commissioner of police, and have made every effort to locate the gang.'

'Well, have you anything to tell us, Mr Holmes?'

Holmes recounted the solving of the address.

'Mr Holmes, before you investigate further I am at liberty to acquaint you with certain facts that may be of help. I regret that I have been unable to confide in you earlier. I must emphasize that Her Majesty's government has been placed in a difficult situation relating to two foreign powers.'

'Russia and Japan, no doubt.'

'Exactly. As I am sure you are aware, relationships between the two are strained to say the least. However, there are two aspects of this. On the one hand, both issue bellicose statements. On the other, at diplomatic level, they endeavour to pour oil on the troubled waters. Japan is not strong enough at present to challenge Russia either on land or at sea. In about ten years from now she hopes to have a powerful navy. This is where we come into the affair. The yards at Barrow, with government encouragement, are building warships for Japan. The Royal Navy is helping to train their officers and seamen. As I said, the present official policy of the Japanese court is a pacific one. Unfortunately a clique of nobles, each being a member of the Samurai warrior class, is determined to confront Russia now. They have agents in many countries including ours. They endeavour to stir up ill feeling between the two nations. We even have information that they may make an attempt on the life of an important Japanese official who is staying in London. If they were to succeed they would then put about that it was the work of Russian agents. Their object being to precipitate war.'

'So the attempt on the bullion is all part of the plan,' said Holmes.

'That is so. It was just one part of their overall scheme. Their principal objective was to weaken Russia's financial standing in the world.'

'Yes, that is the conclusion that Doctor Watson reached.'

'This affair, of course, does not just involve the two countries. As I mentioned, the government is in a difficult position. We do not want to offend Tokyo and thereby jeopardize valuable contracts. At the same time, we do not want to give the czar an excuse to interfere further in Afghanistan. We have only just managed to repair the damage done to our relationship with Russia by that fool Colonel Flashman. Therefore, Mr Holmes, you will understand why we have requested your services, particularly as any action required must be discreet.'

Lestrade and his men kept a surreptitious watch on 38B Cadogan Square. Outwardly it looked no different from its neighbours, except at night it exhibited few lights; on some nights none at all. The servants' entrance at the bottom of the rear steps appeared not to be used. A detective posing as a brush seller could get no answer to his repeated pulls on the bell knob of the servants' door. Inquiries among the local shopkeepers determined that none had been asked to deliver to the house.

After further consideration of the facts and mindful of the need for a quick solution to the case, it was decided that we had to see inside the house. Holmes, Lestrade and I waited on a corner of the square. I had my service revolver with me.

'We've chosen a good night for what we intend. The noise of the wind and rain is on our side,' commented Holmes.

With water finding its way under his collar, Lestrade muttered, 'When I look back on my time with the Yard, my strongest memory will be nights such as this. Villainy seems to go with this sort of weather.'

'Time to make a move,' whispered Holmes, even although the noise of the elements would have drowned a normal voice.

'Remember, Mr Holmes, we have no warrant to enter these premises. If we're caught we'll be disowned until such time as the affair quietens down.'

Holmes just shrugged at the inspector's reminder and led the way to the door of number 38B. There was no sign of life.

I ventured to remark, sotto voce, 'Perhaps they've all gone to a performance of *The Mikado*?'

Holmes gave me a look that implied my levity was not appropriate at such a critical moment. After trying a number of different tools from his roll of house-breaking equipment, Holmes sprang the lock. Once inside the dark hallway, we three 'conspirators' were faced with having to decide on our next move. Holmes pointed upward and we moved slowly and quietly up the stairs. We trusted our leader's instinctive decision, only because Lestrade and I had no ideas of our own.

At the end of the upper hall, the small pool of light from Lestrade's dark lantern moved ahead of us. Suddenly it revealed something that brought us to a halt. Before us was what appeared to be the lower part of a richly embroidered heavy curtain. Lestrade slowly raised the lamp to reveal a broad belt or sash into which were thrust two sword scabbards. Moving the lamp light up further, it came to a fearsome scowling face. For a fleeting moment I imagined they were confronting one of the costumes on display at the current exhibition of Oriental artefacts and dress at the Victoria and Albert Museum.

'It's the dress of a samurai warrior,' I murmured.

In a remarkably calm voice Holmes said, 'It's more than that, it is a very real Samurai warrior.'

As he spoke I remembered reading about the lightning speed with which the deadly swords could be drawn, applied and placed back in their scabbards even before the two separated halves of an opponent's body fell to the ground.

The two swords flashed in the dim light. I fired my revolver close to Lestrade's ear. The warrior fell back in a heap of elaborate brocade.

'Thank goodness you fired, Watson. He could have sliced all three of us up. Mind you, using your pistol against a swordsman is not really cricket.'

The other occupants of the house made no attempt to resist arrest. On being questioned, they were found to be just servants. The samurai warrior was the only one in the country. As for the gang who attempted the robbery, they were petty criminals and were soon rounded up. The small man, whose footprints and manner of mounting a horse had attracted Holmes' attention, was a youth who had badly injured his left hand, which prevented him mounting in the usual manner.

When the affair of the vanishing van was over, I remembered about the Oriental characters written on the other side of the piece of paper.

'Come to think of it, Holmes, have the Japanese characters been translated?'

'Yes, they have. It was apparently some lines of verse. Something about cherry blossom and a dragon breathing fire and steam. There was more about flowers and rivers and mountains and snow. In fact a hotch-potch. The sort of thing an overemotional schoolgirl might pen to her favourite teacher.'

'*The Pirates of Penzance* is now on. Are you interested?'

Holmes grunted and turned to his violin.

* On the railways the 'down' direction is for trains going away from London, 'up' and 'down' having been inherited from the Admiralty visual telegraph chain of stations that extended down from London to Portsmouth.

The Brighton Clown

In which the Indian Mutiny provides a clue.

It was late September; the weather was hot and oppressive. I made one of my frequent visits to 221B Baker Street. Holmes had opened the windows to try and cool his sitting-room but that let in even more overheated air. Below, in the street, people who usually bustled busily about their diverse tasks now moved slowly. My friend was sprawled in his old armchair. His pipe added to the oppressive atmosphere. For me there was one consolation in this uncomfortable weather. It seemed that Holmes was becoming less dependent on narcotics.

'We need a good thunderstorm, Watson, to clear the air.'

'I agree with you. A good downpour would refresh the air and cool the hot streets as well as lay the dust.'

The page boy entered the room. 'A mister to see you, sir.'

'His name, Billy?'

'Didn't give no name.'

'Well, I suppose I must see him. At least it will break the monotony of this, so far, very inactive day. Show the gentleman up.'

The man who entered was very portly and rather short of breath. He had a mottled complexion and his clothes were what I understand are called 'loud'.

Coming towards me he said, 'Good morning, Mr Holmes, I'm glad you have agreed to see me.'

'I'm Doctor Watson, this is Mr Holmes,' said I, inclining my head towards the recumbent figure in the well-used chair.

Holmes stood up, shook hands with the visitor and said, 'Now, sir, why do you wish to see me?'

'Mr Holmes, I'm a – ' Holmes interrupted him. 'You are a man of the circus, I believe.'

'However did you know that? I'd wager we've never met before!'

'Indeed, I have not had that pleasure. How I deduced your profession is not important. More importantly, I can see from your countenance that you have lost no time in reaching me, and that leads me to believe the matter which you wish to put before me is of an urgent nature.'

'Very true. I've come up from Brighton as soon as I could get away from my circus. I desperately need your help. My son is one of the clowns and he has been arrested on a charge of murder.'

'Of course. The affair in which an attendant at the Royal Pavilion was killed.'

'Yes, I'm afraid so. However, it was not my son. It was someone impersonating him. The police will not let him go. They say that he matches in every respect the murderer. Please, I need your help. I'll pay anything you ask.'

'You are, of course, the Great Congreve of the circus of that name. I can assure you I often take on cases more for the intellectual exercise it gives my brain rather than monetary reward. I shall incur expenses but they will not be large. I shall go down to Brighton as soon as I can. In the meantime, rest assured that I shall endeavour to prove your son is innocent.'

When Congreve had left, Holmes suggested that, if it were convenient, he would appreciate my help with the case. As I had few patients in my diary for the next day, I agreed. I was sure that my wife would not object.

The next morning we were in a train bound for Brighton.

'I appreciate your coming with me, Watson, because, as a medical man, you may be able to persuade the police surgeon to disclose more about the nature of the wounds that killed the attendant.'

'I shall try my best. In this newspaper report it states that a very valuable and rare ruby was stolen from the collection of Oriental jewels on display. The murderer apparently took none of the others even though, together, they were of even greater value.'

'That is a singular fact. Why take just one jewel? The answer must be with the ruby itself. Now, what do we know about it? All that we do know is that it was part of a collection loaned from

Windsor Castle to enhance a display of Oriental jewels and artefacts. In fact, this is the first time the particular set of precious items had been seen by the public.'

As the train approached East Croydon, it began to slow down. This prompted Holmes to comment, 'As usual, the railway company is about to extend the time it takes to travel the fifty miles or so between London and the coast as much as possible.'

The London Brighton and South Coast Railway deposited us in the historic Regency resort in just under one hour and a half after leaving Victoria station.

Our first success on the way to proving the innocence of the clown came when I found that the police surgeon had been with me during the Afghan campaign. He was most helpful and I am sure was intrigued to find that I was with my famous friend.

At the mortuary, we examined the victim's head.

'I see he was more than likely struck down by a left-handed man,' said Holmes. 'I presume you examined the accused and did you notice which hand he preferred?'

'I regret, sir,' replied the police surgeon, 'that it is not customary to examine an accused person in such detail other than to ascertain whether he is under the influence of strong drink. I fail to understand why you assume that the fatal blow was delivered by a left-handed man.'

'Because, as you can see, the diagonal wound at an angle across the left temple was more than likely struck by a sweeping blow of the left hand moving across the victim's body, from left to right. I shall demonstrate. If you please, Watson.'

Using me as the victim, Holmes demonstrated to the satisfaction of the police surgeon that indeed the murderer was left-handed.

'You have been most helpful in letting us examine the victim's body,' said Holmes. 'Ah, I nearly forgot. Can you tell me anything about the accused? I understand from his father that he was the principal clown in the Great Congreve's circus.'

'Yes, that is so. In fact he is very well known in the town. He dresses as a clown and hands out playbills to passers-by. He strolls along the promenade and sometimes walks up one of the roads leading to the station. To the town's people and in particular to the visitors at this time of the year, he is a familiar figure.'

'Most interesting.' Holmes paused and then said, 'Yet how strange. Someone in the costume of a clown was seen coming from the scene of the dreadful crime. If anyone is intent on robbery they usually avoid drawing attention to themselves. Yet here we have a murderer dressed as a clown. Not just any clown but one familiar to many in Brighton.'

'I must agree with that, Mr Holmes. It is indeed strange behaviour,' replied the police surgeon.

Despite Holmes' reluctance to be away from London for a night, he decided that we should stay in a hotel. Breakfast the next morning was passable except for the marmalade. Holmes considered it to be of a very inferior quality and told the head waiter what he thought of it. After breakfast we were seated in the window of the hotel, watching the holiday crowd on the promenade.

'Across there, at the entrance to the West Pier, is where our clown often stood. I'm wondering if the murderer sat where we are now and he was watching the people and the clown,' observed Holmes.

'Yes, that is a possibility,' I replied. 'If we were to assume that the murderer was in this room then perhaps he actually stayed here. We could ask to see the names of recent guests. Of course he may not have given his real name.'

'Quite so, Watson. Nevertheless it may be worth a try. Mind you, if he did not stay here then we shall have to visit all the other hotels, of which there are a great many.'

The manager of the hotel was reluctant to divulge the names of guests. When Holmes mentioned that he was a detective the manager said, 'Oh, of course, you are the famous Sherlock Holmes. I have read about the way you help the police to track down villains. Certainly, you may see the guest list. I'm sure your interest in them is in the interests of justice.'

'Thank you. Yes, Doctor Watson and I are very much concerned with justice. Now may I look at the list of those who have registered in the past few days?'

'Have you a particular name in mind, Mr Holmes?'

'Let us start with Smith.'

The manager smiled and said, 'We often have a couple staying with us who register as Mr and Mrs Smith.'

'I understand very well what you mean,' said Holmes. 'No, I am looking for a Smith who stayed on his own on or before the first of this month.'

A search through the list of names of those who had stayed at the hotel soon revealed that just before the day of the murder, a Smith had stayed for three days.

'Although there is only a remote possibility that this Smith is the murderer,' said Holmes, 'we must not dismiss him for the time being. Now, Watson, I must send a telegram to Inspector Lestrade at Scotland Yard. He should be able to verify the address given by Smith.'

That evening a telegram arrived from Lestrade. 'As I suspected, Watson, Lestrade found no such address in London. Now we have to find more about this Mr Smith, or whatever his real name is.'

'We have little to go on. Where do we start?'

With the agreement of the manager, Holmes went very thoroughly over every inch of the room in which our suspect had stayed.

'Watson, I know you are thinking that at least three other people have stayed in the room since the first of the month,' he said, as the back of each drawer was searched. 'However, despite the thoroughness with which the room has been cleaned, there is always the possibility of some minute trace remaining of each person who has stayed in the room.'

He started to lift the paper lining of the drawers that the chambermaid was supposed to have changed after a guest had left. 'Ah, what have we here?' He held up a small laundry bill. 'It has the name Prestot or it may be Prescott. More importantly it has the address. Now all we have to do is re-examine the guest list and if none of the addresses matches this one then we have made the first step in our search.'

He was right. None of the addresses matched that on the laundry bill.

'Well, Watson, who lives at 19 The Blundells, Chelsea? Is it Smith, Prestot or Prescott?'

We devoted the rest of the day questioning shopkeepers and stall holders. Late in the afternoon we took a stroll along the promenade. Near the aquarium there was a large crowd so we decided to join the throng. The centre of attraction was a railway that ran alongside the promenade.

'Of course, this is Magnus Volk's railway on which the carriages are propelled by electricity. A truly remarkable idea,' said I.

'Indeed, Watson. It reminds me that someone from our local electricity supply company has been trying to persuade Mrs Hudson that 221B should be lit by electricity. What I have seen of it does not impress me. As you know, apart from concerts, I care little for theatrical performances. At the few plays I have attended I found that the electrically lit auditoriums, along with the arc and limelights of the stages, provided an unnatural illumination. For the time being I shall remain content with the soft light of the gas and oil lamps.'

The next morning we took breakfast in the coffee room of the hotel. After a further altercation with the head waiter over the quality of the marmalade, we studied our notes of the answers we had received from the people to whom we had spoken. Holmes gave his opinion. 'It is clear, Watson, that the murderer walked, rather than ran, from the Royal Pavilion, toward the seafront. This, we can assume, was to associate his appearance with that of the real clown. However he did not go too close to where the real clown usually stood lest someone saw two clowns. He then more than likely discarded his disguise. And therefore we can suppose that he then went to the station and took a train up to London and so to his Chelsea address.'

These deductions were interrupted by the arrival in the coffee room of a large man of military bearing. He came directly up to Holmes and said, 'Mr Holmes, I'm the chief constable and I object strongly to the way in which you are interfering in the case of the murdered attendant. I must insist, sir, that you stop making inquiries. You are confusing those who may eventually appear as witnesses for the crown.'

I observed Holmes' visage assume one of irritation and determination. He said nothing for a moment. He did not even rise from his chair. Then, opening his newspaper and with a dismissive wave of the hand, he said, 'I shall ignore your request. Good day to you, sir.'

The chief constable looked surprised and then angry and then he turned and, muttering to himself, he left.

'Well, that was a very sociable visit,' remarked I.

'You know, my dear fellow, that abrupt visit from the official police leads me to the opinion that there could be more to this case than we imagine.'

We returned to London. Holmes had decided that there were no more clues to be had beside the sea. Accompanied by Lestrade we went to the address in Chelsea. Outwardly it was little different from the other houses in the road. Without an authority to enter the premises all we could do was observe who went in and out. It was agreed that we should take turns to play the part of loafers outside the public house on the corner. From there we were able to keep watch on the house without revealing our intent. Holmes and Lestrade, of course, found no difficulty in adopting the disguise of someone who frequented a four-ale bar. For my part I had to appear as a distributor of religious tracts that urged those who enjoyed alcohol to abandon the vice. I had to summon what little courage I possessed in order to withstand the verbal abuse to which I was subjected.

During my time on watch, as dusk was falling, I observed two men walking toward the house. They were arguing, although I could not hear what they were disputing. They went inside.

I reported what I had seen to Holmes and Lestrade.

'No doubt our murderer has an accomplice,' said Holmes. 'It appears, from what you saw, that they are in dispute over either the disposal of the valuable jewel or, having exchanged it for money, are arguing over how the proceeds should be divided.'

As I have mentioned before, I always associate Holmes and his cases with breakfast. Once again it was interrupted by Lestrade saying, 'Good morning, I have information that will surprise you.'

'My dear Lestrade,' said Holmes, 'in our long and mutual involvement with the criminal world little now surprises me. If you are about to tell me the Crown Jewels have been spirited away by a modern Colonel Blood it will not affect my enjoyment of this delicious and very rare orange preserve.'

'No, Mr Holmes, not the Crown Jewels. Although from the manner in which they are kept in the Tower, such an event would not surprise me. The surprise is a body recovered from the Thames early this morning. And you may be even more surprised to hear that it was wearing a clown's costume.'

Holmes immediately stopped eating. Although he did not admit to being surprised, I could tell that inwardly he was. 'Lestrade, when can I examine the body?'

'When you are ready, Mr Holmes. The deceased is with the River Police down at Wapping. Papers were found in his pockets giving us the name Prescott.'

I could not help thinking of the fact that in so many of the cases on which I have been with Holmes, we have had to visit the more unpleasant parts of the capital. The police surgeon informed us that the cause of death was by some poison. Holmes examined the body and paid particular attention to the hands.

'Now that is very interesting,' he said, as he placed the third finger of the victim alongside that of the other hand. 'See, the indentation adjacent to the nail of this finger is usually caused by frequent use of a pen. There is also slight discolouration from ink that gets onto the shaft of a pen. This suggests very strongly that the victim is right-hand preferring and is a scribe.'

I hastened to remark, 'However, you deduced that the murderer was left-handed. And we assumed he had discarded his clown's costume somewhere in Brighton.'

'So I did. However, I believe we may have been on the trail of two men, not one. This may not be the Brighton murderer. It could be the body of his accomplice. Is this an attempt to suggest that the case is closed; the murderer having taken poison? The clown's costume is either another attempt to lead a false trail or is a macabre joke. This is not Prescott.'

'Shall we now attempt to see who is in the house in Chelsea?' I suggested.

Holmes turned to Lestrade and asked, 'Is that possible, Inspector?'

'Well, there could be some difficulty in obtaining permission to enter the premises, Mr Holmes. We would have to convince my superiors that we have enough evidence to connect the finding of this body with whoever is in the house. And of course establishing a connection with the Brighton Clown murderer. For a reason that I cannot understand, I have been ordered not to seek the help of the Brighton police with my investigation of this poisoning.'

'What you say, Lestrade, does not come as a surprise. I shall need some time in which to go through my commonplace books. Particular attention will be paid to any cuttings or notes under the headings of Brighton and Windsor.'

That evening after our supper, Holmes turned to those thick volumes in which he noted any items in the newspapers that might prove of value in the future. He also methodically cut items out of periodicals and pasted them on the pages. As the squirrel in its drey, Holmes collected for the future.

'By the by, Holmes, were there any other distinguishing marks on the body we examined this morning?'

'None. Apart from the deceased being right-handed and was a scribe, I found no other clues.'

It was close to midnight before Holmes found what he was looking for. 'Now this is very interesting. These cuttings from the Windsor papers disclose that a number of very valuable pieces of jewellery had been brought back to England from India by an army officer after the Mutiny. Apparently their ownership had been in dispute for a number of years. The government insisted that they belonged to the crown. The officer, at the time a Lieutenant Sandarson, had come across them during the fighting.'

'That was a very singular affair,' said I.

'This report, dated 1860, refers to Sandarson's decision to relinquish the jewels. They were eventually placed in the royal collection at Windsor Castle. They were not put on display. Most importantly, Watson, among the precious items was an exceptionally large and pure ruby of immense value. It was part of a heavy gold chain.'

'I suppose, Holmes, if we find the murderer that should lead us to the gem.'

The sultry weather persisted. Afghanistan had been hot at times yet the air was often clean and less oppressive. Holmes was making his customary diligent reading of the personal columns of the morning papers.

'This small item, Watson, tells us that any person who knows the whereabouts of Simon Small, a clerk with Gadsby, Clawer and Rogers, is requested to communicate with them. Now a visit to those gentlemen may prove of value to our case.'

Messrs Gadsby, Clawer and Rogers proved very helpful. When we arrived at their offices, Rogers had just returned from identifying the body in a clown's costume as that of their clerk Small. He told us that he had failed to arrive for work on the previous Monday. On examining the desk used by Small, it was clear that he was right-handed. Holmes asked if he had taken any documents with him when he last left the office. Gadsby replied. 'I cannot be certain. Although we did find a bundle on his desk that should have been replaced in the strongroom.'

'Did you examine it to see if all the documents were in place?'

'As far as I could tell, Mr Holmes, they were all there.'

'And who is your client?'

'The papers had been left by a client for secure keeping. Confidentiality is the keystone of a lawyer's profession.'

'I fully understand,' replied Holmes. 'Nevertheless, surely, my knowing the name of your client betrays no confidence. I do not need to know what is in the bundle.'

'Well, I suppose it is ethical to reveal his name.' He turned to his partner. 'Do you not agree, Clawer?' Clawer nodded his head and said, 'His name is a Lieutenant Colonel Charteris, retired from a Highland regiment.'

'We are most obliged to you, gentlemen. Good day.'

As we made our way back to Baker Street I said, 'It appears then that this Charteris is connected in some way with the Mutiny jewels.'

'I agree, Watson. However, what connection? At the moment it may be pure coincidence that his documents were perused and possibly some were taken by Small, and that Small was involved with the one who murdered to obtain the jewel. There is, of course, the possibility that Charteris may have been serving in India at the time of the Mutiny. A look in the army or regimental lists for 1857 may prove instructive.'

An inquiry through Holmes' brother Mycroft revealed that Charteris was indeed in India in 1857. As requested, Mycroft provided a list of all the officers who were there at that time. Another important piece of information came from Lestrade, who found out that the clown's costume had been hired to Small.

'This case is becoming more convoluted every day that passes,' said Holmes. 'We still have yet to find Prescott; Lestrade confirmed this as Smith's real name from a visit to the laundry named on the bill we found in the drawer of the hotel room.'

During our next discussion with Lestrade, he agreed that a visit to Small's home might prove useful. The first thing we observed was the open door to the room he rented in a terrace house in Islington.

'I suppose, Lestrade, as the door is open, you can dispense with a warrant in order to enter.'

'Yes, Mr Holmes, there is nothing to stop us.'

The sparsely furnished room revealed at first little of interest until Holmes found a cutting from a newspaper. 'Look at this. Here is a report of the Brighton murder. This is a further clue that indicates that Small is involved.'

He then started to make a careful study of a pile of legal foolscap lying on the table. Small appeared to have been attempting to write a letter. There were four attempts. Each had been heavily inked over. However, on one of them we could make out 'C knows about the true nature of the ruby'.

'Now C is most likely Charteris,' said Holmes. 'This letter we can assume was sent to someone who, on learning about the true nature of the ruby, was prompted to kill for it. Small had taken the document that exposed the murderer's connection with the ruby. Once the gem had been taken he was most likely killed because he threatened to go to the police.'

I interrupted Holmes' deduced account of events by saying, 'What did you mean, the true nature of the ruby?'

'There is one possibility that the words "true nature" could imply that the stolen ruby was a fake, paste in fact, and Charteris knew it. And someone else has known it for over thirty years. We need to find out who the other keeper of the secret is. This copy from a list for 1857 includes the name of Charteris as well as that of a Lieutenant Sandarson, with both gazetted to the same regiment.'

Holmes began to send out messages to his many informants close to the criminal world. At first when I learnt of the way in which he consorted with some of the worst elements of our society I was appalled. However, Holmes assured me that such intercourse was sometimes the only way to elicit clues.

'Just as in our law-abiding society, gossip is the lifeblood of many, so in the criminal world there is gossip. From that gossip we can learn much,' was his reply to my reservations.

Two days later Holmes was able to say, 'Sandarson is definitely associated with Charteris. He is now Sir Edward Sandarson Bart KCB. He is the same who discovered – or was it looted? – the jewels in 1857. He is one of those seemingly very respectable men who sail extremely close to the legal wind. He is, so I understand from my information, another Moriarty. However, on a much smaller scale.'

'Important news indeed, Holmes. Am I right in summing up what we know to be able to say that both Charteris and Sandarson have known all along that the ruby was paste?'

'That is certainly so. Yet why did Sandarson commission a very professional burglar to seize the ruby knowing full well that it was of little value? Another matter, why wait for so many years after the Mutiny? Well, there may be an answer in Small's unsent letters. There are still some sheets that I have yet to study. Of course, it could be that I am maligning Sandarson and he has had nothing to do with the affair. Nevertheless, given his undoubted unsavoury associates, he has to remain a suspect.'

At breakfast next morning I waited to hear if Holmes, who had been up for most of the night, had found another clue.

'I have these telegraph messages, Watson, that were with the papers on Small's table. They are addressed to him. At first I did not think they provided much information. They were from Prescott instructing Small to be at the Chelsea address at certain times. What I had failed to realize at first was that the telegraph office that originated the message was not Chelsea, but Tunbridge Wells.'

'That suggests Prescott was away on some business in Tunbridge Wells. Up to no good, no doubt.'

'The significance of where the telegrams came from is found when you consider that Sir Edward's address is "Lucknow", Fordcombe near Tunbridge Wells. At the time, I did not relate the word luck with a capital L that I found on one of the scraps of paper with the name of a place.

'Now listen to this, Watson, I have been able to bring together enough incomplete letters and sentences to deduce that Small advised Prescott or Sandarson that Charteris's affairs were the responsibility of a relative who had been given power of attorney. Charteris is no longer capable of understanding the world around him. The list on the back of one of the papers is that of the documents in the Charteris bundle. Among the items is a reference to a sealed envelope that on the death of Charteris had to be passed to the commissioner of the Metropolitan Police. When Sandarson or Prescott, or both, were told about the envelope they must have realized that it could contain a confession, one that would expose the crimes of others. Assuming that Charteris might die at any moment, Sandarson persuaded Prescott to commit the burglary at Brighton. By removing the paste ruby it was hoped that it would not be possible to say one way or the other that it was real or a fake.'

'I have another question, Holmes. How could the ruby have remained on display in the Royal Pavilion museum without someone realizing it was paste?'

'That is something we need to determine. And also we need to reconstruct the events at the scene of the crime. Have you still got the times of trains to Brighton? We, that is two visitors to the resort, shall make a close inspection of the exhibition in the Royal Pavilion.'

We spent some time among the Oriental splendour of the one-time royal palace before returning to London. In the train I asked Holmes if our visit to the resort had been of value.

'Very much so. The answer to your question of why the fake remained unnoticed for so long lay in the manner in which it was on view. You will recall that when we visited the display we saw that the most valuable jewels were in a glass case. There was a barrier to prevent visitors getting close enough to detect the quality of the ruby. The murderer, more than likely, had concealed himself close to the display and waited for the moment to strike. That moment was just as the exhibition was closing when there would be few people about. As we know from the newspaper reports, a number of people saw the "clown" leaving the Pavilion at the time when the attendant was killed.'

Lestrade was able to obtain authority to enter the house in Chelsea. The owner opened the door. She was surprised to find a Scotland Yard detective standing there. Holmes and I, as two other detectives, remained anonymous. When questioned, she revealed that she had a lodger who used the front bedroom. His name was Prescott. He had a key to the front door and kept his room locked. His breakfast tray was left outside the door. After breakfast she was allowed in to make the bed and clean the room. Her lodger stayed seated, facing the window, and said little. Apparently he came and went at all hours. He sometimes returned with a companion.

We examined the room and its contents. Holmes stood looking at the desk in the window bay and said, 'Note the position of that heavy silver oil lamp, the way in which the pens in their tray are pointed, the position of the inkwell and the position of the pile of London street directories.'

'He is obviously a very tidy person,' said I.

'More than that, Watson, he is left-handed and so is our suspect. However, we need more than that to establish his guilt.'

Once more Holmes spent the greater part of the night going though his commonplace books and old magazines. His search was rewarded.

'A most important clue has emerged, Watson. I found this account of a cricket match in Kent. Much is made of the tactic employed by the captain of one of the teams in opening with a left-handed and a right-handed batsman. The left-handed player was Sandarson. Now have we just a coincidence or something far more significant?'

When Holmes proposed to Lestrade that we should once again stand watch in turn outside the house in Chelsea, he was very reluctant to do so. 'I can't see any point in it, Mr Holmes.' Nevertheless we stood watch. Lestrade watched first while Holmes and I kept out of sight. Late in the afternoon Lestrade came round the corner and reported on something of interest.

As he spoke he kept looking back at the house. 'Gentlemen, about ten minutes ago a hansom stopped at the top of the road and a tall man in a frock-coat and carrying a heavy silver-topped cane alighted. He walked toward the house and then stopped and stood still for about two or three minutes. He kept looking up and down the road. Then suddenly he turned. Went up the steps, put a key in the front door lock and went inside.'

Holmes pondered this news and then said, 'This suggests that Prescott has given him a key. Now we must watch to see if they come out together.'

Nothing happened for another half hour and then we saw someone leave the house. He was not with the man in the frock-coat. He was dressed in rather nondescript clothes and carried a Gladstone bag. We assumed it was Prescott so we followed him. He walked toward the main road and stood waiting, as if for a passing hansom.

'There's nothing to be lost and much to be gained. I'm going for his bag,' said Holmes. At that he leapt forward, knocked against the man, tore the bag from his grasp and was away round the corner. Lestrade, who was quicker than I in grasping the situation, immediately went up to him and said, 'I'm a Scotland Yard detective. We've been after that lad for some time. May I have your name, sir? I'll try and get your bag back. You'll have to give evidence against him if we catch him.'

At first the man declined to give his name, insisting that the bag was empty and that he did not want to waste his time, or that of the police, in pursuing the matter further. 'It was an old bag. Not worth much. If you have to know, my name is Prescott.'

Lestrade and I went back to Baker Street. Holmes was back before us. His first words were, 'As I suspected. However, I wanted to be certain before I gave my opinion. Prescott and Sandarson are one and the same. This Gladstone bag, as you can see, contains Sandarson's usual attire when in London.'

Following further inquiries, and after Holmes had reconstructed the case, the Metropolitan and the Brighton police had enough evidence to arrest Sandarson for the murder of the attendant. As he had suspected, Holmes was able to show that when Sandarson, alias Prescott, realized that Charteris was likely to die within a few weeks, the will would disclose that he had exchanged the real ruby for a fake. We were unable to determine with any certainty the original part played by Charteris. Possibly he was blackmailing Sandarson. He had either been with Sandarson when the jewels were taken during the Mutiny and was party to the deception, or he found out about it many years later.

As for the great ruby, it had long disappeared and had been turned into the wealth on which Sandarson had established his web of crime. The threatening attitude of the chief constable was nothing more than his annoyance that Scotland Yard and Holmes in particular were interfering in a 'local' matter.

Finally, the real clown was once again walking the promenade or standing outside the West Pier handing out playbills.

A Liquid Mystery

In which Holmes comes closer than ever to death.

What Charles Dickens referred to as a London Peculiar had been settled over the capital for the past three days. In my experience, only snow dulled the noise of traffic in Baker Street during the day. The fog made it difficult to make out the details of the houses opposite. They were just faint grey shapes. As for the sky, that had not been seen for some time. In its place was a strange, copper-coloured glow.

I was staying at 221B for a few days. The sitting room was a warm cheerful island in the midst of the gloom outside. My friend Holmes reclined in his favourite, somewhat shabby chair. His pipe was not lit. Had it been then no doubt it would have added to the fog that had crept through every convenient crack.

After a long silence he remarked, 'My dear fellow, I cannot help other than to conclude that life is infinitely more uncertain and diverse than anything we might conceive. All around us in this great metropolis there are queer things going on; there are strange coincidences, planned happenings; as well as events that are at cross purposes. All these and their results can make all those fictional accounts that are based upon convention and predictable conclusions stale and useless. I'm sure you will agree.'

'Indeed, I do,' I replied.

After spending a few minutes at the window endeavouring to see whether the fog was lifting, I remarked, 'Do you consider that the number of crimes, particularly burglaries, is greater when there is a dense fog such as this?'

'I am not sure, Watson, about burglaries. However, I do know that there are ruffians who take advantage of the fog and assault people. In broad daylight they would never attempt to do so. Ah, that sounds as if it is the front door. Have we a visitor?'

Mrs Hudson entered and handed over a visiting card, saying, 'A gentleman wishes to see you, Mr Holmes.'

'Please show him up,' said he.

A middle-sized man wearing a heavy overcoat with an Astrakhan collar and having, as far as I could see, no particular characteristics of apparel or demeanour, entered. He placed his hat on the table and, at Holmes' bidding, sat down. Having become used to my friend's methods of determining much about a client from dress and mannerisms, I waited to see what he would deduce. Of course, I noted that he first glanced at the inside of the upturned hat and then at the visitor's boots.

'Now, Mr Prendergast, how can I help you? Am I correct in assuming that you have walked from Euston station?'

'Indeed you are, sir. How did you know?'

'Very obvious. The mud on your boots reveals that you have had to traverse the extensive roadworks in front of the station. Now how can I be of help? I anticipate that you have come about something concerned with finance.'

Our visitor gave a surprised look and said, 'In a way you are correct, sir. Yet I cannot understand how you could know. We are not acquainted.'

'Never mind how I know. Tell me why you are here.'

'A mystery, Mr Holmes. As you are reputed to be able to solve the meaning of even the most abstruse and strange happenings, I decided to seek your help.'

'And the mystery is?'

'A house, Mr Holmes, a house.'

'I'm not surprised to hear that. From the exterior many houses display an air of mystery. Where is the house?'

'It is next to mine in Harrow. I have observed some very strange happenings.'

'Have any of these happenings caused you or your family harm or distress?'

'I cannot say they have, Mr Holmes. My reason for coming to see you is the noise as well as the unsightly buildings that have been erected in my neighbour's grounds. They will lower the value of my property. Unfortunately my business affairs have suffered a severe setback recently and I shall be forced eventually to sell up and move to a more modest establishment. So you see, I must sell on the most favourable terms. My agent has already told me that some potential buyers have commented adversely on the noise and on the strange smells coming from the outbuildings.'

'I appreciate your concern, Mr Prendergast. Now, I see from your card that you live in a part of Harrow that I know fairly well. In the meantime, leave things with Doctor Watson and myself.'

When our visitor had left Holmes said, 'Not the usual sort of case. No body nor disappearing heiress. Tomorrow we shall go out to Harrow and view the interesting property. That is if the fog will not disrupt the running of the trains.'

In the train I put the inevitable question. 'How the devil did you deduce that Prendergast had financial problems?'

'His clothes and boots. His overcoat was a very expensive one, as were his boots. However, most of the buttons on the coat had been replaced at some time and the cuffs were shiny at the edges. His boots, despite the mud, were well polished; however the surface exhibited numerous fine cracks in the leather. As for their soles and heels, both had been repaired more than once. His hat, although well brushed, no longer had a pristine finish. I also noticed that his overcoat and his collar no longer fitted him. These indicated that he had lost weight because of worry. Therefore, I deduced that at one time he had been well off. I also deduced that he no longer had the means with which to replace his overcoat and boots. I am not suggesting that he is penniless; rather that he is now having to be very careful with his money.'

'Ah, will he be able to settle your account at the end of the investigation?'

'I have no concern over that, Watson. If, as he told us, he wants to protect the value of his property then I am sure he is prepared to meet my modest fee.'

I knew that Holmes was not avaricious and only asked a client for a sum that he was sure was reasonable and matched their circumstances. The exercising of his special and unique skill was of far greater importance to him than the acquisition of wealth. He would not involve himself with an investigation if the facts were not unusual or the case did not present a challenge. On occasions he had even declined to help the powerful and wealthy; particularly if he considered their case to offer no wothwhile test of his skill.

From the fog-bound station at our destination we took a cab out to a well-wooded hillside on which stood a number of elegant mansions. The houses were close together and each appeared to have a long, narrow garden. We observed that the exterior of the front of the large house next to that of Prendergast's provided no indication that its occupants and use would be any different from those of similar properties in the neighbourhood, except for the distinct and pungent smell that grew stronger the closer we came to the gateway guarding the driveway.

'A strange aroma, Watson. Yet there's something very familiar about it.'

Prendergast was waiting for us. He led us down the side of his house to where we could look over the wall into the next garden. He pointed out the unsightly sheds that had been erected. Without our prompting, he mentioned the aroma of oranges.

'Indeed, it is the aroma of oranges that have been heated,' said Holmes. 'However, I cannot see any point in just looking over the garden wall. We shall have to return to Baker Street and consider a number of possibilities. Do not worry, I am certain that an explanation can be found for the pungent aroma and the presence and purpose of the sheds.'

We did not return directly to Euston because the next and usual step in this type of case was to seek that unfailing source of information, the local shopkeepers. However, we discovered nothing out of the ordinary with the exception of a chance remark by a greengrocer. Apparently two or three dozen crates of oranges were delivered to the house every two or three days. The greengrocer opined, 'They must be making enough marmalade to feed an army.'

'You know, Holmes, if the oranges are being used to make a preserve, I find it difficult to find anything suspicious about such an activity. Unless, of course, we have come across a secret producer who is intent on flooding the market and thereby affecting the business of the well-known and principal makers of preserves.'

'My dear fellow, I believe there is more to the oranges than meets the eye, or should it be meets the nose. And I have to admit that the clues we have are only skin deep.'

I ignored his attempt at a pun and said, 'Then I suppose we must try and find out more about the buildings that have been erected in the grounds next to the Prendergast establishment.'

'Agreed. We must see inside the grounds. Of course, we cannot enter in daylight, or what daylight there is in this fog. We'll come back tonight. If the fog persists it will help to hide our movements.'

We returned to Baker Street. After supper we set out again for Harrow. A Gladstone bag held a dark lantern and Holmes' 'special' tools. I commented, 'Is this wise, Holmes? If we are caught at night with housebreaking tools, we are likely to finish up before the bench.'

'If I thought that we might be caught I should not have started in the first place.'

Prendergast led us to a place where we could climb over the wall into his neighbour's property. By then the fog had become less dense.

'I don't believe there is anybody in. I can't see any lights,' said Prendergast.

The mansion loomed menacingly through the trees and shrubs. To one side was a long, low, wooden shed not in keeping with the formal arrangement of the garden. It had even been erected across one of the original gravel paths. As we came closer, the aroma of oranges was unmistakable. Holmes searched among his 'special' tools, selected one and within a few seconds had manipulated the door lock. We entered. Our senses were assailed by the overpowering smell. Crates of oranges filled the shed, except for a long space down the middle.

By the light of the dark lantern we could make out a long table covered with chemical equipment, such as retorts and distillation apparatus. Further on there was a very large apparatus of great complexity. On the floor in front of this strange collection of pipes and vessels was a carboy into which a liquid was dripping.

'I'm sure this is a laboratory, Holmes. I wonder what this liquid is? It certainly smells very strongly of oranges.'

I let a drop fall on my finger. I was just about to taste it when

Holmes seized my hand. 'Stop, don't taste that, it might prove dangerous. This is a Rumpenkoff distillation apparatus used to concentrate certain elements of a raw liquid to an unimaginable degree. That amber fluid dripping out could be lethal. Hand me that test tube, please. I must take a sample.'

I expressed astonishment by saying, 'What on earth could such a liquid be used for? Surely not for making an unbelievably strong preserve?'

'At this juncture, my dear fellow, I have no clear idea on the subject. However, I do know that what we have to do now is to find out where these carboys go to next.'

We left as we had arrived, unseen and silently.

Using his network of minor criminals, Holmes was able to find the destination of the 'orange' liquor. It turned out to be a small factory on the outskirts of Watford. The nameboard told us that it was Edgar and Sons, makers of agricultural machinery. Posing as journalists researching facts for a series in *The Strand Magazine* on the industries of Hertfordshire, we learnt from Mr Edgar, the proprietor, that a separate part of the factory was rented to K. Stoff and Company.

'It's a strange name. Not from these parts I wager. I reckon it's a Lunnun company,' said Edgar.

'You could be right,' replied Holmes.

The proprietor also mentioned that carboys were often being delivered. 'No idea what's in them. Whatever tis they uses a lot of it. Oh, there's another odd thing. At least one hundred tons of coal is delivered every week. There's often steam about.'

'Well, thank you for your help, Mr Edgar. Should the article be accepted we'll make sure your name is mentioned,' said Holmes. With that we returned to town.

On our way up to Euston, we discussed the case.

'You know, Watson, I am convinced that the K. Stoff company is up to no good. If they are not making an unusual type of marmalade then they must be preparing something else. We shall have to take a look inside Edgar's factory extension. I am afraid it's going to be another "dark lantern night" for us.'

That evening we decided to have supper at an Italian restaurant. We had an interesting meal. Holmes was intrigued by a dish the manager recommended. The dish of strange rubbery white strips, of I know not what, included a thick white sauce into which were added pieces of ham. It was passable. For my part, I would rather have had a more familiar dish.

'Delicious,' commented Holmes as he swept up every last bit on his fork. 'Now why call this dish carbonara? I suppose that it is derived from the Italian for carbon, although the resemblance with that mineral is singularly remote.'

At that moment I recalled the case of the strange events in Naples that had been investigated by Holmes at the request of the Italian government. 'Of course, Holmes, remember the Naples affair: the secret society of Naples, the Carbonari, or something like that.'

'Ah, yes, I remember and I also recall the exaggerated account you published of my involvement.'

We ate in silence until Holmes suddenly exclaimed in a loud voice that made the other diners turn their heads. 'K. Stoff could be a contraction of *Kohlenstoff*, the German for carbon! The company and its strange apparatus has something to do with carbon.'

Choosing a dark night, we made another train journey from Euston station. We hired a cab at Watford and Holmes took the precaution of giving the driver the address of one of the houses scattered along the road leading to the agricultural machinery factory. Holmes had chosen an address at random so that the cabman would not be aware of our intention to visit the factory. We paid off the cab and instructed the driver to be back there in an hour's time. Once the cab had turned and gone back to the station, we walked the short distance to the factory. It was well secured by bars and bolts and it took some time for Holmes to effect an entrance. Inside, by the light of my carefully shielded lantern, we were able to make out a massive brick structure. Passing through the brickwork was a metal cylinder to which a pipe was connected. Another steel or iron cylinder stood vertically up through the middle of the structure. To one side was a small steam engine and its boiler. We were able to determine that it drove a hydraulic pump.

'What do you make of all this?' whispered Holmes.

I could only reply, 'Not much. It is most certainly an apparatus that involves liquor and hydraulics.'

'A singular fact, Watson, is the absence of a chimney,' said he, pointing toward the roof.

'Yes, that is indeed strange. From my limited knowledge of things mechanical, I believe most factories usually have a large tall chimney. The only chimney here is that small one for the steam engine.'

We searched carefully for any documents or reports that might indicate the nature of the peculiar apparatus. There was a complete absence of any. The only thing of note was a small blackboard on the side of the brick and steel structure, on which were scrawled some numbers and words and a recent date.

'Now what can we make of this?' whispered Holmes as he made a copy of the blackboard's information. He then had another look around and said, 'Well I've seen enough. It is time we were going.'

As he said that we heard a door open and a voice saying, 'You fool, you forgot to lock the door.'

'I did not forget to lock it,' said another.

The gaslight was lit. Holmes seized my arm and pulled me into the shadows.

'Not a sound,' he whispered, and we carefully made our way toward the door. I was not careful enough. My foot struck something which made a noise.

'Who's there? Come out.'

Whoever it was followed up their demand with a shot from a pistol, the bullet from which hit some metal and went buzzing past my head.

We made for the door and then ran as fast as my weak leg would allow.

'There's the cab, Watson. Come on. Come on.'

Further shots came from our pursuers as we tumbled into the cab. The cabman needed no encouragement to whip up his horse and away we went. At the station we left him with two sovereigns and the admonition to say nothing of what had happened.

On our return to Baker Street we studied the note Holmes had made of the words and numbers we had seen.

'The date is obvious, Watson, and the words "gals in" and "grams out" must indicate a process of some type. It could be that so many gallons of liquor produce so many grams of something. Of course, that something is a solid substance, not a liquid, otherwise the board would have referred to a liquid measure. More puzzling is the number six thousand followed by the capital letter K. Is that K for carbon?'

Immediately I realized that the K stood for Kelvin, not for carbon.

'No, Holmes, I remember from something I read recently that K refers not to carbon. I believe it refers to degrees on the recently devised Kelvin scale of temperature. Six thousand is as hot as the sun. I'm sure I am right.'

'Of course you are. That is a most important clue, yet it is an enigma. Such a colossal temperature leaves many questions unanswered. Another singular fact is the large quantity of coal delivered. Far more, I imagine, than needed by the small steam engine.'

Anxious to exercise an idea that had formed in my mind, I suggested to Holmes, 'Could there be a connection, or is it just a coincidence, between your attention to carbon and all the coal that is being used?'

'Brilliant, Watson, brilliant. Of course we have it. Coal is carbon. The temperature of the sun and the application of extreme pressure taken together are what scientists have been trying to use to form artificial diamonds. Igniting the orange liquor provides the required temperature. The extreme pressure is produced by the hydraulic equipment. Diamonds are the answer. Of course, on the face of it, they are just the concern of the world of precious gems. Although I do not pretend to understand fully the intricacies of the market, my understanding is that the cost of diamond mining, the annual output of the mines and the market value of diamonds is of great concern to many. Produce enough of them to the required quality and you make a fortune. That is until you have upset the diamond market to such a degree that the price becomes as low as that of a lump of coal. The diamond world will react quickly to stop the company's scheme once we report on our investigation.'

Although I am not a lawyer, I instantly realized that we had not been authorized by anyone to investigate the manufacture of artificial diamonds.

'You know, Holmes, if we disclose our knowledge about the

diamond-making apparatus we might be accused of illegal entry. To start with, has any law been broken? I doubt that there's one that says "Thou shall not make diamonds". This is a commercial matter in which we have become involved by chance.'

Holmes said nothing for a minute or two while he thought about my assessment of our role in the affair. He then said, 'I intend to place the facts we have gathered into Mycroft's hands. He'll know what to do with them. So do not concern yourself. Mycroft will not divulge the source of the information we are about to send him.'

Holmes was able to provide our client with sufficient evidence to bring an action for nuisance against the owner of the garden laboratory. The case was not defended and we learnt later that the unsightly buildings and, presumably, the apparatus had been removed. It transpired that previously the people devoted to producing artificial diamonds had been conducting their experiments elsewhere and had had to move following complaints similar to those made by Mr Prendergast. Mycroft took over the investigation of the diamond-making factory and nothing more was said or heard about our illegal nocturnal activities.

And that was the end of the affair, or so I assumed.

One morning I was in that conscious, semi-conscious state that we all experience at the end of a night's sleep: we are neither awake nor asleep. Afterwards we are never sure whether we were dreaming or lying in bed experiencing voices and images that seemed very real.

Whatever state of consciousness I was in, it was violently interrupted by a loud bang. For a few seconds I struggled to distinguish between a dream and reality. I leapt out of bed and rushed down into the sitting room. The bang was obviously not a dream. The room was full of smoke. As it began to clear, I became aware that what was usually a not very tidy or orderly room was in a state of complete chaos. The pictures hung askew, the carpet was strewn with glass and pieces of paper. The wallpaper was blotched and scarred. And then I realized that the crumpled heap of dark cloth in the corner was moving. It was groaning.

'Holmes, are you all right? Let me help you up. Now sit down. Let me look.'

He slumped back in his chair. His face was blackened. His

dressing gown was torn and his hands and face were burnt and lacerated. Instinctively, as a doctor I set about tending his wounds. After wiping off the dirt and bits of debris, I was able to assure him that he had not suffered any serious damage.

Meanwhile Mrs Hudson had appeared at the doorway. Her face was the colour of whitewash. 'Do you know what happened?' I asked.

'I've no idea, Doctor Watson. I was about to bring up Mr Holmes' shaving water when there was just a big bang and all the pots rattled.'

To alleviate her shock by keeping her occupied, I asked her to fetch hot water and towels.

After attending to his injuries I was able to assure Mrs Hudson by saying, 'Nothing too serious. A few cuts and light burns. He'll survive. Now help me to get him into his bed.'

After about an hour, Holmes revived sufficiently to tell me that he had been up all night experimenting with the orange liquor. Obviously, it was far more unstable than he had anticipated.

The Gong

In which adherence to a habit led to murder.

As I have often mentioned, many of my accounts of the adventures of Sherlock Holmes start at the breakfast table and the arrival of a letter. However, the case of the gong started in the mid-afternoon when Holmes was looking forward to an evening at a violin concert and my wife Mary and I had been invited to visit some friends.

I was just about to take my leave when Holmes' brother Mycroft entered.

'Hello, Mycroft, what brings you to this part of town?'

'Sherlock, your help is needed in solving the murder of a cabinet minister,' was the somewhat abrupt reply. When he mentioned the name I was shocked. The minister was a well-liked member of the government and was held in esteem by the political world in general.

'I read nothing in the papers this morning about a murder, Mycroft.'

'It happened last evening about six. For a number of reasons those concerned have been told to say little about the event. We are trying to keep it from the newspapers. Now can you take on the case? If so, then it is most imperative that you travel down to the deceased's house in Newton St Botolph this afternoon.'

'I suppose I cannot refuse such an important investigation.'

'Now anticipating your favourable response I have already telegraphed the inspector of police who is in charge of the case at Newton St Botolph to book two rooms at the Station Hotel. Two rooms in the event that you wanted Dr Watson to accompany you.'

'You've a visit to friends arranged for this evening, Watson,' said Holmes.

'It was not a definite appointment. If you want me to join you I shall let Mary know and ask her to convey my apologies,' I replied.

'Good. Now, Mycroft, I anticipate that you have even looked up the times of the trains from Paddington to the west.'

'Indeed I have. It is now 5.30 so you can just pack and make the 6.30. It is due into Newton St Botolph at 8.20. Rather late. Nevertheless, I am sure you will agree that the sooner you are able to examine the scene of the crime the better. I instructed the police to leave the body and everything in the room untouched. You will be met by an Inspector Doswell.'

We sped west as fast as the Great Western could manage. At times Holmes calculated that we were progressing at fifty miles in every hour. I regretted that I had had no time at Paddington to walk forward to find out the class of locomotive. After the affair of the missing van I had begun to take an even greater interest in railways. We arrived at our destination thirty minutes late: I was not surprised because the Great Western was not noted for its adherence to the public timetable. The inspector was waiting for us on the platform. We left our bags with the hall porter at the Station Hotel. After a five-minute walk, we reached the minister's house.

There were many lights on in the palatial mansion. Inspector Doswell led us into a large room with a bay window. A greater part of each wall was lined with glass-fronted bookcases. The minister's desk, in the middle of the room, faced the window. The body was slumped forward across the desk. For a minute or two Holmes stood looking around without saying anything. After a few minutes he then asked the inspector, 'Is this the position in which the body was found and, I trust, none of the things on the desk have been disturbed, including this large potted plant?'

'Nothing moved, sir, other than that plant,' replied the inspector. 'It was moved away by the police surgeon in order to examine the bullet wound to the chest and then replaced back in the position it is now. Everything on the table is as I found it yesterday evening.'

'A long piece of string would be helpful at this stage, Inspector.'

When the string was found, Holmes asked me to raise the victim so that he was sitting upright. I then held one end against the side of the body level with the heart. The other end was stretched out past the desk lamp, whose glass shade had been shattered, until it reached the side of a narrow door that interrupted the line of the bookcases.

'I think you will agree, Inspector, that the murderer's gun was fired from some point along this string or through the opening of this door. The door is now shut. Was it open when the minister's body was first found?'

'I'm not sure about that, Mr Holmes.'

'Who came into the room immediately after the shot was heard? That is, I assume it was heard.'

'Mr Waterstone, the minister's secretary, discovered the body. He was in the next room and as the door in between was open he could not fail to hear the noise of the gun being fired. He told me that he sprang up and rushed into this room. However, I didn't ask him about the narrow door between the bookcases.'

Holmes went to the small door and pulled it open. 'I see that this leads to the conservatory and is most likely the way the murderer came, and there is another door leading out into the garden.'

We went into the conservatory. It was narrow and had benches on each side on which stood large exotic plants in pots. Against the doorpost was a large lily to which Holmes paid particular attention.

We returned to the hotel around midnight. My sleep was frequently interrupted by the sounds of trains rushing through the station and by a locomotive that sounded as if it was having a fearsome battle with some goods wagons.

In the morning I joined Holmes in the dining room for breakfast.

I ventured to ask, 'Did you sleep well?'

'Excellent night's sleep. How was yours? No, don't tell me. From your pallid look I see that the activities of the railway conflicted with your repose.'

After breakfast we talked to the minister's secretary.

'How long have you been with the minister?' was Holmes' opening question.

'Just over three years.'

'In that time were you aware of any particular trouble?'

'I don't understand.'

'Was the minister afraid of anyone? I mean of course in the

physical sense rather than the political.'

'As far as I knew, none. Of course he had a number of vocal opponents in the House, but then away from the debates they were among his circle of friends.'

'Now, the minister's daughter, could she help us?'

At that question I became aware of a change in the secretary's demeanour.

'Obviously, my wife is very distraught and I would rather not have her questioned.'

'Oh! So you married his daughter. When was that?'

'A year ago. At first he was very much against a marriage. Not just to me but to anyone.'

'Why was that?'

'Arthur Hastings, my predecessor, had compromised Isabella. It was very embarrassing and I would rather not discuss the matter in any detail.'

'So presumably he was dismissed for making unwanted advances to the lady who is now your wife?'

'Well, not just for that. I understand he was involved in dealings in the City of which her father did not approve. When I fell in love with Isabella we realized that events had made him averse to any man wanting her hand so we had to bide our time.'

'Do you know what happened to Arthur Hastings?'

'I regret I cannot help you. I was told that he left without saying where he was going.'

At that moment a number of striking clocks began to chime the hour. As many of us do out of habit, Holmes took out his half-hunter, glanced at it, and replaced it in his pocket. Then he took it out again, looked at the clock on the mantelshelf and frowned.

'Mr Waterstone, can you recall any unusual happenings up to the time of the tragic event?' asked Holmes.

'Well, it was a typical day. There were only two visitors in the morning and none in the afternoon. That is, until someone unexpectedly forced his way into my office followed by the parlour maid, whose protestations he had obviously ignored. He insisted on seeing the minister. I told him that no one could be seen without an appointment. At that he became abusive. His raised voice caused my father-in-law to come to the door. When he saw the man he said,

"That's all right, Simon, I will see this gentleman". They went in and although the door was shut, I could hear that they both sounded very angry. I was unable to make out what they were arguing about. After about ten minutes the visitor stormed out of the room and before I could escort him to the front door, he had gone.'

'Now, approximately what time was it when he left?'

'About 5.30.'

'Now, this is very important: can you say when the shot was fired?'

'Precisely at six.'

'Precisely can sometimes mean about. Are you certain it was six?'

'The dressing gong had just stopped sounding as I heard the gun being fired.'

'And is the gong always sounded at six precisely?'

'Always. The maid has strict instructions to be punctual. In fact, I now recall that just before I had looked at my watch in anticipation that the time was close to six.'

'Now, Mr Waterstone, when I examined the door to the conservatory from the study, I noted that it could be locked. Was it always kept locked?'

'Always at night, as was the study door. The minister kept the keys with him at night.'

'The inspector was not certain whether or not the door to the conservatory was open when he first entered the room. Yet you were there before him. What did you see? Was the door open?'

'I am sorry, I cannot remember. However, I can tell you that sometimes the door would be left open when the minister was writing his book on exotic plants. You see, it is, I mean was, his relaxation from the affairs of state. He had become a well-known authority on the subject.'

'Then the presence of the plant on the desk suggests that he was studying it and making notes. The door may have been open because he needed to make frequent visits to the conservatory. Would you agree, Watson?'

'Yes, I agree with your reconstruction of the events,' I replied.

After our visit to the scene of the murder we went to the police station. During a review of the case with the inspector, we were interrupted and told that the minister's secretary had observed someone who resembled the mysterious visitor. Apparently, after we had left the house, Waterstone had to go to the railway station in order to send off a great number of telegrams relating to the death of his father-in-law. As he was passing a coffee-room window, he saw the man. He immediately came round to the police station. The inspector lost no time in going out and arresting the man on suspicion of having murdered the minister.

When the suspect was being interrogated, Holmes and I were able to listen to what was being said without being observed.

'Now, Mr Langham, where were you yesterday evening at 6 p.m.?' was the inspector's first question.

'Let me think. Ah, of course, I was at the station sending off a telegram.'

'Can you be sure of the time?'

'Very sure. In fact, let me see.' He fumbled in the pockets of his Ulster overcoat and produced a copy of a telegraph form. 'Look at this. As you can see, the time entered by the clerk is one minute to six.'

The suspect was taken away.

'I cannot hold him for long without more positive evidence. That telegram is a very good alibi, don't you agree, Mr Holmes?' said the inspector.

'In many ways it is. May I have a look at the telegraph form?'

He read the telegram and said, 'It's addressed to someone called Battle at the Crown Hotel, Reading and reads, "CANNOT PERSUADE HIM. MUST FIND IT. BE HERE AT ONCE. LANGHAM." '

'Well,' I commented, 'like most telegrams it is very brief and therefore cryptic. Do you make anything of it, Holmes?'

'At this moment, very little.' Turning to the inspector he said, 'If you are going to release Langham we must observe his movements. As the telegram indicates, he intends to stay here and await a Mr Battle.'

'Yes, I'll let him go. But if you follow him, is there not a danger that he will recognise you? After all, Mr Holmes, you are the most famous detective in the kingdom.'

I sensed Holmes' satisfaction at the inspector's remark. He replied, 'Don't worry, Inspector, even if he should have seen me before, I shall make sure he will be looking at someone else. If you would just hold him for one more hour it will give me time in which to make preparations for the next stage of the case.'

We returned to our hotel and forty minutes later a portly member of the racing world emerged and could be seen in the vicinity of the police station. My part in the plan was to shadow our man at a discreet distance in the event that he made a sudden and unexpected move. Langham came out of the police station and walked along until he came to an inn. He went in and the 'racing' gentleman followed. I waited outside.

Back in the hotel, Holmes gave me an account of what he had overheard.

'I managed to secure a seat against a glass screen on the other side of which sat Langham and a bearded companion, who I assumed was the Battle mentioned in the telegram. I distinctly heard Langham say, "You'll have to come with me tonight. I can't look through the lot alone. Have you brought along the conservatory key?" '

'Obviously, the mention of the key is most significant. It indicates that tonight they intend to enter the minister's house by way of the conservatory.'

'Indeed, Watson, that is certain. I've informed Inspector Doswell and he agrees to let them get into the study so that they will not only be caught in the act, it will possibly show that it is not just an ordinary burglary. He will wait with us in the study. There is something in that room which is so important that it has persuaded Langham to stay here and not abscond before more evidence could be gathered on which to re-arrest him. By the way, I trust you brought your revolver? Langham gives the impression of being a desperate man who will not stop at violence.'

That night, accompanied by the inspector, we secreted ourselves behind the heavy curtains of the study. It was a long vigil. At three in the morning we heard a sound in the conservatory and as the door opened the glow of a lantern illuminated part of the room. As planned, we made no move. Langham and another man entered. The latter opened the glass door of one of the cases and began to take down the books. He opened some and shook them; however, nothing fell out. Apparently he could not find what he was seeking.

His gaze then became concentrated on one particular row of books. Suddenly he reached up and, with a muffled exclamation of triumph, took down a book and out fell a document. Before he could bend to pick it up, Holmes was on him and knocked him to the floor. The inspector seized Langham. I covered both intruders with my revolver. At the same time the study door was unlocked by Waterstone, who had been waiting on the other side with two constables.

On our return to Baker Street, I started to make some notes concerning the case.

'You seemed to be very certain, Holmes, of the guilt of Langham.'

'Indeed, I was convinced from the start that it was he. Although he appeared to have an alibi, I was able to destroy it. The deceased insisted that all the clocks in the house be kept to local time, which I realized when they struck the hour during our visit yesterday. The murderer established his alibi, either deliberately or by chance, when he sent off the telegraph at the station, whose clocks were set to railway time; that is, Greenwich time. We are about ten minutes in time west of Greenwich. In that interval he was able to stride, possibly run, to the house, enter through the conservatory and shoot the minister.'

'Are you satisfied, Holmes, that the evidence about the time will be sufficient to condemn him? I fear a clever advocate will argue to the contrary.'

'Yes, that is a possibility, yet I am certain that, at the time of the crime, he was wearing the Ulster overcoat we saw he had on when he was being questioned. You see, I noted that close against the door leading into the study was a large exotic species of lily. In the police station I observed that the left arm and shoulder of his coat was stained yellow by the pollen. That is where he brushed against the plant as he fired the gun. However, of even greater importance is the fact that the murderer had to be left-handed, otherwise he would not have been able to get a clear shot round the half-opened door. And our man, as I observed, is left-handed. You will remember I stretched a length of string from the body to the door. The shattered lampshade established the angle of the shot and the position of the gun when it was fired.'

'Why do you say the door was only half-open?'

'I am not certain about that. Of course, it is possible that Langham had not the courage to face his victim or get too close.'

'Now what about Battle?'

'I must be getting old, Watson. It took me some time before I realized that we were faced with both a beard and a pun. The beard disguised Arthur Hastings.'

'And the pun?'

'Oh, come on, my dear fellow, Hastings and the battle of 1066. Battle, that is Hastings. During his time as secretary he had obtained a duplicate key for the study so that he could enter during the night and copy cabinet papers. The information was passed to Langham and used to their advantage in the financial markets. After his argument with the minister, Langham decided that some incriminating papers would have to be seized by force. He relied on Hastings' information concerning the minister's habit of studying his plants between five and six in the evening and therefore the door from the conservatory would not be locked.'

'Another matter that raises a question, Holmes, is why did you quickly secret the papers that had been taken by the murderer from the bookcase?'

'Because, although I was only able to read the first page during the confusion of arresting the men, I instantly realized that I was holding a confession written by the minister, followed by a list of prominent people. It also implicated Langham and Hastings. I knew instantly that the next, and possibly the only person, allowed to read those papers had to be Mycroft. The minister had become involved with a number of international financial criminals. Recently it seems he regretted his involvement and had decided to confess. On that afternoon he must have told Langham that he intended to expose them even though he would have to resign from the government. Langham hoped that by killing him and destroying the confession he and the others would escape prosecution. Apparently, the minister preferred to keep his most confidential papers inside a book rather than in a safe. During his time as secretary, Hastings must have observed him secreting papers. Therefore he and Langham had deduced that the first place to look for the incriminating documents would be the bookcase and not the safe.'

Holmes' summary of evidence was handed to the police, and the inspector in charge of the case eventually received a commendation for the way he had tracked down the murderer.

Despite the fact that a minister of the crown had been murdered and that a number of prominent people had been involved with him in illegal affairs, Holmes declined, as was his custom, any public recognition of his part in solving the murder.

Notes

The Great Western Railway had adopted 'London Time', that is, Greenwich time, when it opened in 1841. The Definition of Time Act of 1880 required all railways to set their clocks to GMT.

The 'City' refers to the City of London, which was a separate administration from the City of Westminster, both being the principal elements of London. When discussing financial affairs, the abbreviation 'the City' meant the Bank of England, the Stock Exchange and all the other major financial houses in the 'Square Mile'.

The Tenth Jar

In which stolen jars of marmalade threaten a political scandal and danger to Holmes and Watson.

Part One

For a few days I had observed the gradual onset of a state of lethargy affecting the demeanour of my friend Sherlock Holmes. His recourse to narcotics and the fearsome tobacco he smoked in an old clay pipe tended at times to set him apart from others.

As I came down to breakfast one morning I observed that he was no longer under the influence of a narcotic. He was once again the familiar Sherlock Holmes. His first words were, 'I say, Watson, have you read about the spate of burglaries in St John's Wood?'

'What's that you say?' I replied. 'Something about St John's Wood?'

'Yes, these reports in the papers tell us that in the past few days nine houses have been forcibly entered at night and the contents of their pantries disturbed. Scotland Yard admits to being baffled.' He paused. 'Listen, that's a four-wheeler in a hurry. Ah, it has stopped outside. And, if I am not mistaken, we are about to be visited by Inspector Lestrade.'

'Mr Holmes, Dr Watson, good morning,' said the inspector on entering.

'Good morning, Inspector,' said Holmes. 'Does the minute spot of egg on your waistcoat indicate that you've had a hurried breakfast.'

'Indeed, Mr Holmes, but I've little time for such matters when there are more pressing things on my mind.'

'No doubt you are concerned about the burglaries in St John's Wood.'

'You amaze me, sir. How on earth could you know that?'

'A very simple deduction, my dear Inspector. It is reported in *The Times* and the other papers this morning.'

'I spent most of last night questioning the servants of the last two houses that had been broken into.'

'A singular case indeed,' commented Holmes as he lit his pipe. He slumped in his chair, holding the bowl of his pipe with both hands and obviously marshalling the facts in his brain. We both knew, from experience, that the great detective's thoughts must not be interrupted. Lestrade declined my offer of a second, more leisurely, breakfast of kippers. I could tell that such a dish in combination with the clouds of pungent tobacco smoke was not to his liking. At last Holmes spoke.

'Lestrade, tell me what you gathered from the servants.'

'Unfortunately, they were not able to help very much. In some cases the jars and pots and tins on the shelves had been scattered about. In others, apart from a few signs of someone having entered the pantry, the contents appeared to be in their usual places.'

'Now tell me, can you be certain whether any items in any of the pantries had been removed?'

'I did question the butlers, cooks and kitchen maids and most were reasonably certain that a jar or jars had been stolen.'

'And then did you ascertain what type of jar or jars and what the contents were?'

'Well, no. Does it matter?'

'Of course it matters, Lestrade. A thief is not going to go to all the trouble and danger of being caught if there is not some motive. A motive that made his discrimination among the many and varied contents of each pantry to be of the utmost importance.'

'I confess that I am baffled,' responded Lestrade. 'Burglars operating in St John's Wood are usually after jewellery not victuals. Perhaps you might come with me and examine some of the premises?'

'Oh, surely this case is well within the compass of your abilities. After all it is only a matter of a few provisions. I regret that I am very busy at the present.'

'Mr Holmes, please, I am under great pressure from some of the most noble names in the land. It has been suggested to me that the Queen takes a personal interest, particularly as many of her most trusted ministers live north of Regent's Park.'

'Well, under the circumstances then I will help. You well know that I am always willing to help the official police in any way I can. Come, Watson, the game's afoot.'

We each kept to our own thoughts as a four-wheeler took us north along Baker Street. Soon we were in avenues lined with stately homes, each with its surrounding garden and most with a high wall as a boundary. As expected, the first house we visited belonged to a minister of the crown. The family were away so we were escorted by the butler. Holmes scrutinized the pantry carefully. Mr Pompuoce, the butler, seemed reluctant to talk about the contents. The cook was also unhelpful and one of the maids was obviously in distress. A livid wheal marked her cheek. Holmes appeared not to notice. However, I expressed my concern and said, 'I'm a doctor. That mark needs attending to. How did it happen?' At that the girl looked at the butler and from the expression on his face I surmised that she had to keep silent. I made a cursory appraisal of the girl's face and decided that it was only a minor injury.

To my mind the examination of the pantry shelves and their contents seemed to reveal nothing of importance. We then went out into the grounds of the house. Holmes examined very carefully the place where, obviously, the burglar had climbed over the wall. We then went out into the avenue and studied the other side of the wall. Holmes paid particular attention to the grass between the bottom of the wall and the pavement. He even went down on all fours. We were used to such behaviour and waited patiently. Suddenly he started to sniff the ground and then, taking of his glove, he felt something.

'Most unusual.'

'You have a clue?' I asked.

'Perhaps it is one, Watson. However, it is too early to be certain. I've seen enough here so let us go to the next house on your list, Inspector.'

As we walked to the next property that had been burgled and

were discussing the peculiar circumstances of the case, I remembered the injured servant girl.

'You know, Holmes, I forgot to mention that when I looked at the injury to that young girl's face, she whispered the word "marmalade". Why should she have said just that one word?'

'Oh, oh, did she? You nearly forgot to tell me about something that could be a most important clue.'

We went through the same procedure at the other houses. We questioned the servants, examined the pantry, and made a very thorough examination of the grounds where Holmes sniffed and felt the places where the burglar had passed through the garden.

Back at Baker Street, after leaving the inspector, we were met at the front door by Mrs Hudson saying, 'Mr Holmes, there's a lady and her maid waiting for you. She was most insistent that I should admit her and would wait for your return. She would not give me her name.'

On entering the famous room in which so many baffling cases had been solved with the help of very strong tobacco, we found a tall, veiled women sitting upright on one of the dining chairs. There was another woman standing to one side and holding a large bag. Holmes was all attention. As was his practice, his sharp eyes took in every possible detail of the woman's manner and her dress. The first thing I noticed, as I tried to emulate my friend, was that unlike most clients, even women, this one did not immediately rise and adopt a stance that left little doubt that they were desperate for help. The lady's demeanour indicated that she was not accustomed to rising in order to greet someone.

'Mr Holmes, I have come to you for help with a very delicate and most confidential matter. Before I speak of it, may we be alone?' She spoke in a calm and clear voice, a voice that by its very intonation commanded attention.

'Madam, Doctor Watson is not only a most reliable and trusted confidant, he is often a most essential part of my investigations. This interview shall not continue unless he is present.'

Inwardly I was most surprised and flattered to be spoken of in such terms. Rarely was my help acknowledged in the presence of others. A stately nod authorized my presence.

'Will you remove your veil? I find it hinders an exchange of thoughts.'

'Mr Holmes, as I have said, this is a very delicate matter on which I need to consult you. It concerns an object, not my person. I need to put it to you as a hypothetical situation.' She did not remove her veil.

'Indeed, your Grace,' was Holmes' response.

'How could you. . . ?' For a second she lost her dignified manner.

'Your coachman failed to cover your family crest on the door panel of your coach waiting at the end of the street. I could not help observing it as we walked past.'

'I have been advised of your powers of observation, Mr Holmes. They are indeed remarkable.'

She then removed her veil. I watched Holmes studying the noble face and inwardly I thought about how such beauty had survived generation after generation, ever since Charles II had favoured her common ancestor.

'Not only must I trust you both to keep what I have to tell you within these four walls, above all, no word must reach the duke. His position is already under attack both from within the party and from the opposition in both houses. I cannot bear to think what it might do to him. He has a very delicate constitution.'

'Your Grace's secret, whatever it is, is safe with Doctor Watson and I. Please tell me what troubles you. And, please, I must ask that you tell me everything concerning the matter. Keep nothing back.'

Her reply came as a great surprise to both of us. 'My burden is the loss of the Rainbow diamond.'

'That is indeed a loss,' said Holmes. 'Yet, how strange, for nothing has been reported in the newspapers or from my many contacts in the world of major criminals. So, when was it taken, or perhaps was it just mislaid?'

'Three weeks ago. It was not mislaid. The diamond was taken by one of the servants.'

'How was it taken?'

'Foolishly, I had left it on the table in my sitting room when I went to fetch my tiara from the adjacent dressing room. When I came back I was surprised to see Sykes, one of the footmen, moving out onto the landing. It was then that I saw the diamond had gone.'

'So he of the appropriate name is the suspect?'

'Yes, without doubt, particularly as he rushed from the room. Fortunately he was apprehended by Dudgson the butler, who demanded why he was not at his proper place in the house. Sykes then broke free and sped down the servants' stairs. Dudgson and I followed. The door to the preserves room was slammed in our faces and we heard him trying to open the outer door. When the butler got to him he feigned innocence, saying he meant no harm. I ordered him to be searched. This was done; however nothing incriminating was found on his person.'

'You say nothing was found on Sykes.'

'Nothing, Mr Holmes. We locked him in and I ordered Dudgson to say nothing of what had happened. Inspector Maigrett of the Dorset police was summoned. When I told him that the great diamond had been taken and that I had sent a telegram to my brother the Home Secretary, he agreed with me that Sykes was to have no discourse with others. My brother came down to Tarrant Parva and threatened the local inspector of police with dire consequences were he to divulge any of the facts to others, even to his own officers. That is why you have not heard about this dreadful loss until now. The inspector has worked alone until, when it was realized that he was making no progress, my brother suggested that I seek your help.'

'Where is Sykes now?'

'He was taken to an undisclosed location by agents of my brother.'

During this statement of facts by the duchess, I listened intently to every word. I did not want Holmes chiding me later over some important aspect of the crime that I may have missed. There was silence in the room. Outside the people in Baker Street were unaware of the story which was unfolding in their midst.

Holmes stood up, looked out of the window for a moment and then, turning, said, 'Duchess, I can fully appreciate your concern. As I understand, the Rainbow is not only unique among diamonds, it is the subject of much dispute between the government and that of another country. Its loss, obviously, is not just a matter of its monetary value, some tens of thousands. Its disappearance might even lead to war.'

'You are indeed correct. It must be found, and found before the duke and others in the cabinet, as well as certain foreign agents, learn of the loss. Above all, it must be returned for the sake of political stability both at home and abroad.'

'We will go down to Tarrant Parva tomorrow, if that is convenient, your Grace. Doctor Watson and I will appear as authors of a book on architecture. This will have the object of allowing us to conduct a minute search of your great house and grounds without disclosing the nature of our presence. I presume, as Parliament is sitting, the duke will be staying at your town house?'

'Correct, Mr Holmes. I shall expect you sometime tomorrow. Good day to you.' She swept out of the room as only a duchess could.

When the two women had left, Holmes said, 'Watson, I presume you will be able to come with me.'

'Yes, I am certain I can.'

'Good, then please will you look up the time of a morning train to Wimborne, the nearest town to Tarrant Parva.'

After some minutes of leafing back and forth through Bradshaw, I exclaimed, 'There are no trains from Paddington.'

'Watson, your knowledge of our railways has considerably improved but surely Wimborne is on the South Western and therefore look under Waterloo not Paddington. I trust you are being more careful in those scribblings of yours about my investigations when mentioning the termini of London.'

I replied, 'Yes, of course it is. I must have forgotten.'

This was one of those rare occasions when I was repelled by Holmes' egotism, when he criticized my attempts to record his cases. He sometimes charged me with including too much colour and life into my writing. He wanted me to concentrate on the logic rather than just on the sensational aspects of the crimes. I was, apparently, guilty of turning his intellectual analysis of crimes into a series of popular tales.

Part Two

The next morning we were seated in a first-class compartment of a South Western express. As usual, Holmes applied his mental faculties to determining our speed by counting the number of telegraph poles passed in a minute, or the number of rail joints clicked over each minute.

We then started to discuss the wider aspects of the Rainbow diamond affair and I ventured to comment, 'I suppose our culprit's other name was Bill.'

'My dear fellow, I have never associated you with humour, even of the most banal kind.'

After changing trains at Bournemouth West, we reached Wimborne, where we refreshed ourselves in the Railway Hotel.

'Watson, I always find it of benefit when starting an investigation to listen to the local gossip.'

After the ten minutes or so it took to eat bread and cheese and drink ale, I asked Holmes if he had gathered anything useful from the gabble of voices around them.

'No, nothing of interest, other than it is amazing how often one comes across yet another English dialect. Well, it is time we were on our way to visit the duchess at Tarrant Parva.'

Outside the hotel we found a four-wheeler waiting.

'Watson, note the remarkably large driver and a singularly small horse.' Then to the coachman he said, 'Tarrant Parva, if you please.'

The coachman raised his whip in acknowledgement. We climbed in and away we went.

'You know, Holmes, I seem to have spent a lifetime riding with you in decrepit vehicles along mired roads, under leaded skies, toward stately homes set in the back of beyond. Why can't you confine your cases to London?'

Holmes did not respond. After ten minutes he remarked, 'The last signpost pointed toward Tarrant Magna, yet since then we have passed only two tumbledown cottages.'

At the next crossroads the cab turned in the direction of the sign to Tarrant Bottom and then stopped. The cabman muttered behind the thick scarf wound round his head that we would have to walk for a while. We trudged up a hill. The poor horse wheezed alongside us. At the top, where we got back into the coach, I was not surprised to find a sign pointing down the hill to Upper Tarrant.

Further on, the cab stopped again. The horse had obviously decided it needed to regain its strength. When, after five minutes, there was no movement, Holmes knocked on the roof and shouted, 'Come on, we need to get to Tarrant Parva, not sit in a lane.'

There was no reply from the cabman.

'What is he up to?' said Holmes.

We got out to find that our cabman had disappeared. Further down the narrow lane in which we were stopped was another cab.

'You know, Holmes, there seems to be something very strange going on. What is that cab doing there? I can see no driver.'

'Look out, Watson!' shouted Holmes and immediately I found myself amid a whirl of arms, legs and fists. A heavy stick just missed my shoulder and crashed against the side of the cab. For what seemed an eternity, we had to fight off two ruffians who were intent on doing us severe harm. Despite my weak leg I managed to contribute a few well-aimed blows to add to those being skilfully applied by Holmes, using his fist and stick. By chance one of our attackers swung his cudgel in an attempt to strike down Holmes. Fortunately his companion got in the way of the blow and became hors de combat. His companion abandoned the fight and fled.

We dragged the senseless villain into a hedge and left him. With Holmes on the seat box we continued our journey. Eventually we came to a long, ancient, high brick wall. A mile further on we reached the lodge at the beginning of the long drive stretching in the distance toward Tarrant Parva. Leaving the cab with the gatekeeper, we continued on foot.

As we walked, we discussed the attempt to interrupt our journey.

'Why should anyone want to attack us?'

'I can only surmise, Watson, that they were either gypsies or tinkers intent on robbery or there was a more sinister reason. There are also other facts that could be related to the attack made on us. I may have dwelled in the great metropolis for most of my time but there are nearly as many trees there as in the country. The simplest of compasses is provided by the fact that lichen survives only on the north side of a tree trunk. That driver has taken us north, south, east and west. Why? Could he have been lost?'

'Surely not! He was, I presume, a local man familiar with the roads in these parts. You have told me about lichen many times, Holmes. I admit I was not aware of any particular direction in which we were going, although I am certain we had passed through the same village twice.'

'Furthermore, Watson, why would another cab, seemingly unattended, be standing in the lane where we were attacked? I will have to investigate the day's events more thoroughly. Perhaps there is even a story in all this for you to add to your collection of adventures and mysteries?'

As we came close to the ancient house, I noted in particular the addition of the modern red brick wing with attached, walled kitchen garden. We were received by the duchess in her sitting room on the first floor. There we were shown the small safe in which the famous diamond had been kept. She recounted how it had been on the small table, ready to be hooked in its setting securely onto the front of her tiara.

'Your Grace, why is the Rainbow a separate piece on your tiara?' asked Holmes.

'A good question. You see, it is only worn on the tiara when dining formally. On other occasions, such as state functions, when others are not close to me, it is replaced by a replica of cut glass. This reduces the chances of it being lost. My tiara might even be snatched away.'

Holmes studied the door to the room and then the passageway outside. Leading down from the passage were the stairs used by the servants. We went down to the room in which Sykes had been held. There was a large heated copper vat and the shelves were lined with small jars. The air was heavy with the aroma of boiled sugar and oranges. A door led out into the kitchen garden. Holmes drew my attention to a white apron on the front of which was the ducal crest. There were others but they were not emblazoned.

'I have seen enough, thank you, your Grace. I shall keep you informed.'

With that we took our leave.

As the late-evening train took us up to London, Holmes appeared to take no more interest in our visit other than to remark about the number of books in the duchess's sitting room on the subject of fruit, along with the latest edition of Mrs Beeton.

'Why a book on cookery, Holmes? Surely someone in her position does not need to be concerned with how a dish is prepared?'

'I had the same thought. By the way, have you started on writing up the case of that remarkable submersible machine? I wonder if Jules Verne was more prophetic than we have given him credit for in the past?'

'No, I have yet to find the time. By the way, Holmes, on the subject of writing and books, have you considered writing one on your investigatory methods? You have prepared a number of monographs on different subjects. Surely they could form the basis of a work which could be an inestimable guide for the official police? Consider the popularity of Mrs Beeton's *Household Management*. Your book could be the equivalent in the world of crime.'

'My dear fellow, are you equating my methods with those of managing a household and preparing food.'

'Well, only indirectly.'

'Yes, if I had the time I might write such a book. However, there is one caveat, which is the possibility that it might provide the criminal fraternity with ways of avoiding detection.'

My proposal and other comments and questions passed the time. The train stopped at Basingstoke and a man entered our compartment. I could not avoid noticing that Holmes, as usual, made an appraisal of the stranger's dress, manner and small leather case. After a number of unadvertised stops, we reached Waterloo. For every ten arriving travellers, there seemed to be only one cab.

'Shall we walk across the bridge, Watson? I need to stretch my legs. We can hail a hansom in the Strand.'

My weak leg and I reluctantly agreed.

As a hansom took us toward Baker Street, Holmes put the inevitable question.

'I trust you observed the gentleman who joined us at Basingstoke?'

'I didn't take much interest in him. As it is your custom, I am sure you did and now you are going to tell me all about the stranger.'

'He provided a fairly easy exercise in deduction. Firstly, there was a length of narrow pink tape protruding from his small case. That suggested a lawyer. Secondly, he did not have a drawstring cloth bag of the type in which advocates stow their wig and gown and therefore he was not a barrister, and so must have been a solicitor. Thirdly, he had, most likely, come from the Winchester Assizes at which there is at present a protracted trial for murder. As it was five o'clock and he was going up to town then he was on his way to attend an urgent evening meeting in chambers. Furthermore, you see—'

I interrupted him. 'If you say so. Then it must be.'

I could see that Holmes was somewhat taken aback by the petulant tone of my response.

'Your immediate trouble, Watson, is *The Mikado*. Every time the train was delayed for some reason or other I observed the agitated tapping of your foot and your compressed lips. You were concerned lest the train were further delayed and you would not be in time for the theatre.'

'Yes, that is so. How did you know?'

'Very simple, my dear fellow. Before we left this morning I could not help noticing our housekeeper laying out your dress clothes and your opera hat.'

I replied, 'You are most correct. Nevertheless, how did you know I was going to see *The Mikado*?'

'Simple, dear Watson. You have left *The Spectator* open for a week at the page on which was printed a full review.'

The next visit was to the Home Secretary.

'My Lord, I understand,' said Holmes, 'that for reasons of government confidentiality, only the butler at Tarrant Parva and the police inspector at Wimborne know about the missing jewel.'

'That is correct, Mr Holmes. This dreadful affair has to be kept most secret and I can assure you that my sister and I will be most grateful if you can lead us to the diamond.'

'Sir, there is also the matter of the burglaries in St John's Wood involving the town houses of most of the ministers of the crown. Inspector Lestrade has requested me to become involved with his investigations.'

'So I understand. However, your help must not stand in the way of the recovery of the diamond. That must be paramount.'

'It could be that there is a connection between the two.'

'Come, come, Mr Holmes. How could there be? The St John's Wood pantry burglaries are important only because they happen to involve the town houses of high officials of the government; otherwise they are more of a nuisance. Admittedly, I have been placed under pressure to do something and that is why I gave Inspector Lestrade unlimited powers to clear up the cases, and thereby stop the cynical and scurrilous comments in the press.'

The next day was what I term a 'chemical day'. That is one during which Holmes busies himself with retorts and other apparatus on the long table at the back of the sitting room. Mrs Hudson had long ago abandoned the table's once highly polished surface to the ravages of the noxious chemicals with which Holmes experimented. Unable to suffer the fumes any longer, I went for a walk in Regent's Park. On my return I found the chemical experiments abandoned and Holmes was deep in thought as he reclined in his favourite chair. The chemical fumes were now replaced by those from his pipe. His opening remark revived the Rainbow stone affair.

'The reluctance of many of the cooks and others to divulge the contents of their pantries suggests a visit to the high-class grocers that serve the area.'

When we arrived in St John's Wood, we enquired at each of the grocers whether there was anything unusual among the regular deliveries they made. One of the grocers provided a clue.

'Now you mention it, sir, there are them jars like what I've got to deliver every month.'

'May I see one,' asked Holmes.

' 'Fraid not, sir, they've all been and gone out two weeks or so back.'

'To whom did you send them?'

The grocer leafed through his delivery book and took out a sheet of foolscap.

'Here's the list for this month.'

At the sight of the now familiar ducal crest at the head of the list, Holmes exclaimed, 'A light at the end of the tunnel! A cause yet not a reason. This is interesting. Look, Watson, one name has been crossed off from the list of ten.'

'Surely a grocer's delivery list is of little consequence?' I commented as we drove back to Baker Street.

'Of greater consequence than you might imagine,' was the reply.

Lestrade was awaiting our return and was somewhat surprised to be told that he need not expect any more pantry burglaries in St John's Wood.

'Now, now, Mr Holmes, even though I respect your powers of detection and deduction, I cannot believe you can be certain that our man has suddenly repented of his criminal ways.'

'He may not have repented even if he has, indeed, completed the task he was set. A task that I suspect has been ordered by that master of crime, our old friend Professor Moriarty. As we speak he and his minions have spirited away the stolen jars to some lair where the contents can be searched.'

We were all attention on hearing the great detective's conclusion.

'You mean the jars stolen in St John's Wood?'

'Yes, Inspector, jars of preserve or, rather, marmalade.'

Through his network of street urchins and others, Holmes was usually able to trace the movements of criminals as they moved about the Great Wen. Accompanied by some of the larger members of the constabulary, Holmes, Lestrade and myself burst into a filthy lair, in a filthy rickety house, on the edge of the river in a noisome part of the capital. In the dim light we could just discern the figure of a big, tall man with his back to the window. In front of him on a table were some white stone jars and the discarded oiled paper seals each with its Tarrant Parva crest.

'Moriarty, if I am not mistaken. We've caught you with your sticky fingers in an even sticker mess. Seize him, Constables,' shouted Holmes.

Before any of us could get round the table, Moriarty appeared to vanish. One second he was there, the next he had, with surprising agility for such a massive body, gained the open window. There was the sound of a splash and squelching of mud and he was gone.

'I trust you and your men are fond of marmalade, Lestrade, because what I am seeking may be in one of those jars.'

'What are we looking for, Mr Holmes?'

'Something about the size of a sparrow's egg. Now, let me see, how many jars are there? Ah, yes, there are only nine.'

Nothing was found. At the nearest telegraph office, Holmes sent a simple message to Tarrant Parva. It read: 'Look in the tenth jar.'

The duchess got her diamond back. The duke heard nothing of the affair. Lestrade remained unaware of how close he had been to affairs of state. The inspector at Wimborne trembled every time a letter came from the Home Secretary. He hardly dare speak to anyone lest he inadvertently divulged the secret of Tarrant Parva.

Holmes settled back and proceeded to summarize the steps that led to the recovery of the Rainbow diamond. As was his custom when summarizing a case, his fingertips touched together under his chin. Each point in the case was emphasized by the parting of his hands.

'Every month the duchess sent a jar of her very special marmalade to each member of the Cabinet. Sometimes a member would not be listed because this was a sign of her disapproval of his actions or lack of action. You see, the key to the mystery was the relationship between the dates of what might have seemed to be unrelated events. Now it is important to realize that the precious jewel was removed on the first day of the month. On the third day the grocer distributed the jars in accordance with the duchess's list. On the fourth day the pantry burglaries started. Nine days later occurred the last of the attempts to secure one of the jars. A minor clue was the grocer's distribution list on which I observed that one name of the ten had been crossed out. Recourse to an earlier copy of *The Times* revealed that a member of the government had resigned a month before. Therefore, the grocer had been sent only nine jars for the month.

'When Sykes was confronted and cornered in the preserves room he managed to thrust the diamond into one of the open jars of marmalade. These were being allowed to cool before being sealed.

The next day the girls responsible for securing the jars, packing them in a wicker basket and despatching them to the station carried out their tasks unaware that one of the jars might have held such a valuable jewel. You will recall, no doubt, the size and the noncommittal manner of the coachman at Tarrant Parva. That was Moriarty. I suspected from the beginning that he would be the instigator of the robbery. His plan had gone awry because, presumably, he had intended that Sykes, his accomplice, would have been undetected and been able to hand over the diamond. And, of course the vicious attack made upon us may have been instigated by Moriarty. Although for the time being I cannot think what his real intention was, other than to injure us.

'Moriarty somehow may have gained access to Sykes before the latter was removed to London. Or he was outside looking in through the window and saw the diamond being secreted in one of the jars. He was unable to intercept the basket of jars because both the carter and the railway officials were extremely vigilant. Any mishap to the basket would bring down the wrath of Tarrant Parva on their heads. Eventually he traced the destination of the precious cargo. However, it was too late: the grocer had distributed the jars.'

I interrupted the story: 'Holmes, there is something missing in your reconstruction of events. Surely the diamond could have been discovered at any time after the third day when the marmalade was being taken from the jar at a breakfast table in one of the houses?'

'A good point, Watson. I am pleased that you have followed my reasoning so attentively. The answer lies with the relationship between the duchess and the Cabinet. You will recall that in her sitting room there were many books on fruit growing and preserving, and an open copy of Beeton's book on household management and cookery. However, I suggest you failed to notice also that there were as many on law and on our unwritten constitution. The duchess has long been known as the "power behind the duke". Were it not for the equivalent of the Salic Law in our political world, she might even have become First Lord of the Treasury. She indicated her approval or disapproval of decisions taken by a member of the Cabinet by the sending or withholding of a jar of her homemade marmalade. Each month the arrival of the stone jar with the ducal crest signified approval. Its absence would prompt a telegram to Tarrant Parva apologizing or seeking an explanation. No doubt you observed the apron hanging in the preserves room and the books in the duchess's sitting room that suggested she prepared the marmalade with her own hands. You might say the Cabinet was tied to her apron strings. A further imposition on each member was the strict injunction that under no circumstances must each month's jar be opened before the twentieth day of the month. That is why, Watson, the diamond could remain undetected until that date. The recipe was kept a secret even from her own servants. As is your nature, you expressed concern over the mark of a whip or crop on the face of the maid in one of the houses. I deduced later that she had been caught helping herself to the special marmalade.'

Again I interrupted the reconstruction of events.

'Why did you smell and touch the grass outside one of the houses in St John's Wood?'

'Only because my eye caught sight of a glistening substance. The aroma of oranges and my sticky finger suggested that whoever had come over the wall had dropped some marmalade. I confess, Watson, that among all the investigations with which I have been involved never has such a seemingly small observation proved so difficult to relate to other facts. Indeed I even went as far as dismissing it from my mind. And then when studying a map of roads around Tarrant Parva, I noticed that on the direct route between the Station Hotel and the lodge gates there was the Orange Tree Inn. Perhaps Moriarty, knowing my powers of observation and that the inn sign could provide a clue, deliberately took us on a circuitous route and was not, as we first assumed, lost. However, on reflection, I am inclined to believe that that would have been too clever, even for him. I should have mentioned that it was likely that whoever the burglar was knew what might have been in one of the jars, and tried to get at the diamond and outwit Moriarty. Hence the traces of marmalade.'

I then mentioned the sticky end to the search.

'Holmes, the Rainbow stone was not found in the marmalade in Wapping.'

He gave one of his knowing smiles and said, 'Because it never left Tarrant Parva. The laws of probability decreed that there was a one in ten chance that it was in a particular jar. It was, and the particular one was the unsent tenth residing on the shelf in the preserves room. Had the particular minister not resigned then we may never have seen the diamond again.'

A few days after the end of the affair, a messenger arrived from Tarrant Parva. He handed over a handsome cheque along with a large hamper, inside of which were enough jars of the duchess's marmalade to last for many weeks.

The Deerstalker

In which a cricket bag holds a clue.

Holmes and I were on our way back to London. We were seated in one of the sumptuous first class compartments of the Central British Railway. Whenever the train stopped at a station I observed very closely the people on the platform. My reason for doing so was to anticipate that moment when Holmes would suddenly say, for example, 'Do you remember that commercial traveller we saw at so and so? You noted, no doubt, that his business was in the seed trade?' I was often mortified by appearing to be so unobservant that I made every effort to become as skilful as Holmes.

Holmes directed my attention to a man walking along the platform of a provincial town station at which the train had stopped.

'It is incredible, Watson, the lengths to which a man will go to adorn his person with some strange item of dress. Look at that absurd headgear. It has a peak both back and front and ear flaps tied together on top.'

For once had I discovered a flaw in my friend's encyclopaedic collection of information?

'Holmes, surely you recognize a deerstalker's cap?'

'Come to think of it, I have seen one before. I still say it is an odd hat to wear in this part of the country where there are few, if any, wild deer. Nevertheless, it is far too eccentric for my tastes.'

Of course, I was not certain whether or not one of my legs was being pulled.

As the guard blew his whistle there was a commotion at the

ticket barrier. A tall man dressed in a frock-coat and carrying his hat was forcing his way past the railway officials, who were trying to restrain him. He burst free just as two policemen appeared. The train had started to move. I leaned out of the window and watched the presumably 'wanted man' run alongside the train, wrench a door open and fall into the compartment next to ours. We heard the bang as the door was shut.

'He's in the next compartment!' exclaimed Holmes. 'For a gentleman to be in such a hurry to escape the law suggests a major crime has been committed.'

'Should we pull the communication cord and stop the train?'

'No, Watson. If we do that he will no doubt jump out and disappear. Better he stays where he is. The next stop is not for another twenty minutes. No doubt his presence on the train will have been telegraphed ahead.'

As the train sped on its way, Holmes sat in deep thought. His thin fingers were pressed together under his chin. I was not sure what facts needed to be gathered about the tall man.

'Have you reached any conclusions about the man in a hurry, Holmes?'

'All we have is a supposed criminal. We need a crime before we can reach any positive conclusions.'

'We may not know of the crime yet we can reach some conclusions straightaway.'

'What do you mean?' said Holmes.

'Simple deduction, as you would say. Our subject has a robust constitution. He is, or was, most likely an officer in the army and has spent many years east of Suez.'

I could see that Holmes was taken aback. Never before had I ventured opinions from so few facts with such obvious assurance.

'My dear fellow, I can appreciate why you say he has a robust constitution because of the speed and agility with which he gained the train. However, your surmise about the army and the years in the east?'

'Fairly simple. I might even say elementary, except that word is far too common among writers of detective stories. I will tell you. Firstly his handkerchief was half out of his sleeve. Officers, such as myself, had no pockets in their uniforms in which to stow a handkerchief. And so at one time he certainly held the Queen's commission. Secondly, his swarthy and raddled complexion exhibited the ravages of the diseases and fevers to which so many white men, including at one time myself, are subject in hot and humid climates.'

'I must admit that I have to agree with your deductions, Watson.'

As the train began to slow down on the approach to the next stop, we looked out of the window. As expected, the door of the next compartment swung open. Before the train reached the platform, the supposed criminal leapt out and disappeared into the bushes alongside the line. Some policemen who had, as we had anticipated, been alerted by the telegraph, were waiting on the platform. Holmes beckoned one of them.

'Constable, your man has slipped away before we came to the platform. That is if he is the tall one-time army officer who has served in the east.'

'Are you a friend of his, sir? You seems to know rather a lot about 'im.'

'Certainly not. I am just expressing opinions based on facts.'

'I advise you, sir, to keep your 'pinions to yourself and let us decide.'

Holmes was not best pleased at being rebuffed.

A few days after the event of the fleeing man, Holmes was reading the proceedings of the Royal Society of Science.

'I'm reading a most interesting report. You may also find it so.'

'What is it about?'

'A Professor Heinrich Hertz of Karlsruhe Polytechnic has demonstrated that electric waves can be reflected, refracted, diffracted and polarized in the same way as light. The other day at the Royal Society he demonstrated these effects. I confess to failing to understand the principles involved. Nevertheless, I can appreciate that they may lead scientists along entirely new paths of discovery.'

'Most intriguing,' I replied, 'although I cannot really grasp the concept of electric waves.'

Some time later I was startled from my reverie by a loud exclamation from Holmes. 'I say, what a coincidence! Having just read of this Professor Hertz and his waves, I am now reading about a disturbance at a Cambridge laboratory in which the name Hertz is mentioned. So what can we make of that?'

'As you say, a coincidence. It may be nothing more than that.'

A few mornings later, I found Holmes sprawled in his chair. His countenance displayed the effects of the strong narcotic with which he had injected himself. As usual I had tried to dissuade him from drugging himself. For over a week there had been few calls upon him to exercise his deductive powers. A lack of intellectual activity made him irritable and subdued. Mrs Hudson entered and, with a resigned look at the wreck of a man by the fire, she said, 'Doctor, there are two gentlemen insisting that they speak to Mr Holmes. What shall I tell them?'

'You will have to say that he is not available for a consultation.'

'I cannot lie.'

'You will not have to. Now help me get him into his room. You can then say that he is not here: that is to say, in this room. Which indeed he will not be.'

Once Holmes was out of the way, Mrs Hudson showed the visitors into the famous room that served as study, sitting room, dining room and laboratory.

'Good morning, gentlemen, I am sorry that Mr Holmes cannot meet you today,' said I. 'If you will state your business I will let him know and then I am sure he will communicate with you. I am Doctor Watson, his confidant in all matters obtaining to his investigatory practice.'

The two men exchanged glances. One shook his head and said, 'Doctor Watson, we appreciate from all that we know about Mr Holmes and his work that you are indeed a most trustworthy keeper of secrets. However, our commission involves matters concerning the safety of the realm and it states most specifically that no one, including you, may be party to what we have to discuss with Mr Holmes. I can assure you that, as such, no aspersion is cast upon your character. Under the circumstances therefore all we ask you to do when Mr Holmes returns is to impress upon him that we must speak to him. It is not only most important that we do so, it must be as soon as possible. Even a day's delay may prove disastrous. Please request him to telegraph us as soon as he has read this letter. Our address is on the envelope.'

I took the letter and assured the visitors that I would make sure to give it to Holmes. Once they had gone, I summoned Mrs Hudson. 'Once again I must ask that you help me to revive him. Apparently his presence in the real world is urgently required.'

The next morning, after a night of hot baths, cold baths and numerous concoctions that I had devised, Holmes was nearly his usual self. A message was sent inviting the emissaries, whoever they were, to an early meeting at Baker Street.

'You know, I have been thinking about the two gentlemen who are so anxious to talk to you. I am certain they are naval officers.'

'Indeed, Watson. You are becoming more of a detective every day. Tell me about the reasons for your conclusion.'

'Their boots gave me the first clue. You are always reminding me that one of the most important and indeed the first observation to be made of someone is their feet, or rather their footwear. I noted immediately that their boots had the very square toes that are characteristic of the boots of a naval person. However, I did not jump to any conclusions based on just one fact. I recalled your advice. I then observed their countenance. Both exhibited what I might term "weather-beaten" faces and the eyes were surrounded by a myriad of small lines denoting many years of peering into the distance. Another feature that confirmed my first observation was the way in which their cravats were tied.'

Holmes received the two men who, obviously from their bearing and manner, had come about business of the realm. They would not disclose their names. However, when they produced a letter to Holmes signed by his brother Mycroft, their names did not matter. At that point I moved to the door, saying, 'I believe these gentlemen would prefer that I withdraw.'

One of them spoke. 'No need, Doctor Watson. Please stay, because since we were last here we have been instructed to say that, if Mr Holmes desires it, you can be privy to the matter.' Holmes nodded his agreement.

'Mr Holmes,' said the other visitor, 'as your brother indicates, we must have your help in tracing a valuable item and in catching the person or persons that stole it. A famous laboratory at Cambridge is conducting experiments on behalf of the Admiralty. The experiments involve Hertzian waves and a device that may be of vital importance to the navy. The work is most secret. Regrettably, the national press came upon an old local newspaper report about research into Hertzian waves at the university. Otherwise it had been hoped that the work would not have been mentioned.'

The other nameless man took up the story.

'Apparently the thief gained access somehow to the laboratory, although there were no signs of forcible entry. Also, at the time, the only keys to the only door were on the person of the head of the laboratory, a Professor Rains.'

Holmes interrupted him.

'Is that the Professor Rains of the Department of Philosophical Science?'

'Indeed the very one. He is most perturbed by the loss of something called a Boswell Concentrator, particularly as, should the research programme be delayed, then the government might withhold financial support. I have to tell you that within certain circles the project is being termed a solution looking for a problem. None of the admirals privy to the work can see any use for the device even if it were perfected. However, my own opinion is that it may prove extremely useful. There is always the possibility that the secrets of the device might pass to a foreign power. If that were to happen and the device were to work, then the Royal Navy could be at a great disadvantage in the event of a war.'

'We will have to inspect the laboratory and its surroundings as soon as possible. Clues have a habit of fading with time,' said Holmes.

'Of course, Mr Holmes. We both hoped for and anticipated your cooperation to the extent that a carriage is already at your door and tickets to Cambridge await you at the barrier at King's Cross. There is a train at 9.30.'

'We have yet to have our breakfast,' said I.

'May we suggest that it will save time if you refresh yourselves in the station breakfast room at King's Cross? I have always found the service to be most prompt.'

*

We were met at the laboratory by Professor Rains who showed us round. He led us to a small enclosure within the laboratory. Unlocking the door, he said, 'This is where we conduct the very special experiments and this is where the concentrator is tested, and from where it was taken. By the way, Mr Holmes, did you enjoy your breakfast at King's Cross? I could not help observing a faint trace of marmalade on your waistcoat; a very distinctive brand is served up in the station breakfast room.'

Holmes ignored the comment and I surmised was wondering, Why so many people and, for that matter, writers, try to play the detective? He then asked, 'Professor, may I see a drawing or illustration of the concentrator?'

'Certainly, Mr Holmes.' He unfolded a drawing marked '*Most Confidential*'. 'As you see, it is two foot in length and conical with a base diameter of six inches. There are two threaded terminals with nuts to which wires can be secured. More than that I cannot tell you.'

Holmes studied the drawing for a few minutes and then remarked.

'I presume the secret is within its body otherwise it appears to be nothing more than a decorative finial?'

'Correct. However, what is in the interior must remain a secret even from you, Mr Holmes, though I cannot see that it will hamper your investigation. I wish I could tell you more.'

'I hope it will not. Now we need to look for something that will lead to how entry was effected, how the concentrator was removed, and by whom.'

Holmes made his usual meticulous inspection of the scene of the crime. As was his custom he did not confine his activities to the immediate vicinity of the bench on which the concentrator had been lying. He made sure that there were no marks to indicate that the door locks had been tampered with or picked.

'At this stage of the investigation,' said Holmes, 'the only reasonably certain conclusion to be reached is that only one burglar has been inside the laboratory. Now, am I right in assuming, Professor, that the object in question is not too heavy?'

'I regret, as I said, I'm not permitted to disclose such information. Even to you.'

Under one of the benches, Holmes' keen eye revealed a small heap of tobacco ash, which he carefully scooped into a fold of paper. Further on there was another heap of ash. The bench on which the concentrator had lain, and the two heaps of ash, formed a line pointing toward the end wall of the laboratory. Ten feet above his head, as he stood at the wall, was one of the oriole windows with a fanlight. He observed that the fanlights for all the windows were operated by a system of rods high up under the roof. They were all operated from one lever and, as the professor informed us, it was always locked in the closed position when the laboratory was shut for the night. Furthermore it was interlocked with the door.

'It appears,' said Holmes, 'that the only way out is through one of the oriole windows, yet how? The benches are bolted to the floor and, as you said, Professor, when you left the laboratory there was no ladder inside. However, these marks are of a chair being dragged across the polished floor. It could have been used by the burglar to gain the window. Even so he must have been very tall and very strong.'

He tested his theory by standing on a chair yet he could only stretch to within an inch of the window.

'Professor, may we have the windows open, please?' When the lever was operated, all the windows opened except the one above Holmes' head.

'I can just make out,' said he, 'that the rod which should have been connected to its crank is not. Somehow the thief was strong enough not only to gain the window ledge, he was also able to force the mechanism. The window had fallen shut behind him.'

Inspection at the foot of the wall on the outside disclosed two deep footprints.

'These footprints and the window mechanism that had been forced clearly indicate how the thief left the laboratory,' said Holmes. 'Having satisfied myself concerning the method of leaving, I shall turn my mind to working out how the thief had entered this seemingly impregnable laboratory. As we can see, there are no signs of footprints pointing toward the wall and neither are there any marks of a ladder or rope having been used.'

I ventured to say, 'I am inclined to think that this is another Trojan Horse case.'

'You mean the criminal was already inside the laboratory when it was locked up for the night.' He paused and then said, 'You could be right. I agree, some of the signs suggest that that is what happened. What we have to do now is find the hiding place. What about the cupboards and the work benches?'

The professor replied, 'As you can see, they are full with shelves and the benches have drawers underneath and thick supporting frames. There is no space for anyone to hide.'

Holmes looked around and then asked, 'What about this tall narrow cupboard? A man might just be able to fit in there. Let's open it and see. Ah, it's locked. Have you the key, Professor?'

'Well, no. This cupboard came from the Royal Society of Science. It contains a surprise gift on my becoming Professor Emeritus. Apparently, it holds some special apparatus that I have always wanted to have for my particular interest in science, and which I shall continue with in my remaining years. I had a letter from the society advising me that I was to be honoured with a gift. It also requested that I might allow a small ceremony to take place in the laboratory at which I would be presented with a key to the cupboard. In agreeing to this I was very aware that when that happened the concentrator would have to be locked away and that no mention could be made of it.'

'Who signed the letter?' asked Holmes.

'The secretary of the society.'

'Are you familiar with his signature?'

'I cannot really say. I have had very few letters from him.'

'If you will allow me, Professor, may I see the letter?'

'Certainly. I happen to have it with me.'

After reading the letter Holmes said, 'So, the society's representatives failed to arrive?'

'Yes. I was so concerned over the loss of the concentrator that I forgot all about their pending visit.'

'And, of course, the cupboard arrived the day before the burglary.' commented Holmes.

'That was so.'

'May I keep the letter for the time being?'

'Certainly if it is going to help your investigation.'

It was then that Holmes started to pick the lock of the cupboard.

'I say, you must not do that. As I said, this is a gift that. . . .'

Holmes waved aside the professor's protest.

'I am sorry, I must. Turn your back so as not to spoil the surprise, though I doubt that will be necessary because I expect our bird has flown.'

There was nothing inside. Holmes made a careful inspection of the interior of the cupboard. He found nothing of interest other than a row of large ventilation holes. Moving the cupboard away from the wall revealed a small brass plate at the base of the back panel.

'His or their first mistake. This is the maker's plate on which we have an address. I can tell you, Professor, that such a seemingly mundane clue often provides a significant pointer toward a solution. How was the cupboard delivered?'

'By a common carrier. Two men used a porter's trolley and I directed them to bring it into the laboratory.'

Holmes then made a further examination of the bench from which the concentrator had been taken.

Back at Baker Street, Holmes settled in his chair and, amid a cloud of tobacco smoke, set his mind to sorting through the facts of the case. I anticipated that eventually he would start testing various hypotheses on me.

Eventually, I ventured to interrupt his thoughts about the case. 'Why didn't you inspect the ground outside the wall first?'

'Because, Watson, I might have been prejudiced in my judgement over other clues. Footprints outside a crime scene more often than not can be saved for later, just as a child saves the icing on the cake until last. However, sometimes they can lead one to very wrong conclusions.'

At this point in our discussion a telegram arrived. Holmes looked at it and exclaimed, 'Capital! Watson, your conclusions were correct. This message from Mycroft tells us more about the affair, and reveals that the two gentlemen were indeed naval officers. Events have now moved on. You recall the references to Hertzian waves in the papers. Well, it seems that Professor Rain and his team have developed a method of harnessing these waves in such a manner that they can be formed into a beam similar to that of a beam of light. The more enlightened officers in the navy support the project.

The ability to detect the presence of an enemy vessel without revealing your own position, as would a searchlight, would be most advantageous. However, do not ask me to explain how it works. Like you, the concept of ethereal waves composed of electricity is beyond my mental powers.'

'An astounding device. No wonder its presence is so secret,' said I.

'We are charged with two things. One, and of the utmost importance, recover the device and two, track down the thief or thieves. I have now been told that, as was suspected, a certain undisclosed foreign power may be behind the burglary at Cambridge. We now need to visit the cabinet maker that made the cupboard. Mycroft has arranged for Inspector Lestrade to accompany us.'

At first the owner of the small furniture factory, located in the East End, refused to answer questions about his customers. Lestrade produced a warrant that unlocked both tongue and memory.

'Yes, there was two gen'lmen that ordered a queer cupboard.'

'Queer, you say. How?' asked Holmes.

'Well, sir, they wanted it six feet and six inches tall, twenty inches wide and two foot deep. They wanted ventilation holes in it.'

'Can you recall, in any way, the two men who placed the order?'

'The one that give me another five guineas on top of what I was charging them was a very big man. The extra was to make me say nothing to nobody about the cupboard or them. The other was a beanpole of a man. I can't say I liked the look of his eye. Now you mention it he had a dark face an' a black moustache. He had a silver-topped cane. When he also said like I was to keep my mouth shut he prodded me 'ard with his cane.'

'And to where was the cupboard to be consigned?'

'You mean where 'ad it got to be sent to?'

'Yes. Also the name of the addressee?'

'Adressy? Oh, you mean the man what wanted to 'ave it. The name was I think Millard and he lived at a place called something like Grenchester.'

Holmes was losing his patience with the protracted extraction of vital information.

'You have an order book, no doubt. The name and address should be in there.'

'Yes, 'er tis. Now let's see. It was about a week ago. Maybe longer. Wait a minute! The page's been torn out. It was there when the railway carter came for the cupboard.'

'I'm not surprised. Never mind. You have the carbon copy?'

'That's been an' gone as well.'

Holmes looked closely at the dog-eared book and said, 'I will take the next page with me.'

On the way back to Baker Street, Holmes drew attention to the sequence of events involved in the case.

'On the first day the professor receives the letter advising him of the delivery of the cupboard. On the fourth day the cupboard arrives at the laboratory and the thief emerges from it after the laboratory has been locked for the night. That was also the day when the moon was at its brightest, so he did not need a dark lantern. On the fifth day the loss is discovered. That is also the day we witnessed the event of the fleeing man at Midshire.

'The description of that man matches one of the two at the cabinet maker's. You recall that the cabinet was six foot and six inches high. An average-sized burglar would have fitted in a much shorter cupboard. Although, I have to confess, there is only a thin thread connecting the two. However, there are two new facts that have emerged relating to the thief. Firstly, the papers this morning carry reports about a search that is continuing for a man who violently attacked another in Meadborough. The poor fellow succumbed to his injuries. The date given matches that of our fleeing man in the train. And that was at Meadborough. Secondly, my habit of reading the first class passenger list of steamers arriving at these shores disclosed the name of a Major Raymond Tresscot-Jones of Hodges Light Horse of Bengal. A request to my brother disclosed, from the regimental lists and from the India Office, that the major was no longer a major. He had been cashiered for embezzlement of the mess funds. He had also, somehow, avoided being incarcerated by the civil authorities for the brutality with which he punished his servants. His singular name led me to my commonplace books. There I found that, some thirty years ago, a young officer of the same name in the 11th

Hussars had been ordered by Cardigan to sell his commission. Apparently, Tresscot-Jones' brutal and uncaring treatment of his men was even too much for the earl himself. You will remember how the notorious earl often had a man flogged close to death for some trivial offence.'

'Well, Holmes, it seems then that the identity of the probable criminal is more than likely Tresscot-Jones. Could the other man who was at the cabinet maker's be Moriarty?'

'Possibly. The description tends to suggest so. The nature of the crime is such that he could be the mastermind.'

Lestrade nodded agreement.

Holmes continued, 'In the meantime, I have another line of inquiry to pursue. It concerns tobacco ash. I found ash in the laboratory and this evening I shall refresh my memory on the subject by going through the notes and observations I made some time ago when writing a monograph about how to identify the different types of ash.'

After supper Holmes sat at the big table used for his chemical and forensic experiments. An hour passed before he exclaimed, 'Watson, I think I have come closer to our man! The ash is that of a Bengal Thin cheroot. Until now I've yet to find anyone in this country who smokes them. However, now we have the major who more than likely acquired a liking for them in India. In the morning I shall repair to Salmon and Gluckstein in Piccadilly. If anyone has a Bengal Thin it will be they. Now for this blank page from the cabinet maker's order book. Will you assist me, please?'

Holmes selected from one of the many flasks on the table one containing a black powder.

'I say, Holmes, you are not going to use that carbon powder? It gets everywhere and Mrs Hudson will not be too pleased. It will mean that our meals will be served without comment and may not be very appetizing for at least a week.'

Nevertheless, Holmes was always ready to incur Mrs Hudson's wrath in the interests of science. As instructed, I carefully poured the powder down the surface of the paper. Gradually an address emerged.

'There it is. I can just make out the *Archers Grantchester*. That's enough. We now know the cupboard was consigned to Grantchester and it is more than likely that is where the thief, who may be the major, set off for the laboratory.'

'Not much to go on, surely, Holmes. Who are the archers?'

'Not who but what. It is the name of a grand house, and immediately we have another confirmation that Moriarty is behind all this. When I was up at Cambridge a fellow student was Guy de Beaumaine, whose distant ancestor had waded ashore with William the Norman. One lovely afternoon we took a punt upstream to Grantchester. Beaumaine had invited us to tea at ten to three at the Archers. We were accompanied by none other than Moriarty, who at that time was our tutor. In those years, before he turned to crime, he was a renowned academic.'

'That suggests that Moriarty has some hold over Beaumaine and, as you say, it was from the Archers that he and the major set out for the laboratory.'

'My thoughts exactly. I imagine my commonplace book may provide a clue in that direction. By the way, the name is often pronounced "bowmen". You see the connection between the name and the name of the house?'

'Not really. However, if you say so, Holmes.'

Holmes gave a resigned shrug and did not reply.

He took down one of the thick books, each full of cuttings from newspapers and journals as well as letters and other ephemera. For over an hour he pored over book after book. Suddenly he jumped up, waving one of the books, and said, 'I have it. There are a number of reports of Beaumaine losing large sums when gambling. One newspaper item from the past suggested that the estate had been heavily mortgaged at one time. A favourite device of Moriarty is to encourage the scions of noble and rich families into gambling. He then takes over their debts and thereby is able to keep such a strong hold on them that they cannot resist helping in some criminal activity. Remember Beaumaine holds an important government position, as do others who have been weak and foolish. I am certain that, through one of them, Moriarty has been able to learn about the concentrator.'

The next morning, to the surprise of a passing policeman and a road sweeper, Holmes was standing against the doorway of the cigar and cigarette shop at 7.30, a time when few gentleman would be expected to be about. The mention of Inspector Lestrade's name was sufficient to satisfy the constable that he was not loitering with intent. As soon as the shop was opened, and even before the manager had time in which to light the small gas jet on the counter, he was inside.

'Good morning,' said he.

'Good day to you, sir,' replied the manager. 'You are a very early customer.'

'For good reason. I need urgently to find some Bengal Thin cheroots. I believe your reputation is such that you will have some.'

The manager lit the small gas jet on the counter and pondered the question.

'Let me think. Ah, do you know that it was only about two weeks back that a gentleman bought ten bundles. In fact they were nearly all we had. I have had to send for more in case he pays another visit.'

'Excellent. Now, can you describe the man?'

'Difficult. We have over a hundred customers each day. Admittedly I and my assistant – he's late again – know the regulars, of course. The purchaser of the cheroots was not one of the regulars.'

'Perhaps I might help you. Was he very tall and very thin and had a swarthy complexion and a dark moustache?'

'Why yes, I do recall him. He lit one of the cheroots and I noticed that he had to step well back from the counter so that he could bend to reach the flame.'

'He took the cheroots with him?'

'Well, no, he asked me to send them to his hotel.'

'As I had hoped. May I see your delivery book? By the way, you say he bought nearly all the cheroots.'

'It so happens, sir, I do have some among these odd ones in the drawer. Here they are.'

'I should like to have a few. How much?'

'To you, Mr Holmes, nothing.'

'You know who I am?'

'Of course. Some years ago you came into the shop and to my surprise bought one of every brand of cigar, and samples of all the different cigarettes. Later Inspector Lestrade of the Yard was inquiring about some cigars found at the scene of a crime and he mentioned that you had written a small book about how to identify tobacco ash.'

The name and address in the cigar shop delivery book led Holmes and I to Green's Hotel in Buckingham Palace Road. The manager immediately recalled a Mr Millard staying there.

'A most difficult guest. He browbeat my staff into letting him have a room even though he had sent no telegraphed request. At the time we were very full because we abut onto the Royal Society of Science. The members were holding their annual founder's day ceremonies.'

'Most interesting. Can you recall anything else about him?'

'He is not likely to be forgotten. I caught him in an, er, well you know, embarrassing situation with one of the chambermaids. She had to go. We have a reputation to maintain.'

'Anything else. Did he smoke?'

'The housekeeper showed me the dreadful state in which he had left his room. There was cigar ash everywhere and the grate was full of stubs. She had had to open the windows in order to clear the room of the strong smell of his tobacco.'

'Cheroots, no doubt!' said Holmes.

In the secretary's office at the society, Holmes produced the letter that had been sent to the professor at Cambridge.

'Is that your signature or indeed did you write this letter?'

'It is a reasonable facsimile of my signature. However, this is certainly nonsense. I never wrote such a letter. The society has not planned to award the professor with any gift delivered to his laboratory. The fact of the matter is that, yes, we have planned a ceremony to honour him, but it will take place here and later in the year.'

'How was the society's headed paper obtained?' was Holmes' next question.

'Not too difficult. There is headed paper and envelopes on the desks in the members' reading room.'

'Does the doorkeeper know the members by sight?'

'The majority, I should say. They have to sign the register when they come in.'

'On founder's day I presume there were many guests?'

'Many.'

'So the staff would not be surprised to see a stranger in the reading room?'

'Not really. On that day, of course, some of the members were staying at Green's and the passageway connecting us with the hotel is open to allow the waiters to move between the hotel kitchens and our banquet.'

In our discussion on the way back to Baker Street, I suggested, 'Undoubtedly Millard is or was Tresscot-Jones and he stole the society's headed paper and envelopes without difficulty. Do you not agree?'

'Yes, that appears so.'

'It seems we have reached a point in the case at which it is difficult to see a way ahead,' said I. 'I suppose we have to decide now between looking for the concentrator or the thief. Do we pursue the object or the man?'

'In many ways, Watson, the concentrator is the more important. However, the man might lead us to the object. Yet the concentrator will not necessarily be with Tresscot-Jones. Without doubt Moriarty is behind all this. Why was the major in Meadborough on the day after the robbery?' He reached for his pipe and thought for a moment before saying, 'Of course, the town is on the line from Cambridge and not far from Grantchester. We are faced with the possibility that the concentrator is either with the major or it is still at the Archers. Although the major did not appear to have it with him when we happened to watch him from the train. So it is either at the Archers or somewhere between Grantchester and Meadborough. The question is, where. He left no instructions at the hotel about forwarding any letters.'

When we got back to Baker Street, Lestrade was waiting for us. Holmes gave him a résumé of our visit to the hotel.

'I agree with your reconstruction,' said the inspector. 'As you requested I have been in touch with the police at Meadborough about the man who was found murdered. They told me that he was a well-known local character who was, more often than not, the worse for drink. He had a habit of accosting strangers begging for money. Unlucky for him he may have accosted, of all people, the major. So far they have found no trace of him.'

We arrived in Grantchester. Lestrade was armed with authorization from the Home Secretary that ensured access to any premises and the right to call upon the help of any police force.

'I suggest we enquire at the station first,' said Holmes. 'We cannot march up to the Archers and demand that the premises be searched. Moriarty is too wily for that. He will have hidden his prize somewhere else.'

'Agreed,' responded Lestrade.

At the station, when Holmes described our quarry to the booking office clerk, he replied, 'Yes, sir, on that day I do remember a man looking like that who bought a ticket to London via Cambridge.'

'Did he have a bag with him?' asked Lestrade.

'Can't really say.'

'Can you recall anything else?' asked Holmes.

'Well, come to think of it, I was surprised to find a gentleman buying a ticket at that time of the morning. Not many gentlemen come for a train at six in the morning.'

'Now, are you sure that he was alone?' asked Holmes.

'Yes, very sure.'

'Another question – did you see him get into a train?'

'Sorry. You see, it's always very busy at that time of a morning. There are always a lot of workmen and also women taking fruit and vegetables to market. Both platforms get crowded. We get both an up and down train stopping at the same time.'

'At the same time, you say. Most interesting.'

'Ah, wait a minute. There's another odd thing. After he had gone, two gentlemen came and asked me if a tall thin man had caught a train that morning. They also wanted to know where he had booked to.'

'Now this is very important,' said Holmes. 'Was one of the two men very large?'

'Quite right, sir, he was a very big man.'

'Thank you very much. You have been most helpful.'

Holmes spent some time studying the timetable before saying, 'I believe that he may have crossed the bridge when the train to

Cambridge arrived in order to get to the other platform and board the Meadborough train and not the one to Cambridge. The two trains, according to the timetable and as the booking clerk mentioned, happen to cross at that time of the morning. It was not us who he was trying to throw off the scent. He was leading a false trail for Moriarty.'

'Why should he want to do that?' I remarked.

'It could be that he sneaked out of the Archers at dawn carrying the concentrator. Do not you agree, Lestrade?'

'Yes, that's quite likely. The major may have suddenly decided to leave in a hurry because he had thought of a devious plan of his own to outwit Moriarty. He was double-crossing the others.'

'Double-crossing, I understand, is some criminal jargon that has entered the language in recent years,' said Holmes.

On the assumption that the major was in Meadborough and that he may have had an accomplice waiting for him, we travelled there and inquired at the town's two hotels. At the temperance hotel, to our surprise, because it was an unlikely place to be visited by an ex-army officer, the manager remembered the major.

'Yes, a Millard stayed here on that date.'

'You are certain?' asked Lestrade.

'Certainly. Here is the register. I also recall that he smoked in bed. There was ash all over the room.'

'Cheroots, no doubt. Did he have any luggage when he first arrived?'

'Well, he only had a Gladstone bag. He said his other luggage had been deposited at the station.'

'Very interesting,' said Holmes. 'Our man seems to depend a lot on the railway, and that supports the idea that all along he intended to outwit his accomplices.'

The manager turned to a shelf and said, 'He may come back to collect these gloves. Or he may have discarded them because they are not very clean.'

'May I see them?'

Holmes examined them closely, sniffed at them, and said, 'If he returns it is most important that you inform the police. This is Inspector Lestrade of Scotland Yard – he will confirm what I say.'

'Yes,' said Lestrade, 'and it is most important that you do not mention that we have been here. He is a dangerous man.'

We stood outside the hotel debating our next move. Holmes said, 'Now we have to consider where the major may have left the concentrator, or even consigned it to an accomplice. The most likely place to look, I suggest, is at the station. He may have decided to send it by train to somewhere else for collection.'

We went across the market square to the station opposite the hotel.

'There is a good chance,' said Holmes, 'that what we are after is in the left luggage office. Of course we may be too late and it has already gone. Lestrade, this is where you come in. Use your powers to have all the bags examined. We need not concern ourselves with any that are less than two feet in length.'

After an hour nothing was found. The porter who was helping us muttered, 'lucky we ain't doing this in the West station. They've three times this lot.'

'Watson, you're the one who's supposed to know all about railways,' said Holmes. 'Why did you not speak up?'

'I assumed, like you, my dear fellow, that it would be here. The hotelier did not specify which station. But this is the closest. However, it so happens I am well aware that there are four stations for this town: South, West, Central and Meadborough Road. You see, in the fifties and sixties the town's people strongly supported a number of railway bills that would connect them to the outside world. Three companies entered into cut-throat competition and—'

Holmes interrupted me saying, 'Yes, yes, the names of the stations will suffice. We will now try the West station if that is the next nearest.'

Once more, a searching of bags took place. This time, however, Holmes had only been inside the luggage office for a minute or two when he pounced on a cricket bag, saying, 'This looks like it.'

After insisting that the station staff leave the office, the bag was opened. Sufficient to record that that was the end of the quest for the Boswell Concentrator. However, we still had to trace the perpetrators of the crime. And that is another story.

We three, who between us had recovered one of the nation's most precious secrets, were relaxing after a splendid 'victory' dinner in the dining car of the southbound express. Holmes and Lestrade were going over the facts and events. There were still some unanswered questions.

'Why,' asked Lestrade, 'did you go straightaway to the cricket bag at the West station, Mr Holmes?'

'The gloves, the gloves. You remember the manager of the hotel drew attention to the marks on the discarded gloves. Well, my nose detected linseed oil. At the time I was not sure it was important. Not until we were among the luggage and saw a cricket bag did I apply the clue. The major must have found the bag in the house and decided that it would make an unobtrusive way of carrying the concentrator. Also he must have used a cloth that had been wrapped round the cricket bats to protect the concentrator. They must have been recently oiled, and when he threw them out to make room some of the oil must have got onto his gloves.'

'Your nose saved us much time.'

Holmes tapped his nose and said, 'It can be most useful on occasions to be a human bloodhound.'

I raised the matter of Beaumaine and his part in the affair. We all agreed that he would be arrested and that because of his high position in government the resulting scandal would precipitate a political crisis. As for Moriarty and the major, they were, unfortunately, still at large.

My attention began to wander. The soft roar of an express speeding through the night and noise of the wheels all added to the effects of the claret and brandy. The voices of my companions faded and faded. . . .

Diamonds at Sea

Or

The Missing Bridesmaid

In which the Baker Street Irregulars play an important part.

When looking through the notes of Holmes' investigations, one is faced with many which present strange and interesting events, so that it is difficult to know which to choose and which to leave aside. Mindful of the criticism of the manner in which some have been narrated, a careful choice has had to be made. Some cases appear to have baffled his analytical skills and therefore should not be published; particularly if they have had no obvious beginning and no end. Some would have their explanations founded upon conjecture alone, and on surmise, rather than on the logical proof which Holmes considered absolutely essential.

The following account may not meet the above criteria; nevertheless, it is one which emphasizes the importance Holmes attached to his sources of information, and in particular the Baker Street Irregulars, an army of boys of various ages who lived by their wits and without the benefit of soap and water and schooling.

I made onc of my customary calls on Holmes and found him leafing through the morning papers. Mrs Hudson was clearing away the breakfast table.

Holmes greeted me by saying, 'I wonder, could this be a singular coincidence? If so, an important one.'

'A coincidence, Holmes?' I replied.

'Yes. This account in the *Morning Post* for the fourth of this month reports that, on the first, a Miss Hortense de Vere and her maid were drugged in their hotel in Holland. When they recovered from, it was assumed, a stupefying agent they realized someone had entered their room. Their possessions had been riffled yet the only things taken were some papers concerned with Miss de Vere's journey.'

'Sinister rather than singular, I would say.'

'Indeed. The name de Vere sounds familiar. I must have read about her recently. Let me see.' Holmes searched through the pile of recent newspapers that cascaded across the carpet. 'As I thought. This report of a wedding at St Margaret's between Sir Simon Downlea and the Honourable Cynthia Cloudsly tells us that the bride was most disappointed that her friend Miss Hortense de Vere, who should have been one of the bridesmaids, was forced by circumstance to miss the wedding. Miss de Vere was travelling on the continent. The packet boat she intended to take from the Netherlands could not sail because of a severe storm. For some reason she was not able to board the boat when it eventually sailed on the second of the month.'

'And the second was the day of that strange affair when someone carrying a quantity of diamonds was forcibly taken off the Hook to Harwich packet boat in the middle of the German Ocean.'

'Just so, Watson. Are we to assume that there is some connection between a missed wedding and an abduction at sea?'

'If there is, then it must be a very tenuous one.'

This discussion was taking place a week after the day on which Inspector Lestrade had called to seek Holmes' help with solving the disappearance of five thousand pounds' worth of cut diamonds.

The diamonds were being carried by a Julius Vanderpole. He had boarded the steam packet *Anglia* at the Hook. An hour into the voyage two men had come on to the bridge and, at gunpoint, ordered the master to stop the ship. When the *Anglia* lost way a steam launch came alongside and a number of men came on board. The passengers and other crew members were herded into the saloon. The pirates, for that is what they were, must have left on the launch, which steamed away to the south taking Mr Vanderpole with them. None of the other passengers was harmed or robbed.

When the *Anglia* reached Harwich, all the passengers were held on board until the harbour master and the local police could take statements from them. None of the crew or passengers was able to provide any useful information about the pirates. At the time the master, Captain Anderson, and the purser were not aware of the valuables being carried by Vanderpole.

Scotland Yard, in the person of Lestrade, responded to the request from the Netherlands police for help. They had been led by an informer to where Vanderpole was being held prisoner. He was not able to say with any certainty whether or not the diamonds had been taken aboard the steam launch. If they had remained on board the *Anglia* then they could have been taken ashore by one of the passengers, if that passenger had been an accomplice of the pirates.

At the time, Lestrade had commented, 'If only we had been at Harwich when the *Anglia* docked. The trail has now gone cold.'

'I agree, Lestrade,' had said Holmes. 'We have lost much valuable time; a whole week in fact. I assume the *Anglia* has been searched?'

'It was only searched two days later, because in the meantime it had been allowed to sail the next day.'

'I doubt, Lestrade, that you would have found the diamonds on board. No, the thieves must have planned to take them ashore at Harwich. At the time no one was aware of their loss. The Waterguard would not have been alerted to the possibility of someone smuggling in the diamonds.'

Since Lestrade's visit, Holmes and I had been endeavouring to solve two questions. One, why did the pirates go to all the trouble to steal the diamonds when Vanderpole was on board the *Anglia*? They could have waylaid him before the vessel sailed. The second question was far more daunting. Who carried the diamonds off the vessel at Harwich and where were they now? These questions would have to be put to Lestrade during his next visit to Baker Street.

Lestrade arrived the next day and was able to tell us that he had received a communication from the Dutch police. Apparently, Vanderpole had an escort of armed police officers on his journey from Amsterdam to the Hook. They stayed with him until the last moment before the *Anglia* sailed.

'Gentlemen, as for who took them or where the diamonds are I've no idea where to turn,' said Lestrade.

'Well, Inspector, I suggest the first thing we need to do is to determine which of the passengers was the one most likely to have carried the diamonds off the vessel. If we can solve that problem I am sure it will lead us to the next clue. Now, did you bring the passenger list?'

'Yes.' He handed over the list.

'Oh, it is not a very big list. There are only thirty-six names.'

'The *Anglia* is a "butter boat", as they say, and can only accommodate about forty passengers. Its main purpose is the carrying of dairy products from Denmark and the Netherlands.'

'Thank you, Lestrade. Now what have we here?' He glanced down the list.

'Just as I expected. Miss de Vere's name is listed.'

'That is odd. Surely she missed the sailing time,' I asked.

'She did indeed, Watson. Her ticket and her travel papers, however, did not miss the boat. And so we can now be certain that it was a woman, posing as the missing bridesmaid, who carried the diamonds off the boat at Harwich. Furthermore, it is more than likely that she took the train to London.'

'I wonder why they chose a woman for such a vital task?' asked Lestrade.

'Because there was always the possibility that the Waterguard might decide to search some of the passengers. As you told me, Lestrade, during the Bancroft affair, they stop people at random. However, the pirates may have relied on the fact that females are rarely searched.'

'Oh, of course, and I follow your deduction, Mr Holmes. Now Scotland Yard has to find one particular female out of the two or three million that live in London. That is, if she is in London.'

'I'm fairly certain she is somewhere in our sprawling metropolis. I shall ask through my special sources within the criminal world if there has been any word about the diamonds. The word does get around, as you know. Particularly when such a valuable haul is involved. Disposing of five thousand pounds' worth of cut diamonds is not going to be easy. I also deduce that the criminals had someone in mind in London who can handle the diamonds for them. Otherwise they would have taken them on board the launch that intercepted the *Anglia* and taken them back to the Netherlands. Do you agree, Lestrade?'

'I am sure you are right, Mr Holmes.'

After the second visit by Lestrade, Holmes took up his violin and that made me decide to take my leave. I returned later in the evening and expected to be told that he had deduced from the few clues available who the woman in the *Anglia* was and where she could be found. Holmes was standing at the window watching the people and the vehicles moving along Baker Street.

'Any progress with the *Anglia* affair?' I asked.

'I regret to say, little. As you know, I am extremely confident in my ability to solve all manner of mysteries. I have been able to name many a villain and have had the satisfaction to see them being put behind bars. I have even outwitted, with your help, of course, that villain of villains, Moriarty. However, this time, like Lestrade, I cannot think how to proceed further.'

'I'm certain you will find some seemingly unrelated fact on which you can reconstruct completely the chain of events that started aboard the *Anglia*.'

'I'm grateful for your expression of confidence. Apart from the obvious sequence of happenings between the hotel in Holland and the pirates boarding the ship, I am finding it very difficult to imagine what happened thereafter. What we may assume, with some certainty, is that the woman who passed herself off as Miss de Vere left the *Anglia* with the diamonds concealed in her clothing. She then caught the train to Liverpool Street. And there at the terminus my mental trail ends. I have come to a brick wall. To a blank page. To an impenetrable fog.'

'Come, come, Holmes, you must have some idea on how to proceed further?'

'I wish I had, my dear fellow. I have stood at this window for most of the afternoon in the hope that the sight of someone or something passing below will give me inspiration.'

At that despairing admission I realized that, indeed, the great detective had, on one of the few occasions in his distinguished career, met his match. That night I could not sleep. I tossed and turned. The *Anglia* affair troubled my thoughts. That amount of diamonds would have been a heavy burden on the carrier, I mused. Other questions passed through my thoughts. Each time I arrived at an answer, it had to be discarded after rigorous analysis.

The next morning Holmes' only response to my greeting on arrival was a grunt. I perceived that he had ignored breakfast. I ventured to suggest that we might go down to Harwich and question the police and the Waterguard.

It was some time before Holmes spoke. When he did I could see that a determined look had returned to his eyes. 'Excellent suggestion, Watson. Of course you are right. We will go closer to the start of the trail. I shall telegraph the shipping company and Lestrade.'

We walked to the Baker Street Metropolitan station and took an Inner Circle train to Bishopsgate. From there we walked to Liverpool Street station and studied the timetables. Fortunately there was a train for Harwich about to leave. There was as much smoke in the station as down in the underground railway. There were numerous locomotives. Their air pumps panted in and out of beat with each other.

The Great Eastern carriage was spartan, not very clean and the wheels sounded as if they were octagonal rather than round. It was an instructive if somewhat laborious journey. The railway company allowed its passengers plenty of time in which to admire the architecture, the activity on its platforms and the minutiae of railway operation at Chelmsford, Colchester, Marks Tay and Manningtree. It was raining heavily when we reached Harwich.

The *Anglia* was lying alongside the quay and we lost no time in going aboard. Captain Anderson welcomed us in his tiny cabin.

'Good afternoon, gentlemen. I'm honoured to meet you, Mr Holmes, and you, Doctor Watson.'

'Thank you, Captain Anderson, for giving us an opportunity of inspecting the scene of the crime and being able to talk to you about the events that occurred at sea. May we start with a description of the pirates who boarded your vessel.'

'They were dressed in pea jackets. Each wore a heavy scarf that hid most of the face.'

'Were there any marks on their faces or anything out of the ordinary?'

'Yes, Mr Holmes, I recall that I could just make out a white scar across one cheek and the end of the nose of the one who gave the orders. His companion had a pallor close to that of whitewash. He was sweating profusely and his hands and body were shaking.'

'As I understand from the police report, you said that they suddenly appeared on the bridge.'

'That is so, Mr Holmes.'

'What did they say?'

'The heavily built one pointed his gun at me and said, "Heave to. If you don't then the mate gets it". As he made the threat he pressed a gun to the mate's head. I had no choice. I rang down "stop engines".'

'What else did he say?'

'He ordered the mate, the helmsman and myself to move right over to the larboard wing of the bridge. It was then that a launch, that had been keeping station on our starboard quarter, moved in. I felt the bump as it came alongside. Unfortunately, from where I stood, I could see only the mast and the top of its funnel.'

'So while you were held on the bridge, the pirates abducted Mr Vanderpole. And then they left you and boarded the launch.'

'Yes, that's so, Mr Holmes. When they had gone the mate and I went below to see if anything had happened to the passengers. They had been held at gunpoint by two other pirates. Apart from witnessing Mr Vanderpole being forcibly dragged out of the saloon, they were unharmed.'

'One other thing, Captain Anderson. When the one who gave the orders spoke, did his English pronunciation sound strange to you?'

'Now you mention it, he could have been a Dutchman or a Low German. I have sailed to and from ports on the Ems and the Weser where the local dialect is not far removed from English and nearly sounds the same.'

Our next call was to the Waterguard, where Holmes questioned them about the females that had come ashore from the *Anglia*.

'Can you recall anything about their appearance?'

'Well, sir, as the list shows, there were only two that day. One was the wife of one of the passengers who frequently travels in the *Anglia* with her husband.'

'And the other?' asked Holmes.

'Well, she seemed to be unwell and I heard one of the passengers, who was helping her, say, "Now don't worry, we are on dry land now and you'll soon feel better". Or something like that. She must have been seasick. The butter boat rolls about a bit.'

'So, you did not stop her and question her?'

'Didn't think it necessary. She was not one of the women we have stopped in the past who wind long lengths of contraband about them under their clothes. I wished I had, now that we know she may have smuggled in a great hoard of diamonds.'

'An expensive decision, my man. In fact, a five thousand pound decision. Well, at least do you remember her face?'

'No chance, sir – she had a veil. Five thousand pounds, you say? Well, well.'

On our return from Harwich we sat down and went over what we had learned.

'Holmes, I hope you will agree with me that my suggestion that we should visit the scene of the crime has proved of value.'

'I'm not certain whether it has, Watson. The recollection of the Waterguard concerning the veiled woman certainly suggested that she was the one carrying the diamonds off the boat.'

'It was most unfortunate that he let the woman get away. Come to think of it, Holmes, in one of your cases the villain escaped the country in a female disguise. Could the woman at Harwich have been a man? Now, how about the description and voices of the pirates?'

'I've been thinking about what the master of the *Anglia* told us. I suggest you look through the notes you have made of past cases and find what I remember you intended to call the Borkum Mystery. I recall vividly the sinister villain with a duelling scar. On that occasion I only confronted him once. He said little although I recognized the accents of the Frisian Islands.'

'Of course, Holmes, I do remember. You were confronted by, let me think, ah, yes, it was a Herr Karl Norden. A moment while I fetch my notebook for that year.'

I found my notebook.

'Here it is. Norden attacked you with a sabre. After a desperate fight back and forth in a boat shed, in which he cut your walking stick in two, you dealt him a fearsome blow on the jaw and he fell senseless at your feet.'

'Your account, Watson, greatly dramatizes the fight. It was over in a few seconds. He dealt only one sweeping cut with his sabre that I parried with my stick. He was already off balance when my fist connected with his jaw. When he fell he hurled abuse at me in Plattdeutsch. I detected among the words he used, "Not cricket".'

'Well, then, although there may be many others with scarred faces, you may have identified the villain.'

'With your help, Watson. With your help.'

'Is there a possibility that this Norden has now come to London?' I suggested.

'Yes, and I am certain he was the leader of the gang who abducted the diamond courier. He, or someone, will be arranging to collect the diamonds from the woman who, we assume, carried them ashore at Harwich. He will try and sell them and, therefore, there is a good chance that he will be found in the vicinity of Hatton Garden and its many dealers in diamonds. I doubt that he will attempt to sell them to any of the reputable members of the diamond trade. They are now well aware of the robbery and, as I said, anyone offering a large quantity will be under suspicion.'

'What is our next move, Holmes?'

'Obviously, we have to start looking for Norden. Admittedly he has a distinctive duelling scar yet even so we are looking for a needle in a haystack of six million Londoners. I shall have to bring in my Baker Street Irregulars.'

He rang for Billy and gave him instructions. Within two hours the hallway and the staircase was a mass of jostling boys of varying ages. Holmes described to them the man we were looking for. He emphasized the scar and suggested they start to search an area centred on Hatton Garden. Each was given sixpence and the one who found Norden would receive half a crown.

They left, buoyed by the thought of the reward to be gained if Norden were found.

'Holmes, I fail to see how just twenty or so boys can scrutinize all the thousands of people around Hatton Garden?'

'I'm relying on the fact that the sixpence which each has received will be shared by one or two others they may meet on the way. It is possible that the original twenty will multiply until there are one hundred pairs of young sharp eyes looking for the man with the scar. A half a crown reward is a great incentive.'

We heard nothing from the searchers for two days. Eventually the leader of the Irregulars and another boy arrived. 'Mr 'Omes, sir, we got 'im. 'e's art side the Blackfriars Inn. If you 'urry you'll catch 'im. Tommy 'err sawed 'im abhaat an hour back.'

'Well done, Tommy,' said Holmes. 'Now if you are right and lead us to the man with the scar there's half a crown in it for each of you. Now cut along and hail a growler. We'll be down in a minute.'

On our way down the stairs to the hall, Holmes gave Billy a shilling and a message to take to the telegraph office. Ignoring the cabman's protestations about having two filthy urchins in his cab, we urged the driver to take us at the fastest possible pace toward the bottom of Farringdon Street. Once in the cab, I soon realized that the boys were most obviously strangers to soap and water.

As we drew up outside the Blackfriars Inn, Tommy pointed and said, ' 'e's still 'er. That's 'im. The tall bloke wots 'aving a barney with the laidy.'

'Now, boys,' instructed Holmes, 'keep back and be ready to follow them if they scarper.'

'Don't rush, Watson. Have your pistol ready.'

At that moment a cab stopped and out stepped Lestrade and another inspector from the Yard.

'Which one, Mr Holmes?'

'Glad you could get here, Lestrade. The tall one talking and gesticulating to the woman with the floral hat. That's your man and I suspect the woman is an accomplice.'

We closed in from four sides. After a short struggle the two suspects were bundled into a cab and taken to the nearest police station. I forgave the boys their filthy appearance when I saw the broad grins of pleasure on their faces as Holmes gave each half a crown.

Later, as we discussed the day's events, we both fell silent when we realized that the whereabouts of the diamonds still remained a mystery.

'As Norden did not have the diamonds on him then we shall have to question the woman very carefully. It may be possible to trap her into revealing where they are,' said Holmes.

*

At the police station, where the woman was being held in custody, Lestrade allowed Holmes to put questions to her.

'Your name is?' asked Holmes.

'Mary Spencer,' was the reply.

'Oh, that is a remarkable coincidence. It's the same as that on the wall calendar advertising Spencer's footwear for the constabulary. However, it is not the same name as that on the envelope found in your possession. Why should you have a letter addressed to a Miss Mary Hammond of number twenty-five Leinster Row?'

'Isn't mine,' replied she.

'Oh, I'm sure it is. The letter instructed you to be at the Blackfriars Inn at midday yesterday.'

I could see from her expression and resigned droop of her shoulders that she realized she had been identified.

Holmes continued his questions and then said, 'Miss Hammond, for that is your name, I expect that you have lost some weight since you stepped off the butter boat at Harwich. It is those lost pounds which interests us.'

'I've no idea what you are talking about.'

'Well, I am sure you do. A visit to twenty-five Leinster Row may prove rewarding. Agreed, Lestrade?'

'I'll need to get a search warrant, Mr Holmes. I should be round at Baker Street by ten in the morning.'

Armed with a warrant, we examined the woman's small terrace house. Lestrade and his men searched all the 'traditional' hiding places. Nothing was found out of the ordinary and certainly nothing that would lead to the diamonds. The linoleum flooring showed no signs of having been disturbed. Holmes was able to verify the fact by observing that all the depressions made by the legs and feet of the furniture were old and none had been made recently. We did not examine the loft because the paint round the edges of the trap door was old and had stuck the trap door shut. The small paved yard at the back showed no sign of any of the slabs having been lifted.

Holmes started to pay particular attention to the door into the parlour. He pointed to the hinges and said, 'Someone has been removing these screws. See the slots are burred. Push that chair over, will you, Watson?'

He climbed up onto the chair and was able to feel the upper surface of the door. 'Lestrade, will you get your men to remove the door?'

Lestrade supervised the removal of the door. Once it was off Holmes borrowed a knife and started to scrape away at the top edge. Within a few minutes he had uncovered four holes plugged with newspaper. In the holes were packets of diamonds.

Later, as I was writing up some notes of the salient facts of the case, I put the question, 'What led you to the door? Unless the door was open the hinge screws could not be seen.'

'Your memory is not what it was, my dear fellow. Recall one of the cases involving the Fenians. You remember? They hid their bullets in the top of a door.'

'Yes, now you mention it, I do remember. You know, Holmes, this appears to me to be a very unsatisfactory case. One that has not exercised to any great extent your powers of observation, other than the damaged screws. I am inclined to subscribe the successful outcome more to two half a crown pieces than anything else.'

'I agree.'

Nothing more was said.

The Sycamore Seed

In which sycamore seeds and circles in the corn play a part.

Part One

A letter arrives

The letter that Holmes received one autumn morning was obviously of great interest.

'I've had a most interesting letter,' he said. 'It's from my cousin Charles Wellbos, the chief constable of Wessex. Apparently, a body has been found with no means of identification. The clothing is that of a fisherman. The injuries that caused death are strange. He asks if I can spare time to investigate,'

'Do you want me to accompany you?'

'Certainly. Your medical knowledge could be of value. Can you see if *Bradshaw* lists a convenient morning train to Dorchester.'

'We will need rooms at a hotel?'

'No need. My cousin has invited us to stay at his manor house.'

The next morning we were in a comfortable South Western railway compartment speeding west. At each stop Holmes carefully scrutinized people on the platform. I did not interrupt his studies because, from experience, I knew he was storing impressions of individuals in his mind for future use. I did not doubt for one minute that the portly man wearing stout boots and gaiters and a low-crowned hat was a farmer. I was well aware, of course, that Holmes had already filled his card index of a brain with much more information, such as: a farmer on the way to market; is a widower; has both arable and livestock interests; is careful with his money.

At Dorchester we hired a four-wheeler. It was most refreshing to the mind and the senses to be in bucolic surroundings and away from the stifling heat of the city. An hour after leaving the station and having passed many prosperous-looking farms, a gaunt Norman castle increasingly began to occupy our view toward the sea. I commented on the sight.

'That's strange, Holmes. The castle is Norman. Yet I understood that few were built in these parts.'

The closer we came to the great pile of stones, the more we could discern the out-of-character additions made to the eleventh century original. The eastern side was a jumble of low-roofed outbuildings. The walls surrounding the bailey were surmounted by the Tudor domestic quarters.

On our arrival at the manor house we were welcomed by Holmes' cousin and his wife. The house was itself a mixture of old and new. Some parts were Stuart and others Georgian. I could not help noticing the Holmes' family likeness when we were greeted by his cousin. His first words were, 'Cousin, I am very pleased to see you. I am faced with a strange affair that is most baffling. My men are at a loss to know how to proceed further. Now, enough of the problem for the time being. We shall discuss it after dinner. By the by, I have not mentioned to anyone that you are here.'

That evening we were joined by Doctor Hedges, the county coroner, and his wife, to whom we were introduced as a Mr Pallisser and a Doctor McCloud. Nothing was mentioned during dinner about the case. When the ladies had retired, we settled down to talk about those subjects that are normally forbidden at the dinner table. The coroner raised the subject of the body on which there was no means of identification. Holmes said nothing. He sat with his long fingers together under his chin. Only his eyes betrayed his attention to points of interest.

The coroner turned to Holmes and said, 'Forgive my intrusion on your privacy. For you see, ever since you were introduced to me as Mr Pallisser I was certain that you were a relative of Wellbos. You both have the same distinctive features. I will go further in my deductions. If I am not mistaken, you are the famous detective Sherlock Holmes. And,' turning to me, 'that makes you, sir, Doctor Watson, alias Doctor McCloud.'

The chief constable laughed and said, 'You are correct. This is indeed Sherlock Holmes and this is his friend, Doctor Watson, who records his cases. I have requested their help. You are most observant. I considered it prudent to keep their identity a close secret. The fewer people, other than yourself, who know that they are about to come under the fearsome scrutiny of Sherlock, the better.'

'Watson and I are most happy to assist,' said Holmes.

He then put some questions to the coroner.

'Doctor Hedges, you say that a body clothed as a fisherman was found lying in the long grass at the side of the road. I have met cases before where there has been nothing to indicate who the deceased had been. It would be most helpful if you could show me the place where the body was found.'

Early next morning the coroner arrived and we drove in his carriage through the lanes for about two miles.

'This is the spot, Mr Holmes. As you see, the grass still bares traces of where the body lay.'

Holmes made his usual meticulous examination of the surroundings. I was somewhat surprised when he picked up a small branch that had fallen from an oak tree, whose limbs reached over the road. He also examined a number of other small broken-off branches.

'Mr Holmes, do you think these branches have something to do with the deceased?' asked the coroner.

'At this stage of my investigation it is far too early to reach such a conclusion.'

We returned to the manor house.

Part Two

A newspaper report

At breakfast the following day I passed the *Wessex Times*, that I had brought to read in the train, over to Holmes.

'There is a report in here that may be of interest.'

Holmes read through the item and commented, 'It seems that a local newspaperman went down to Stourminster Regis to investigate a strange phenomenon. Among those he interviewed was the Reverend Seymour Chase who has very firm views about phenomena of all types. His views are in marked contrast to those of the farm labourers and servants who were questioned. Oh, this is amusing: the reverend gentleman dismissed their reports as hallucinations and pointed out that the men questioned were on their way home from the public house. Nevertheless, the recollections all had one thing in common. The night was dark with low cloud and light breeze, when each experienced a rushing wind and hissing sound. The wind appeared to blow straight down upon them. Where they differed one from another was in the descriptions of what they saw. Some said they saw a vast dark shape. Others mentioned a dark cloud low overhead.

'You know, Watson, there was a similar report two months back of unaccounted-for phenomena in Dorset. However, I do not place too much trust in newspaper accounts. I am inclined to accept the clergyman's explanation. For the time being I shall cut out the story and put it in my commonplace book when we are back in Baker Street. That is if you have finished with the paper?'

I agreed and no more was said of the matter.

The evening was sultry and from the distance came the grumbling of thunder. I had left the door ajar and the window of my room open. Two of the servants were on the landing. Their conversation was more than the usual below-stairs gossip. I distinctly heard one say, 'Last night my Gabriel felt that great wind and the rushing noise when he crossed the long bottom field.'

'What you on about, girl? Of course it's windy down there,' replied the other.

'No, it's like 'e said. A rushing noise and wind. He swears he zor a huge black bird o' prey like the devil come from the sky. Just 'is telling of it makes me shiver.'

Instantly I recalled the newspaper report we had been discussing. In the past, under the influence of Holmes, I had acquired an interest in strange phenomena. At the same time I agreed with his opinion that there is a simple explanation for all we see, feel and hear in this world. All the same, the servant's tale was intriguing. I ventured to mention the subject to our host. He was not surprised and said, 'For the past year I have been receiving stories about some very strange happenings around here, such as noises, disturbances of the air and dark shapes.'

'I have read the newspaper report,' said Holmes. 'Charles, tell me, are there any common facts among the different tales other than a dark night and low cloud?'

'Only that I happen to know that most of those to whom the reporter spoke are not only tenants of mine, they are also of a sober disposition,' replied the chief constable. 'Of course their experiences are passed from ear to ear and it is natural that the events become somewhat embellished by the time they reach the other side of the county.'

The next morning we accepted the coroner's invitation to examine the corpse. The skull had been fractured from the eyebrow on one side to the occipital region. Furthermore, the skull had been subjected to great heat. In my many years in the army I had never come across such a strange wound. I could only construe that the victim had been violently struck by a cylindrical object that was very hot. Even if the blow to the head had not proved fatal, the fracture of all the major bones in the body would have eventually resulted in death.

I thought for a moment and then ventured my opinion.

'The injuries are consistent of his having fallen over a cliff. That is with the exception of the burn mark on the head. Yet the only cliffs near here are on the seashore a few miles away.'

I became aware that this was one of the very few occasions when Holmes appeared lost for comment. He did not even venture to say, 'A most singular set of injuries.'

As we were about to leave the mortuary, Holmes stopped and said to the coroner, 'May I examine the deceased's clothes?'

When the clothes were laid out on a table, he spent some time carefully examining them.

'Certainly, these appear to be those of a fisherman,' said Holmes. 'However, this heavy jersey, the tarpaulin jacket and the close-fitting woollen cap are not often to be seen being worn so many miles from the sea. Even more puzzling, though, is this pair of plimsolls. They are those of a yachtsman, yet the garments are those of a rough fisherman. I need to re-examine the body.'

Holmes paid particular attention to the hands. After a few minutes he said, 'These are not the hands of a fisherman let alone a yachtsman. See, there are no calluses. However, you will observe the discolouration of the forefinger and thumb. If I am not mistaken the skin has acquired a permanent black hue from being in contact with the ink of a pen. Our victim is more a clerk than a fisherman. I might even venture that the lack of any blue tint suggests that he was a draughtsman using dense black drawing ink.'

Holmes made another study of the clothing. He searched through the pockets. 'Ah, what have we here?' he said, holding up a sycamore seed with its characteristic shape. 'And here are some more. Now, the question is why this particular botanical item? Are these the clothes of a botanist who is also possibly a draughtsman?'

The next day we told the chief constable that we were going to walk along the high ground leading to the castle. 'I for one should like to look inside. From the exterior it gives the impression of being a most interesting example of its kind,' said I.

'I must warn you not to get too close,' was the reply. 'They are a very strange lot in there. They keep to themselves and employ a number of brutal gamekeepers. Furthermore, the shrubbery and the copse and spinneys close to the walls are strewn with mantraps. I have sent warnings to the owner about the illegality of the methods he employs to keep trespassers away.'

As we walked along the high ground toward the castle, Holmes discussed the problem of the unidentified body with which we were faced. Suddenly in mid sentence he said, 'Now that is rather odd. Look over there, Watson, at that wheat field. Can you see it? The one to the right of the village down in the vale.'

I could see clearly that the expanse of golden grain was marred by a large circular depression.

'Come on, Watson, that is a strange sight. Let us investigate further.'

We set off down into the vale. After walking and, despite the pain of my old wound, half running to keep up with Holmes, we arrived at the edge of the wheat. We could see no further into the field than the nearest stalks.

'Are you any good at climbing trees, Watson? No, I'm sorry, of course your damaged leg will not allow such exertion.'

Before I could comment, Holmes, as lithe as a cat, climbed one of the oak trees at the edge of the field. When he came down from the tree, brushing the dirt from his clothes, he said, 'I was only just able to discern the location. Ideally, we need to be either on the ridge or up with a bird to see clearly. Let us hear what my cousin has to say before we go trampling through the crop.'

Wellbos was surprised at our finding. None of his tenants had reported such an event. He decided to accompany us to the farm. The farmer was also surprised when we met him and said we would like to inspect his field. He agreed that we might make a path through the standing wheat.

'Well, I never,' he said when we examined the scene. 'Who'd do such a damn silly thing? That's a few bushels lost.'

We could see that the stalks had been blown down. They were completely compacted in the middle of the circle. Toward the edge it was less so. We appeared to be standing in the middle of a saucer of disturbed wheat. Holmes paid particular attention to three depressions in the soil. Each was about a foot in diameter. After pacing between them he said, 'Each is the same distance from the other two. Together they form a triangle. Another thing to note are the marks made by the hoofs of two horses. Two riders must have entered the field and approached whatever made this saucer-like depression. For some strange reason one of the riders has galloped round in small circles. First clockwise and then anti-clockwise.'

As we stood there, thinking about what we were seeing, I ventured to suggest, 'Could this be some ancient pagan ritual?'

'Pagan ritual my foot,' replied the farmer, 'it's some fools a be larking about. I'll give 'em pagan ritual if I catch 'em at it. It's all very well young couples a cavorting in the crops, cos they don't make much damage. But this is something different.'

On our way back from the field we met another farmer and when he heard of our find he said, 'That's odd. One o' my lads says the long bottom field 'as been trampled on.'

We went over to the field. Within a rough circle the crop had been flattened and there were three deep depressions in a triangular formation. There were also clear signs that a number of people and horses had been moving about. Holmes went down on his knees, oblivious of the effect on his trousers. He sniffed the ground. After dinner that evening he retired to his room saying that he had to forego our company because he needed to think deeply about the events of the day and set down his preliminary conclusions.

Part Three

An appeal

The chief constable requested that we should stay for a few more days because he hoped we would solve the mystery of the unidentified body and, at the same time, determine the cause of the strange effects on the crops.

The next morning at breakfast Holmes was opening a letter.

'Watson, this is from my brother Mycroft. Something of great interest, no doubt. He only writes when absolutely necessary. I did not tell him I would be down here. Little escapes him, you know. He also tells me that he has sent a copy to Charles.'

From experience I knew that Mycroft was a man of few words, both spoken and written. His urbane nature belied the veritable dynamo of his brain. As I have mentioned, his position and role in government were never discussed. He answered to no one particular department. He was, in effect, the grey eminence of Whitehall, always ready to advise and to seek out information for others to use. From the expression on my friend's face, I assumed the matter to which the letter referred was both important and of a singular nature.

Impatient to know what the letter contained, I interrupted Holmes' thoughts as he read the correspondence for the second time. 'I know I sound like Buckingham disturbing Richard Crookback. Nevertheless, please, what does your brother want?'

'He says that information has been received which suggests that an unusual machine is being developed in great secrecy. Apparently, it could prove a threat to our country's security if it fell into the hands of an enemy. It seems he wants me to find this machine. That is, of course, if it actually exists and is not just a pipe dream. Jules Verne has much to answer for by putting ideas into inventors' minds.'

'This is all very well, Holmes, because it raises the question of where does one start to look. More importantly, what are we to look for?'

'Obvious questions. However, Mycroft does provide a clue, or he believes it is a clue. He has intelligence of unusual happenings at a castle in Dorset.'

'Surely not the castle that we went to look at? This is all too much of a coincidence.'

'A singular coincidence indeed, Watson. Mycroft writes that the informant could not say what sort of machine, and may have been motivated by jealousy, greed or anger and therefore is not to be relied upon. However, when his information was put alongside that gathered from our agents in a certain foreign country, then it became certain that it was absolutely necessary to look into the matter further. Now this is very interesting, Watson. Apparently about six months ago an agent of the government was sent to investigate the castle because it seemed certain that a strange machine might be found within its walls. Only one message was received and that conveyed little. Regrettably, soon after his body was found washed ashore in this part of the county. It is assumed that someone from the castle had murdered him. He goes on to say that relationships with the foreign country involved are at a delicate position and therefore no mention of the affair must be made public. Furthermore, obtaining a warrant to search the castle might result in the device being deliberately destroyed before it could be examined. If it is as lethal as is reported then the British government is anxious to get hold of it. All this means that any attempts to seek the device and its custodians by a direct approach will fail. Mycroft wants me to use my deductive powers without entering the castle. As I said, my cousin has been sent a copy of this letter.'

'As you would say, this may prove to be a singular case.'

'Indeed so. This is not the first time I have had to determine what was afoot inside a building or guarded enclosure without being able to see inside. It is then that I have to rely on clues from the surroundings. As Donne wrote, "No man is an island", and neither is that castle. It impinges on its surroundings and in turn they affect the castle. Therefore we must make the customary inquiries among the local people; in particular the tradesmen, the postman and the railway goods yard office. In the meantime we will keep the castle at a safe distance.

'Yes, I agree. Discretion being the better—' I was interrupted.

'Good morning. I see you've read Mycroft's letter,' said Holmes' cousin as he strode into the breakfast room waving the letter in his hand. 'I've had to deal in my time with a murder or two, a big bank robbery and the disappearance of a large herd, yet never have I been involved directly with Whitehall. This may also explain the unidentified body that was washed ashore. Now, Sherlock, what can I do to help? I cannot supply detectives because we have none.'

'Nothing immediately, Charles, thank you. Watson and I will do some old-fashioned detective work ourselves. In other words knocking on doors and asking questions, yet at the same time not disclosing the reason.'

That day we made inquiries among the local tradesmen. At the railway station in Dorchester we learned that a great number of casks and metal containers were frequently delivered to the castle. The nature of the contents could not be determined; although there was a faint aroma of oranges. In other circumstances a covert examination of the goods would have been undertaken. However, that was not possible because of Mycroft's insistence that we avoided, whenever possible, giving an indication that the castle and its secret were under investigation. As we seemed not to be gaining any worthwhile information, other than that concerning the casks and containers, I said, 'How about a balloon, Holmes? You could ascend above the castle and look down upon its inner courtyards. You could also examine those depressions in the wheat and see if there are any more. You might even be able to take a photographic impression.'

'Splendid idea, Watson. Let us waste no more time. We must go immediately to the local post office.'

Off went a telegram to Mycroft saying, 'Urgently need flight in a balloon. Please arrange.'

Knowing Mycroft, I knew that such a terse and unusual request would hardly ruffle his demeanour and that he would immediately respond.

Within a few days a major from Her Majesty's Balloon Factory at Aldershot rode up to the manor and announced, 'I have orders to provide an aerial reconnaissance of a local castle and that a Mr Holmes and a Doctor Watson are to accompany me.'

At that moment I wished I had not suggested the idea of a flight in a balloon. I have been with Holmes in many strange situations and in some tight spots. Nevertheless, always with my feet firmly on the ground. I did not sleep properly that night. By dawn I was feeling distinctly, as they say, 'under the weather'. Over breakfast, although not over mine, the major explained the wonders of ballooning. He also explained that he had been instructed not to tether the balloon and that a free flight had to be made starting some distance upwind from the castle. Therefore, the voyage would be very much at the mercy of the wind. Holmes agreed that tethering the balloon near the castle would certainly alert the occupants that they were being observed. Our flight had to be made to appear to have no interest in the castle.

We travelled west to the border with Devon and from there we ascended in a balloon. I clung to the edge of the basket. As we rose up from the ground, my regrets at having agreed to this plan of action increased. It was a most unnatural place to be in, although I had to admit that the vertiginous effects on the senses I had experienced when climbing the mountains of Afghanistan were absent. All the same, I feared that the balloon might burst or the ropes that joined it to our basket would part, and we would be dashed to the ground. The major announced, 'The aneroid barometer tells me that we are at one thousand feet.' In the circumstances, I would have been happier not to have known this fact. Holmes, in contrast, was absorbed in the passing scenery.

'We shall be close to the castle in a few minutes,' said Holmes. 'In this wind there will only be a few minutes to make our observations.'

Now we were passing over to one side of the castle. Unfortunately for our purpose too far to one side. Holmes pointed his binoculars and said, 'I cannot see much of the inner bailey from this distance.

Ah, yes, it appears to be covered over. I regret that you cannot cast out the anchor, Major, so that we can hover like a hawk, even for only a moment.'

'If we were to do that I might not be able to release the anchor from whatever it may have hooked on to. Then I would have to release the gas and descend.'

'And, of course, that would alert the castle's owner to our presence. We must carry on, Major, as if this is a military exercise whose movements are entirely dependent on the wind direction. Watson, can you Kodak the castle, or are we too far away?'

'There is a chance.'

I pointed the camera, in hope rather than certainty, and pressed the trigger. By now we had passed away from our target and being at the mercy of the wind we could not, as a sailing vessel could, beat into wind and fly over again. This limitation prompted me to ask, 'Major, did you read that article in *The Strand Magazine* about Hiram Maxim's intention to build a flying machine? Apparently it will be driven by steam.'

'Too clever by half,' he replied scornfully. 'I cannot see how he is going to carry enough fuel for the boiler in order to sustain flight for a reasonable time. All the same, I can tell you we are also investigating a number of proposed flying machines with engines that can be steered in any direction. Not just dirigible balloons, but machines that are heavier than the atmosphere, that can proceed in any direction and be independent of the vagaries of wind and weather.'

I will not attempt to burden the reader with the remaining events of the flight, other than to report that our progress suddenly became more rapid and it started to rain. We were not able to observe the crops in the vale and to see if there were any other marks. Sufficient to record that after a stormy passage in torrential rain we had to come down in a field ten miles to the north east. Those who followed our progress on horseback only just managed to find us before night set in.

Back at the comfortable manor house at the break of dawn, I was about to retire to my room when Holmes, undeterred by the arduous flight we had survived, insisted on reviewing what we had discovered.

'I conclude that there could be two reasons why the inner bailey is covered. Obviously there is something in there that has to be protected from the weather. And, two, whatever is inside has to be kept very secret. Which leads to the conclusion that the owner of the castle is well aware that the inner bailey can be seen from a balloon. From the look of this morning's weather, we are in for a dark night. Dark enough, I wager, for stalking the mystery of the castle.'

That night, after supper, we walked along the lane that led to the north of the castle and waited. As Holmes had predicted it was a dense black night. A thin drizzle reduced visibility even further. As we stood there it reminded me of many other nights I had had to keep vigil in the cold and the wet as we waited for the appearance of a criminal.

'I can just make out a light from the castle,' whispered Holmes, although why he had to whisper I could not understand. After all, we were not a couple of poachers in fear of a gamekeeper. I could just make out the light. When we moved a mile to one side we could see two lights. We came to realize that when we stood to the north of the castle we could see one bright light. When we moved round to the east we could see two lights and when to the west three lights. If we were to move sideways from, say, the east, the two lights would dim and be replaced by a single light when we were north of the castle. As we continued to move, then that light would gradually dim and be replaced by an emerging set of three lights until they were at the fullest intensity. We discussed the lights with Wellbos, and we mentioned that there was, at the same time, a steady light on top of the castle that could be seen in all directions. He said they were obviously similar to the leading lights positioned to guide seamen when approaching a harbour.

Part Four

Intelligence

The postman arrived at the manor punctually at nine o'clock, as he did every day. Among the letters was another from Mycroft. After studying its contents, the letter was handed to me. I was surprised at the information it contained. Apparently, correspondence from the castle had been intercepted which indicated that the secret machine was a flying vessel. I read the copy that had been made of a letter to a General X (as I mentioned earlier, the names of the country and its personages must remain a secret).

Your Excellency,
I have the honour to report that Professor Bactrac's flying machine has been completed and that during the past two months a number of voyages have been made. The machine performs well in the vertical plane. Unfortunately, I regret to have to report that we have yet to achieve satisfactory forward motion and the ability to steer at will.

The power for rotating the lifting sails is derived from a Hero type of engine whose effluxes are arranged as the arms of the Indian religious symbol, the swastika.

The downward flow of air from the revolving sails (sic) causes the body of the machine to turn slowly in the other direction of rotation. Because we have to minimize the weight it is not practicable to increase the area of the stabilizing fin and its movable portion that acts as a rudder. You will recall from an earlier report that we had tried installing the Hero engine in the body of the machine and driving the lifting sails by chains. Unfortunately when we tried that method the sails remained still and the body of the machine spun round.

We are convinced that once we have achieved sustainable movement for a number of hours the machine can progress to Z. There, in your splendid scientific establishment, the present shortcomings will be overcome. Then, Your Excellency, our country will have an aerial weapon against which there is no defence.

I remain, Excellency, your most obedient and most humble servant.

'Undoubtedly, then, we have been pursuing the flying machine mentioned in the letter. What is our next move, Holmes?'

'In my opinion too early to say. I had understood that such a machine has to achieve forward motion on the ground before it can rise like a bird and—'

I had to interject at that point, saying, 'What about Jules Verne and the aerial vessel he describes, that is lifted by rotating paddle blades on the top of masts? And this letter mentions lifting sails.'

'Of course, Watson, you have pointed to a possible answer. Yes, the machine in the bailey would have to rise vertically from within the confines of the walls. The swathes of flattened crops are where it has alighted. Furthermore, why has it chosen or, possibly, been compelled, to seek the ground on so many occasions after only a short flight?'

'Now I recall what the major said about Maxim's machine. You remember he referred to the need to carry sufficient fuel in order to sustain flight for a reasonable distance.'

'Indeed, the fuel is possibly an important clue. Now, let us look at this copy of the map that was enclosed with the original letter. The line marked could indicate an intended voyage from the castle to a point near Dover. You will also note the column of numerals. They appear not to convey any meaning. Mycroft's covering letter admits that the experts in codes and ciphers he has consulted are baffled. What do you make of it?'

I examined the numbers yet could not discern any pattern. I handed it back to Holmes, who was leaning on the mantelpiece. He happened to be holding the map close to the mirror as he re-read the letter.

After a few moments he said, 'Very simple, Watson. As I look into the mirror I find, staring me in the face, the numbers on the map. They are of course reversed. When read in that order they provide the longitude of each of the points marked on the map. Have you a pencil and paper? I'll call out the numbers.'

I thought, So much for the so-called black art of cryptography.

We used the numbers to provide positions on a map. It became clear that they were intended to be places where the machine could have its fuel replenished.

'This is interesting,' said Holmes, as we marked in the last position. 'It is alongside Dover Castle. Could it be that he, or they, are attempting to traverse the Channel in the machine? We must act immediately. Borrow the trap and hasten to the post office. A telegram must go without delay to Mycroft. It should read: "Machine may attempt to alight into open space either to the north of Lyndhurst or outside Hurstmonceux Castle. Last chance to apprehend will be in meadow to the east of Dover Castle. Suggest welcoming parties attend for the next few days".'

Part Five

Bird in hand

Only after three unsuccessful all-night vigils to determine the meaning of the strange events occurring near the castle were we rewarded. We were waiting at the edge of one of the fields to the north of the castle. There was no moon and few sounds. Suddenly Holmes grasped my arm, saying, 'Listen, can you hear it?'

At first I heard nothing and then I began to hear a hissing and threshing sound. The noise grew louder and louder and a great wind beat about our heads. A menacing black shape passed above us and then alighted in the adjacent field. 'Now's our chance!' cried Holmes. 'Come on, Watson.'

Our progress was arrested by a formidable hedge and it was some time before we broke through and rushed toward the strange shape that stood amid the wheat. It loomed dark and foreboding. I could not really understand what I was seeing. There was an arrangement of posts and bars surrounding a number of cylindrical shapes. However, the most remarkable features were four great arms that curved outward and downward from the centre of the machine. I could have been looking at a monstrous four-legged spider. A figure all in black was on top of the strange contraption. It was holding a large can and pouring a liquid into a container mounted at the juncture of the four great arms.

Holmes cautioned silence and we started to creep toward our goal. Suddenly we were spotted. The can was hurled to the ground. A lever must have been pulled and before we could advance further the great arms began to whirl and straighten up. Holmes was well ahead of me. The machine began to rise. Holmes made an athletic leap and gained a handhold on one of the bars. I was too late. I stood breathless beneath the machine as it rose. A fierce wind from the spinning arms beat against my head. I could just see Holmes clinging on as the awesome machine rose higher and higher, moved away and was lost from sight.

The dark of night had swallowed the machine and Holmes. There was nothing I could do to save my friend. I returned to the manor. There a search party was formed and set out at my direction toward where I assumed the machine had gone. Not until dawn did we come across Holmes. He was staggering across a field. His clothes were torn and he had a number of cuts and bruises. He said little as we carried him back to the house.

Later in the morning Holmes recovered sufficiently to recount his aerial adventure. 'When I grasped the machine I had to gain a firm hold because I realized that it was leaving the ground. I had hardly achieved a safe position when I was set upon by the occupant. He was lithe and strong. We struggled together. He was intent on hurling me from the craft. I knew that if for a moment I were to relax my grip, I would be doomed. As we fought, the machine plunged and rolled alarmingly. Without its master's hand on the levers it was possessed with the desire to dash itself onto the ground. I cannot recall what happened after that. All I remember is finding myself lying on the wet grass and feeling rather ill used.'

I listened intently to Holmes' amazing account of his fight in the sky.

'Did you have the opportunity to observe how the machine managed to rise from the ground and then, as it were, fly across the fields?'

'No chance, Watson. I was far too occupied in frustrating my opponent's attempt to evict me from the machine. However, I could not fail to be aware of the whirling and glowing mechanism just above my head and that I was being forced toward it.'

'Have you any idea where the machine is?'

'None. Now if we could return to where you found me I imagine it is not far away from there.'

Mindful of Mycroft's warning that the nature of the device should not be revealed as public information, Wellbos suggested that only he should accompany us in our search. We retraced our tracks and arrived at the place where Holmes had been found. From that point onward, despite his injuries, he was able to exercise his undoubted skill as a tracker. He followed his own very faint footsteps and other clues until we reached the place where he had found himself lying on the ground. From there we spread out and moved in the direction indicated by Holmes. I was not surprised to note that we were moving toward the castle. A little further on we found a heap of tangled metal. The pipes, bars, rods and cylinders were all mixed up together. However, there were no traces of the man who had tried to kill Holmes.

Holmes moved from clue to clue. A spot of blood, a footprint, a broken branch and other signs that indicated that someone had moved away from the wreckage and toward the castle. His cousin held him back, saying, 'No, it is much too dangerous to go any further. We shall either be shot at or caught in mantraps. Even worse, we could be set upon by ferocious dogs. We must wait for reinforcements.'

'Yes, I agree,' replied Holmes. 'It is not so important now that we know the machine will never reach Dover.'

Part Six

Explanations

A number of officials from Horse Guards and the Aldershot balloon factory examined the wreckage of the machine. Its tangled remains were gathered up and taken away.

Later that day we stood outside the castle gate. We were accompanied by the county police and the detectives from Scotland Yard who had been instructed to work under the direction of Holmes. At the shout, 'Open in the Queen's name,' the great gate of the castle was opened. Only a few servants were to be found. Of those who had devised and built the flying machine there was no trace. However we discovered a great quantity of different chemicals and machinery of various types.

'The one person we must find is the Professor Bactrac referred to in the letter that was intercepted,' said Holmes. 'Mycroft tells me that he is a most distinguished scientist. At the same time he is a recluse which is why his absence from his home has not been noticed. It is surmised that he has been kidnapped and held in the castle and forced under duress to develop the flying machine. We are now faced with the question of where he is now.'

During our search of the apartments of the castle, Holmes observed a number of sycamore seeds lying on the stone floors. He stood looking down at them for some time and then said, 'Observe that the seeds form a line leading to the wainscoting under that large painting.'

Not unexpectedly, considering the Tudor origins of that part of the castle, a secret entrance was revealed leading into a series of windowless rooms. We found many machines and materials.

We also found Professor Bactrac.

In reply to our questions he explained, 'I was kidnapped and forced to develop a flying machine. I have no idea who my captors were. They threatened me with dreadful consequences if I did not obey them. I was given some notes written in German. From them I had to develop the design into a practicable machine. Apparently it was the invention of a scientist at Gõttingen. I was never told his name. I am most grateful to you gentlemen for rescuing me.'

'Professor, you owe your deliverance to the acute observation of none other than Sherlock Holmes,' said Lestrade. 'It was he who observed the trail of sycamore seeds leading to the panel in the wainscoting.'

'Indeed! I have been most fortunate,' he replied.

As I was examining one of the many engineering drawings and documents we had found, I observed that written under the title and number on some of the drawings was the name James Fastnett; on others there was just a set of initials.

'Professor Bactrac,' I said, pointing to some of the drawings, 'who is Fastnett, and whose initials are those appended to some of the drawings?'

'Fastnett was an engineer, and the initials are those of the other engineer who translated the inventor's notes and prepared the necessary engineering drawings, though I was never told his name. In addition to building the machine, they were both charged with venturing into the air with it. I believe that Fastnett met with an accident when testing the machine.'

Later we reviewed the case.

'Well, Holmes,' said I, 'this appears to have solved the mystery of the unidentified man found under the tree, although we have not accounted for his fatal injuries. Also, I suppose we must presume that the fellow who tried to kill you survived the terrible crash to earth and has fled.'

Holmes replied, 'They say that when your life is threatened and the end is near you recall many things from the past. When I wrestled with the driver of the machine, and death came close in the form of the hot whirring machinery, I remembered the dreadful injury to the man's head. My head was about to suffer the same fate. I would be struck and hurled overboard. That is most certainly what happened to Fastnett. The poor fellow must have inadvertently raised his head too high. He was more than likely dead before he crashed through the branches of the oak tree.'

'That explains much. Except there is one point I do not understand. Why were you so interested in the sycamore seeds found in his pockets?'

'At the time I had no possible idea. It was only when I saw the machine for the first time did I notice that the lifting sails, even though bent in half, were identical with the shape of a sycamore seed. The seeds scattered about the castle had most likely been discarded during experiments with different shapes of lifting sails.'

'Then we were correct in assuming in the first place that the machine was capable of rising vertically from the ground, and you mentioned the need to alight at intervals in order to replenish its container of fuel. I know little of mechanical matters although at least I can appreciate that, were the fuel supply to be suddenly empty, the machine would fall violently to the ground.'

'Yes, Watson, that is quite so. This is where the seeds played their part in our adventure. You see, the professor had obviously observed what we all know: namely, that a pair of sycamore seeds spins round as it descends so as to slow its fall and allow the wind to disperse it away from the tree. When deprived of the power from the engine, the lifting sails of the machine behaved as if they were sycamore seeds, thereby lowering the machine gently to the ground.'

'It was most observant of you to detect the line of seeds pointing toward the secret door.'

'Indeed they did provide a clue but only to remind me that the wainscoting in old houses often have panels, projections and other decorative features that when pressed cause a hidden door to open. We would no doubt eventually have found the door after a systematic examination of the woodwork. I just happened to come upon the opening device purely by chance.'

'Chance indeed,' I commented and raised another point. 'I recall you deduced that some horsemen had added to the flattening of the crops by making peculiar traces.'

'Again a chanced observation. It had little to do with the saucer shape made by the machine. I deduced that one of the horses ridden by someone from the castle had been frightened and the rider had had some difficulty in controlling it.'

'And another thing, Holmes. Why did you pay particular attention to the ground in the second field? Was that an important clue?'

'Indeed it was. I detected traces of the aroma of oranges. Although I was not sure at the time, later I recalled the distinctive smell of Kohlenstoff's powerful liquid used to produce artificial diamonds. That is what provided the immense power needed to elevate the aerial craft.'

Needless to say, Holmes received a letter of commendation from the Prime Minister along with a suggestion that he should consider accepting a title. The latter was greeted with a laugh and the comment, 'Even if I were to be offered, however unlikely, a dukedom, I would refuse. If people wish to add just "Mr" to my name let them. Whatever I am called or will be called is of little interest to me. I doubt that it would affect my powers of deduction.'

This was a particularly remarkable case which Holmes had successfully solved, one in which he wrestled with a criminal up in the air, and realized that mankind was about to conquer the skies.

Notes

'Horse Guards', a location, refers to the offices of the commander in chief of the army and his staff. Not until ten years later would extensive reforms result in the establishment of an army council headed by the chief of the general staff.

Tracks in the Snow

In which a serpent is confronted.

Part One

High pressure steam

When I awoke I could see through my bedroom window that it was very dark outside. I glanced at the clock and was surprised how late it was. Looking again, I saw that London was enveloped, or rather was being suffocated, by one of its notorious fogs.

As I went down to breakfast I could hear Holmes and Mrs Hudson having, as they say, 'words'.

'Mr Holmes, I am not at all pleased to find such a mess in my kitchen.'

'Come, come, I was only trying out a new formula that I am certain will revolutionize the detection of adulterated milk. As you must well know, there are unscrupulous dairymen who add chalk and water.'

'Adulterated milk, Mr Holmes! You'll find no such thing in my pantry.'

I stopped on the stairs until both parties had come to an agreement over Holmes' use of the kitchen as a laboratory. My friend said very little as we breakfasted. I could tell from his manner that he had not prevailed against all of Mrs Hudson's severe reservations concerning using the kitchen. Outside, the dense fog muted the usual rumble and clatter of vehicles and the shouts of people in Baker Street.

For more times than I can remember, breakfast was often that time of day when a letter or an important visitor arrived which would prove to be the starting point for another of our adventures among the webs of crime and mystery that had to be untangled. This was to be another such breakfast.

Mrs Hudson brought in a card. Holmes took one glance and said, 'Please show Mr Ashendon up.'

Our visitor was a small rotund person of uncertain age. His ulster and hat were well worn and not particularly clean. Holmes, for a reason I could not understand at the time, was most deferential to our visitor and they were obviously well acquainted. He offered him one of his best cigars and some cognac. Despite his appearance, he appeared at ease in lighting the cigar and savouring the bouquet and regarding the colour of the cognac. He settled back in my favourite chair and said, 'Holmes, your help is needed and needed quickly.'

'Ashendon, I see from the name written against yours on this card that your visit and request for help is concerned with a matter of state.'

'It is indeed. Charles Woolnough has disappeared. He must be found. It is now over a week since he left his house.'

'Woolnough! I am not familiar with the name. Who is he?'

'A scientist who is consulted by many companies when they have problems with steam engines. He has not been seen or heard from for two weeks.'

'Steam engines, you say?'

'Not just any steam engines. They are a type that uses steam at extremely high pressure. He is the foremost authority on the subject and that is why he must be found, presuming he is still alive, because he is working on the development of engines for Her Majesty's ships that will enable them to steam halfway round the world without the need to stop to take on more coal.'

'Serious, indeed,' remarked Holmes. 'Surely he is not the only engineer involved? There must be others with whom he works that could carry on the important development in the event of anything untoward happening to him?'

'None, Holmes, none. The ideas are his alone. He does all his research in his house in Hampshire. There is great concern at the Admiralty that he may have been kidnapped by agents of a foreign power who would very much like to get their hands on the details of his engine, and in particular its revolutionary boiler. In the meantime there are warships in the yards whose machinery is only half finished. Every day that Woolnough is away the greater the chance that a foreign power may learn the secret and will gain an advantage over the Royal Navy.'

'My brother's name on your card is sufficient incentive to offer my services without delay. Shall we start our investigation at Woolnough's house? If he agrees, I should like Doctor Watson to come with us.'

'Yes, the house is the best place to start and Doctor Watson is most welcome to come along. The Hampshire constabulary will be advised of our intention.'

I indicated my willingness to accompany Holmes and Ashendon and, once again, have the opportunity to be a Boswell to Holmes.

Part Two

Sand and pines

The next morning we met Ashendon at Waterloo station. Despite, as he told us, being an experienced traveller by train, he was as baffled as we were by the confusing arrangement and numbering of the platforms. We had to spend some time going from platform to platform in order to be certain we had found the Southampton train and would not be carried to some remote branch line terminus in the wilds of Surrey or even Dartmoor.

Once started the journey was uneventful. We alighted at a station some twenty miles to the south of Winchester. A short cab ride and we arrived at the house of the missing scientist where we were welcomed by Mrs Proud the housekeeper and by Inspector Andrew of the local constabulary.

The first questions put to the housekeeper elicited that the scientist had had a visitor whose visiting card had disturbed him.

'Mrs Proud, you say that your master was very upset when he looked at the visiting card,' said Holmes.

'Yes,' she replied, 'he went white and for a moment seemed to hesitate before telling me to show the visitor in.'

'Did you see what name was on the card?'

'There was no name, just a picture of a snake. Here's the card.' She handed Holmes a normal-size calling card.

'There's something I must tell you. Something he forbad me to mention to anyone. However, under the circumstances, I feel free to speak. You see, he was in fearful dread of serpents. Even a picture of one in a book would produce convulsions. He was going to move from here as soon as he could. He inherited the house from his father who died six months ago. He came to settle his father's affairs. He told me he intended to leave as soon as he could and let his brother have the house.'

'Why did he want to move?' asked Holmes.

'He did not like living close to the Great Heath because there's so many vipers there and he feared that they might get into the house.'

While Holmes was making a careful perusal of the room, the inspector asked the housekeeper if she could describe the visitor who had the left the card that had so agitated the missing scientist.

'He was a gentleman.'

'Yes, yes, but was he bearded or have any outstanding features?'

'Not really, Inspector, just like others who visit Mr Woolnough. I mean did.'

'What happened next?' asked Holmes.

'I was told to fetch the bag in which he had sufficient clothes always ready for when he was suddenly called to go to some works where they wanted help.'

'So you were not surprised that he suddenly left with a stranger?'

'No, not at all.'

'Surely, Mrs Proud, he told you where he was going?'

'Well, that's the strange thing. Usually he always tells me where he is going. He seemed confused. It was the visitor who told me they were going to Newcastle. That's where he often went. So at the time I was not surprised or even worried. It was only after three days and when I had not heard from him that I became concerned. I decided to telegraph the big shipyard company at Newcastle. They replied that he had not been there. They must have told someone in London about the master's disappearance and that's why I suppose you gentlemen are here today.'

'Mrs Proud, your information is most helpful. Ah, I nearly forgot. Did you see what the unnamed visitor arrived in? Was it his own carriage?'

'No, sir, it was one of the cabs from the station.'

We then made our way to the station. One of the cabmen remembered taking someone to the house and then returning with him and Woolnough, who was well known to the cabmen. The booking office clerk also remembered seeing Woolnough with another man on that day. 'They bought tickets for Summerfield, a station about ten miles down the line. No, they didn't ask to be booked through to Newcastle.'

We left Ashendon and returned to Baker Street to study the facts we had gathered and to consider where the scientist may have gone after arriving at Summerfield. Telegrams were sent to all the companies with whom Woolnough dealt. Their replies confirmed that none had been visited by him for at least three weeks. We had just decided that an entirely different approach had to be made when the morning papers carried the news that the body of Woolnough had been found less than half a mile from his house. The reports gave no indication of the cause of death other than it must have been from natural causes because there were no signs of foul play.

Holmes telegraphed Ashendon and proposed that together we inspect the place where the body had been found. During our train journey down to Hampshire, Holmes explained to Ashendon that 'the place where his body was found could provide clues to where he has been in the past two or three weeks'.

'But he died from natural causes, Holmes. The police report I have received confirms that there are no signs of foul play. We may be wasting our time.'

'Not at all. I should also like to examine the deceased's clothing. Can that be arranged?'

'The body and effects are in the mortuary at Winchester.'

The lane where the body had been found was narrow and muddy and the wide grass verges suggested that at one time it had been part of a Roman road.

Inspector Andrew led us toward a stile. 'This is the step on this stile, Mr Holmes, where Mr Woolnough was found sitting, but dead. As you can see, his house is only about a quarter of a mile off. The postman, who uses this lane as a short way back to the town, said "good morning" as he passed. As the deceased, who knew him well, did not answer and was slumped forward, he went up to him to see if he needed help. The rest you know.'

Requesting that we should not follow him, in order not to add more footprints, Holmes walked slowly along the lane toward the house with his head down, intent on the ground. At a gap in the hedge he walked across the field toward a line of Scots pines.

When he came back to where we were waiting by the stile he said, 'There are three items of immediate interest. Firstly, there are no recent wheel tracks of wagons or carriages in the lane. Secondly, there are the footmarks of two men, one of whom was walking backwards, which appear to lead from that gap in the hedgerow. And thirdly and most intriguing are the wheel marks of some vehicle that has come across the field as far as the gap in the hedge. It, apparently, could come no further because of the deep fosse. Watson, if you have your notebook I should be much obliged if you will make a sketch of the wheel tracks for me.'

We went along the lane to the gap in the hedge and I made a drawing as best I could of the tracks that Holmes pointed out with his walking stick.

'As you can see, gentlemen,' said Holmes, 'the wheels are unusually broad. They are very similar to those of the wagons or carts that plied the unpaved roads of the last century. Also, and most strange, are the ridges at intervals across the tracks. Inspector, I note that away across this field there is a distinctive change in the appearance of the countryside.'

'Yes, Mr Holmes, that is the Great Heath. It stretches for over twenty miles from here and goes right over to Sablchester. The land is neither fit for crops or beasts. As the housekeeper mentioned, not many folks around here will venture on to it because of the snakes. They like the dry, sandy soil and some of them are deadly. There's supposed to be more vipers here than in any other part of the kingdom.'

At the station none of the railway men or the cabmen, who knew Woolnough well, recalled seeing him arrive by train and walk up the lane. At the mortuary the police surgeon was only able to give the cause of death as heart failure.

'There were no marks or wounds on the body then?' asked Holmes.

'None. Would you like to see the body?'

'No, thank you. However, I would like to examine his clothing.'

Holmes made a careful scrutiny of the deceased's clothes and in particular his boots. From the latter he took a sample of the dirt around the toe of each. Among the personal effects from the pockets was the return half of a ticket for Summerfield, the station some ten miles down the line from where Woolnough had last been seen.

'Now why would he have an unused return half? See, it has not been clipped. Unless, of course, he did not go back home by train. I could find no footprints that indicated someone had earlier walked along the lane from the station.'

'Do you think then, Holmes,' said I, 'that he was carried to the stile and left there to give the impression that he had collapsed as he walked home from the station? As you say, there are sets of footprints that may indicate that he was carried by two men from that gap in the hedge, where you asked me to make the drawing of the tracks of a cart or wagon.'

'That, Watson, appears to be what most likely happened. He was carried in a vehicle of some sort as far as the fosse.'

'Holmes, if that is what happened then should we trace those tracks back to their starting point?' said Ashendon.

'That would obviously be the next step. Unfortunately, as I discovered, once the wheel tracks passed onto the sandy soil they could no longer be followed.'

'Why? Surely, Holmes, sandy soil accepts and retains tracks and footprints as well as wet soil?' said I.

'Indeed, Watson. However, it is possible that wind and rain may have obliterated any tracks. We are now forced into finding another way of tracing the place at which the vehicle started, carrying, as I am certain, Woolnough. Although whether he was alive or dead at the time is another unanswered question. You will recall that he and the stranger left the house in a station cab and, when questioned, the cabman and booking clerk remembered that they had caught a down train. What we need to do is to make a fresh start by going to Summerfield, the station named on the return ticket found in Woolnough's pocket. In the meantime I'll return to Baker Street to consider the clues we have gathered so far. Ashendon, I'll telegraph you when we are ready to pick up the trail again.'

Part Three

The sounds of snow

I suppose the activity in a street is one of those background sounds to which we become so accustomed that only when it suddenly stops do we realize that it has been there all the time. Holmes and I had been so absorbed in the Woolnough case that it was not until Mrs Hudson entered the room and said that there had been a heavy fall of snow did we realize that the usual rattle and rumble of cabs, carriages and wagons in Baker Street had been deadened.

After luncheon Holmes, who was standing at the window, said, 'Watson, have you the drawing you made of those vehicle tracks?'

I found the drawing and gave it to him.

'As I thought. Look, you see those tracks being made by that horseless carriage down there? See, it is backing out of the mews. The tracks in the snow are the same as in your drawing.'

'Of course, you are right, Holmes. Woolnough was more than likely carried across the heath and as far as the side of the lane in a vehicle having a similar arrangement of wheels.'

'Therefore, we now have two important facts to consider in this case. An engine, similar to the one in that carriage now leaving a cloud of steam up Baker Street, and an unusual four-wheeled machine. They may be connected. This suggests that Woolnough was willingly or, more than likely, unwillingly involved with a steam driven carriage. Now the question that remains is why was it equipped with very large broad wheels?'

In response to a telegram, Ashendon joined us at Waterloo station and once more we travelled down to Hampshire. I confess that, as we stood on the platform at Summerfield, I had no idea what we were looking for. I wondered if the others had reached any conclusions.

Ashendon broke our silence by saying, 'Can we assume that Woolnough may have gone with the stranger to a house or farm somewhere on the edge of the Great Heath?'

'An excellent suggestion, Ashendon,' answered Holmes. 'Let us study your map Watson. It may give an indication of where we should look.'

The map showed that there were only a few villages on the edge of the heath that were within a mile or two.

'I am of the opinion, gentlemen,' said Holmes, 'that had the mysterious vehicle started any further away then Woolnough would have been taken by a different route. For example, by a stopping train going up to London and alighting at a station close to the northern side of the heath.'

'An acceptable conclusion, Holmes,' said Ashendon. 'Perhaps we should visit the local agent who deals with property in this area. We could pretend to be interested in buying a house so as not to draw attention to our quest?'

'I agree. We could assume the disguise of a committee looking for a large house and grounds in which to establish a sanatorium,' said Holmes.

We visited two agents and explained that we were looking for a large house with spacious grounds that would be suitable for our purpose. We emphasized that the health of the residents would benefit if they were on or close to heath land. Three properties were recommended to us. We declined an offer to have a visit arranged to each of them because, as we explained, we did not want to alert the neighbourhood of our intention, and thus be forced to pay more than was necessary. Therefore, we would, for the time being, just survey them from the outside.

Armed with details and the locations, we hired a horse and trap and surreptitiously studied the three properties from a distance. Each looked like any other private dwelling. Two appeared to be unoccupied and in a state of disrepair.

'There is a possibility,' said Holmes, 'that Woolnough was in one of these three houses at some time, and that he was then taken by the vehicle whose tracks we investigated across the heath to within a short distance from his home.'

'I cannot understand why you have reached such a conclusion.' I said. 'You have always been most insistent that one should not try and make the facts fit the anticipated or wished-for result.'

'You are quite right, Watson. I have to confess that I am making an exception to my own rules because, at this moment, I have absolutely no clear idea of what we are looking for, or even of how to proceed further.'

Such an admission on the part of Holmes was unexpected. However, his doubts and those of Ashendon and myself were dispelled somewhat when we observed the largest of the three houses, which did appear occupied. It had an unusual number of crude extensions and in a secluded part of the grounds was a large barn-like edifice partly hidden by shrubs and trees.

'Those sheds are out of character, I would say,' said Ashendon. 'There's no sign of any animals that would indicate that this is a farm.'

'The largest of the unusual buildings is, I suggest, the first one we should try and penetrate,' said Holmes. 'However, I am still questioning why the tracks of the strange vehicle are so broad and why they are so difficult to follow. If, as I conjecture, this is its lair, then we should find its tracks nearby.'

We then made our way through the garden of one of the unoccupied houses and approached the grounds at the back of the house that appeared to be occupied. We kept as far as possible behind trees and shrubs so as not to be seen. Holmes examined the sandy soil at the boundary of the heath. 'As I anticipated, there are traces of wheel tracks leading from the heath and they are similar to those we saw in the lane where the body was found.'

'I recommend that we return after dark,' advised Ashendon. 'We do not want to attract too much attention. Otherwise those who abducted Woolnough will be warned that they are being watched. It is most important that we find out who they are and what they are doing before any direct action to apprehend them is attempted.'

Part Four

A charmed snake

That night we returned to the suspect house and its unusual outbuildings. As we stood close to the barn-like structure, we became aware that someone was approaching. We quietly slipped back out of sight and watched. Whoever it was stopped in front of the barn, stood still, and gazed across the heath. After a few minutes he turned to the doors of the barn and swung them wide open. As far as we could see there was nothing of interest inside. He then continued to look out across the heath.

Holmes gripped my arm and whispered, 'Listen, can you hear a strange whistling and rumbling? It's getting louder. It's coming from the heath.'

I did and nodded my head. Ashendon indicated that he also could hear it.

The sound increased and then to my astonishment an apparition loomed out of the darkness. It resembled an upturned boat. There was a large gun barrel pointing forward and on top of the hull a cupola from which projected the barrels of a Gatling gun. Underneath were very large and broad wheels. Low down at the front was the menacing shape of a pointed ram. It slowed down as it came closer and I could see that the wheels at the front were swivelling and guiding the machine into the barn. It passed within a few feet of where we stood behind the bushes. I felt the intense heat that radiated from it. As it moved, it made a sound similar to that of the engine of a steam ship. I smelt hot oil and metal. Once it was in the barn the doors swung to and were closed behind it.

Keeping my voice low, I said, 'Those wheels at the front turned after the manner of the Ackermann steering on horseless carriages.'

After waiting to make sure that all activity in and around the barn had ceased, we started to explore. We managed to find a way into one of the sheds. Once inside and, by the light from my dark lantern, we could see that there were many pieces of complicated machinery. 'These are lathes, if I am not mistaken,' whispered Ashendon. All around were many cylindrical objects and numerous pipes.

The sudden very loud shout shattered the silence.

'Stop! We have guns and we will shoot if we have to. Keep absolutely still. Secure them hand and foot.'

We were, as directed, bound hand and foot by unseen persons.

A voice then said, 'Sherlock Holmes, I have been expecting you. What took you so long to find me?'

Out of the dark came Holmes' reply: 'You have the advantage, sir. Have we at some time been introduced?'

'Indeed we have. Five years ago, before I became detained for an indefinite period at Her Majesty's pleasure, our paths crossed on the road to Epping Forest. You had the advantage then. Now I have the advantage.'

'Lempschone, of course. The villain who cold-bloodedly shot and wounded two police officers. Thanks to a soft-hearted judge you avoided the hangman's noose and later escaped from the Moor.'

'I am sure you now expect me to exact revenge on you and your companions. You would be right. However, first I need to know how you found me and how much you have learned about this place. I expected that Doctor Watson would be with you but I must know the identity of the third member of this gang of midnight burglars. You realize that I would be justified in shooting all three of you on the grounds that I was defending my property and, of course, had no idea who you were. However, that would be such a crude ending to your adventure. Fortunately, I have the means of eliminating you without leaving any clues. However, before taking that step, I am certain I shall be able to force you to divulge how much has been determined about my recent activities.'

We were then roughly marched along passageways and into a

small room. There our captors tied us each to a chair set before a high bench. I recall how helpless I felt and how apprehensive. What did the villain mean when he said that he had the means to make us divulge our intentions? In Afghanistan I had at all times been prepared to suffer the appalling tortures that would be inflicted on me should I fall into the enemy's hands. I realized this was a very different situation to be in. The unknown is perhaps the greatest fear of all.

By candlelight I could see that, for some reason or other, we were seated so that our heads were just above the level of the bench.

'Now, gentlemen, I will show you why you will tell me all I need to know,' said Lempschone. With that threat, a door in a box on the bench opened and out slithered a large snake.

'I am sure you will recognise the very deadly Indian Cobra. Doctor Watson, from his service in that part of the world, will be able to enlighten you about its lethal abilities. With this wand I'll provoke it so that if anyone struggles, or even sneezes,' he laughed, 'it will strike.'

The wand came over my shoulder and its tip was brought close to the flickering tongue of the serpent. 'Gentlemen, are you now convinced that I am in earnest when I demand that you tell me what has been discovered about my work here?'

Considering our dire straits, Holmes' voice was extremely calm. 'Lempschone, even if we do know we will not oblige you. And knowing your disdain for human life, without doubt you intend to dispose of us whether or not we meet your demands. In a similar situation, in a penny dreadful, the victims would curse you and warn you that you will not succeed other than to the hangman's rope. So further words are of no avail.'

I wanted to shout out, 'Holmes, what are you saying? Stop. I'm no hero. Even if that's the part you want to play.'

The wand touched the head of the snake. It struck at it. I wish I could recount that, at that moment, I was calmly analyzing my state of mind. If the truth be known, I was rigid with fear.

Lempschone's voice was full of hatred and menace. 'I will now leave you to consider your fate and, of course, to face the terrible choice of either telling me what I want to know, in the hope that I might spare you, or perish. As I said, any sudden movement or even any movement, however slight, could invite being struck by our angry friend.'

We were left alone. The cobra's gaze seemed fixed upon me rather than on my companions. We tried to converse in the manner of a ventriloquist by not moving our lips. The presence of the hooded menace only two feet from my face prompted visions of my time in India. I had only seen a cobra in the native market as it swayed to the music of its keeper's pipe. To this day I have no idea why the strange tune should come to mind. I began to purse my lips and imitate, to the best of my ability, the sound of a snake charmer's chant.

At my side Holmes was trying to speak through compressed lips. 'What are you doing?' I ignored him and continued. The cobra began to sway from side to side.

I realized that as long as I imitated the sound with which the cobra was familiar, we were safe. However, only, of course, until our captor returned. And then out of the corner of my eye I saw a grey creature scuttling on to the bench. It was a rat. The snake's head, in a flash, seized the unsuspecting rodent and its fangs delivered a lethal injection. The jaws began slowly to envelop the limp body. The cobra slithered round and went back into its box, to digest its meal.

Holmes was struggling against his bonds. Somehow he managed to free his hands and then was able to release his ankles.

We conversed in whispers.

'Can you hear any movement on the other side of this door?' Holmes asked.

'I can hear some sort of hissing noise and a number of people are arguing,' I replied.

'We will have to take a chance. Let's get out of here and face the consequences,' suggested Ashendon.

We crept out of the room and stealthily approached a half-open door at the end of the passageway. Peering through the door, I could just make out a mass of convoluted pipes. The heat was intense and there was steam hissing out of valves and out of joints in the pipes. There were four men standing close to a cylindrical vessel, whose massive bolts suggested they were intended to resist a great pressure. They were gesticulating and shouting. One called out, 'We'll all be killed. Release the pressure now.'

I recognizsed Lempschone's voice as he shouted, 'It's safe. The last thing Woolnough said before he died was that it would stand a pressure of fifteen hundred pounds. We're only at one thousand. Get on with it.'

As he spoke I turned toward the others, who were just behind me. There was a terrible cracking sound; a fierce blast of intensely hot steam threw us to the floor. I was faintly aware of the pungent aroma of peeled oranges.

When we composed ourselves we found, amid the wreckage, the bodies of Lempschone and his companions. They had perished in a most terrible manner. In another part of the grounds we came upon many documents and drawings.

As Ashendon gathered some of the documents together he said, 'Woolnough was not forced to go with them just because of his knowledge about ships' engines. He was obviously wanted by them because they needed advice on how to develop a compact and powerful enough engine to drive a military vehicle. A machine that would be able to lead the van of an army and be immune to shot and shell. One such machine was the one we saw entering the barn.'

We went to the barn. It was indeed an awesome machine. The thick metal plates of its body appeared able to resist all but the largest of shells. As for rifle bullets, they would have been scattered away. Of particular interest was the Gatling gun in the conning tower in which we found the levers used to control the machine. In one part was an arrangement of cylinders and pipes similar to the one that had just exploded.

'Yet why build the device, or machine, in such secrecy?' Holmes asked.

'Because,' said Ashendon, 'and I regret to have to say this, His Royal Highness, the commander in chief, and his advisers, are firmly committed to the horse. When the inventor, Stevenson, tried to gain their interest he was, as we say, shown the door. He was not even given the opportunity to show the generals any of the details of his proposed machine. The idea of a self-powered vehicle is, apparently, an anathema to them. Even the suggestion of a battalion of soldiers on bicycles, that has been raised recently, is looked upon with a jaundiced eye by many in the army.'

I commented, 'Yes, I read about that most interesting innovation in *The Strand Magazine*.'

Ashendon continued. 'The colonel in chief of the Household Cavalry expressed himself to me on the subject in no uncertain terms. He said that the horse had served the army perfectly well for hundreds of years. Even if such an outlandish device were acquired it would frighten the horses. In any case its use in battle would be contrary to all the rules of war.'

'A somewhat head in the sands attitude,' remarked Holmes.

'When Stevenson was rebuffed,' explained Ashendon, 'he was not heard of again until we began to gather bits of information that, together, indicated that he had decided to proceed on his own and build his self-propelled, steam-driven land machine. We could not be certain whether he intended either to test its effectiveness in secret and then sell the plans as a military vehicle to a foreign power, or even use the machine for some criminal purpose, such as forcing a way into a bank. Even though we had no idea how it worked, other than it would be driven by an engine supplied with steam at an enormous pressure, we were immediately suspicious when we heard that Woolnough was missing. Only he had the knowledge concerning boilers and engines that worked at extreme pressures.'

'A most singular train of events indeed,' said Holmes. 'I think we can assume, with a degree of certainty, that Lempschone heard about the invention and, realizing its awesome power for criminal purposes, stole the plans and may have killed Stevenson.'

'I presume that Lempschone also killed Woolnough, but how?' asked Ashendon. 'As we know, there were no marks on the body to indicate a lethal wound or, according to the post mortem, any indication that he had been poisoned.'

'I have given some thought to that,' replied Holmes. 'I have concluded that he died from his fear of snakes. Lempschone must have subjected him to the same ordeal as the one we had to face. The sudden appearance in front of him of a cobra was all that was needed to induce a fatal convulsion and seizure of the heart. I doubt that the intention was to kill him. His murderer only wanted to gain information that would enable him to use an extreme pressure of steam. At some time, perhaps at the very last minute, Woolnough exacted his revenge by leading Lempschone to assume that a pressure greater than one thousand was safe.'

Ashendon arranged with Inspector Andrew to have the bodies removed and a strict guard placed on the machine.

Back in Baker Street, I began to jot down some of the essential details of this extraordinary and very dangerous adventure.

'Holmes, who exactly is Ashendon?'

'I've known him for many years. All that I can tell you is that he is a colonel in military intelligence and that Ashendon is not his real name.'

'Now, what will happen to the machine we examined?'

'I understand that it will be taken to the Woolwich Arsenal. I doubt that it will be looked upon, other than as a curiosity having no place on the battlefield.'

'Another question that comes to mind is, why did Woolnough agree to go with Lempschone? Surely he could have refused?'

'I pondered that question for some time and it was only after I had looked through my index of names and my commonplace books that I think I found the answer. It seems that both were up at Oxford and in the same college. Lempschone had founded one of those absurd undergraduate clubs that involved an initiation ceremony.'

'Of course. Snakes.'

'Just so. A candidate had to stand naked in a small room in which there were snakes. I am not sure whether they were lethal or not. All the same, the ordeal left Woolnough ever afterwards in dread of serpents. You recall the visiting card with the picture of a snake.'

'Yes, I follow all that.'

'I regret to have to tell you of something I discovered. You see, the Serpent Club's members were inclined to certain perverse behaviour. An activity that is never referred to openly in polite society. In the police courts, where they often find themselves, their practices are referred to using euphemisms. Had he not gone with Lempschone then, no doubt, the latter would have threatened him with the exposure of his youthful indiscretions.'

'I think I understand. However I fail to see how you were able to free yourself so quickly from your bonds? Mine were like bands of tight-fitting iron.'

'I suppose I shall have to let you into a secret. You must not divulge it to anyone lest I find myself again in the same predicament. I am sure you are aware that I have always kept my muscles in good order. When my wrists were being bound I exerted the utmost effort to keep them apart so that later, when I relaxed the muscles, the bonds became sufficiently slack for me to force my wrists free.'

'An important secret indeed and one which I certainly will not reveal.'

'By the way, my dear friend, had the rat not appeared we would have been dependent entirely on your snake-charming ability. Your imitation of the sound of the charmer's pipe was very good, considering the great danger to which you were exposed. However, snakes have only rudimentary ears compared with ours. They are sensitive to vibrations transmitted through from the surface on which they are lying. The cobra responded not to your vocal effort but to the slight vibrations transmitted from your head and lips. At the time I did not consider that imparting such important information would have been any comfort to you. Come to think of it, did you detect the smell of oranges when the engine exploded?'

Fair Play

In which Holmes reluctantly deceives a widow.

Sometime in July of 1896, Holmes and I were just about to start our breakfast when Billy, the page boy, announced that a gentleman, who did not give his name, wished to see Holmes.

'A very early visitor,' he commented. 'To arrive at this hour suggests a matter of either great urgency or of great importance. Or perhaps for both reasons. Show the gentleman up, Billy.'

On entering the sitting room the visitor addressed Holmes, saying, 'My apologies for descending on you at such an early hour and without the courtesy of writing to you first. Of the matter, on which I am only the messenger, I can only say that it is of great importance. The Prime Minister instructs me to tell you that he has complete confidence in your abilities and he believes that there is no other detective or detectives who will be able to undertake what may be a very sensitive investigation.'

'Lord Marsham, you say?'

'Yes, Mr Holmes. He requests that you go down to Osborn House at Tring immediately. His private train is already waiting at Euston to convey you there. I am also instructed to say that if you wish Doctor Watson to accompany you that would be in order.'

I looked at Holmes and said, 'I am ready if needed.'

'Good. Certainly I should like you to accompany me. Now let us gather our things together.'

Addressing the emissary he said, 'You say you are not able to tell us anything about the matter? I would wish to have some facts before meeting Lord Marsham.'

'I am sorry, Mr Holmes, I have no idea of the nature of the problem that is troubling the Prime Minister. You will have to wait until we get there.'

The special train, which was always kept in steam to rush the Prime Minister at any time of the day on his way to the Palace of Westminster, had been sent up to Euston. As soon as we had taken our seats in the one and only carriage, one of Mr Webb's engines was hurtling us through the tunnels and out and away from London.

At Tring station a well-turned-out carriage and pair, with the Marsham coat of arms on the doors, was waiting to take us to the house. On entering I was overwhelmed by the sight of the numerous portrait paintings. The history of England crowded in on me.

The Prime Minister greeted us. 'Gentlemen, thank you for coming so promptly and for foregoing your breakfast. As you see I am about to have mine. I prefer to breakfast alone and away from the family table. However, circumstances are such that I welcome your company.'

He did not immediately raise the subject for which we had been summoned. Breakfast was not usually the time to discuss serious matters. We ate in silence.

Breakfast over and the servants dismissed, Lord Marsham produced a letter and handed it to Holmes. I could see, on the single sheet of paper, the words 'GIVE IRELAND WHAT SHE DESERVES'.

Holmes studied the letter carefully and then said, 'There is no address or signature or anything to indicate who sent it.'

'It may have come from the Fenians,' responded the Prime Minister.

'I am inclined to agree with you, my lord. Although we have not heard much from them since they committed those outrages on the underground railway in London.'

'That is so, Mr Holmes. I had also hoped that the bomb at the Palace of Westminster seven years ago was the end of their long campaign of terror. You may have heard at the time that the chief constable for the county received a letter from Ireland that contained a threat on my life.

'It so happens that the letter in your hand coincides with a document that is also concerned with Irish affairs. That document, at the moment, is of great importance and which requires your renowned investigative skill.'

'A document, you say. I assume it is also anonymous and you want me to trace the author.'

'No, Mr Holmes, the problem we are faced with is not that of knowing who wrote it. You see, I was the author. I have to tell you that, some time ago, I wrote an appreciation of the Irish problem. It was intended to be a private document in which I set down the principal threads that formed the tangled web of Irish politics. I did not hesitate to voice my own opinions. These opinions were formed early in my life when they used the potato famine to vilify us, despite the large amounts of money sent from England for their relief. I also included my strongly held view that the church in Ireland meddles unhelpfully in politics. The murder of Cavendish and Burke in Dublin was a dastardly act.

'However, despite that, and my opinions, I acknowledge that successive governments have failed to encourage or support the establishment of industries and railways which could relieve the abject poverty of most of the people. That poverty is the root cause of much of the trouble. Unfortunately my appreciation was stolen by someone who could use it to serve a particular political purpose, such as promoting Home Rule. And, of course, it could be the Fenians.'

'As you say, my Lord, they are just your opinions, yet why are you so concerned that they might be disclosed?' said Holmes.

'Because there is more in the document than just those opinions. I also set down a prediction which suggested that the activities of the Land League, the Fenians and the numerous murders committed might force Her Majesty's government to impose draconian martial law and to limit the activities of all males between the ages of sixteen and sixty; except, of course, members of the Ascendancy. I have learnt that somehow James Powall, the Irish politician, acquired the document. Now that he is dead we will never know what he intended to do with it. However, if the Fenians were to get their hands on it they will make public the martial law paragraphs to stir up even more trouble. The most likely use of the document is to pass it to Gladstone and those who continually urge the granting of Home Rule. He would, of course, only accept it as a political weapon if he had the original written in my own hand. He could not use just a copy or hearsay when campaigning for Home Rule. Now, Mr Holmes, may I assume you will take up this case?'

'So you want me to recover the document?'

'As soon as you can.'

'I am reluctant, my Lord, to take on the task because I do not agree with your administration's opposition to Home Rule. I consider it a pointless attitude. Nevertheless, I will set aside my political objections because I appreciate the seriousness of the problem with which you are faced. Therefore I am going to have to take on what may prove to be a most daunting of tasks. However, I absolutely insist that my name must under no circumstances become associated with the investigation. It is most important that I maintain my independence from political affairs.'

'Certainly, Mr Holmes, I understand.'

'Sir, have you any idea where the document might be?' asked Holmes.

'As I explained, I did not discover it had been taken for some time and that Powall had somehow acquired it. Since his death, his widow Frances, as I understand, has kept all his correspondence and papers. That is the first place to look. I am not certain what use he might have made of my words. As I explained, if the Fenians were to get their hands on it they could cause even more trouble. Irrespective of who has or has not got the document, it remains a petard with a short fuse already burning. It must be found, and quickly, before it literally explodes relationships between Ireland, the government and the opposition, and particularly with those who advocate Home Rule. I am relying on you, Mr Holmes.'

A few days later I was aroused from my reverie among the mountains of Afghanistan by the appearance of a bowed and scholarly figure at my side. Once again my friend was adopting a disguise in order to penetrate a problem.

'I'm off to visit the widow Powall. She has invited me, Patrick Flyn, to research among her late husband's papers. I am writing a book about the more important Irish politicians. She is ready to help anyone, such as myself posing as a scholar, who could show, from a study of her late husband's papers, that he had no direct involvement with the Fenians, nor had he anything to do with the murder of Cavendish and Burke in Phoenix Park, Dublin. What of my brogue?'

'It will just about pass. Can I help?'

'Thank you, not at the moment, Watson.'

Within four days the 'scholar' arrived back. With a triumphant gesture, Holmes produced a sealed envelope.

'Are you going to open it?'

'No. What it contains, I am sure, is not for our eyes.'

He then recounted all that had happened.

'When I arrived at the house in Godalming, Mrs Powall was obviously most anxious to help me in my research task. She let me work in her late husband's study amidst his books. I suggested that if there were diaries then they would be the first place to start. She agreed and opened a small safe in which the diaries were kept. Each day when I had finished with the diaries, she locked them back in the safe. To my surprise, she even allowed me to read the more intimate letters that had passed between them. Eventually I came across one particular letter that Powall had written to her. When I read it I realized that it was one I should not have seen. What I considered to be a significant part was where he had written that if anything should happen to him, then she should remember the "Double Seal" that he had entrusted to her for safekeeping with "Athlone". Should anyone approach her and ask for it, they would say "Kilmainham" as their authority to let them have it. In turn she had to say to them that the key was in the Dark Pool. They would understand. Under no circumstances was she to let the Fenians have it.

'The words "Double Seal" and "Athlone" exercised my brain for some time. Who was Athlone? Was he a friend of the family? It was not until the next time the safe was opened by Mrs Powell that I realized that an envelope with a double wax seal lying with the diaries could be the one I was seeking. The remaining problem was that of taking it. I had, obviously, to try and find the numbers for the combination lock on the safe. As you know, Watson, for the benefit of thieves, the owners of safes often disguise the sequence of numbers in the form of alphabetical characters. "Athlone" might be such a code.

'I waited until I heard Mrs Powall leave the house and, trusting that none of the servants was likely to disturb me, I tried the numbers revealed by the code word. I was frustrated. The safe would not give up its secret. Then, after further thought, I tried another common subterfuge of safe owners. I reversed the numbers, and the safe opened.

'It was at that point that I realized that if I went off with the envelope its absence would be quickly noticed. I sat at the desk, looking round the room, seeking inspiration. And then before my eyes on the desk alongside the stick of sealing wax was Powall's gold signet ring. Quickly I took an empty envelope and applied a double seal and put it in the safe. Thus, the real and the counterfeit were exchanged.

'The next morning I said farewell to the widow who, unwittingly, had been so helpful with my quest. I confess to a feeling of great guilt that I had deceived her. However, I had been charged with a task in which there was no room for human feelings. Here is the copy I made of part of the letter which led me to the location of the document. See what you can understand of its intended meaning.'

I read the extract from the letter two or three times before giving it back to Holmes.

'Well, Watson, what are we to make of the mention of Kilmainham and Dark Pool?'

'I've no idea other than they are, possibly, the most important words in the letter.'

The document remained sealed until we were once again in Lord Marsham's study.

'I trust, my Lord, this is the document?' asked Holmes.

The Prime Minister slid a paper knife under the seals, opened the envelope and took out a sheet of foolscap.

'What's this?' he exclaimed. 'This is not it!'

'May we see?'

The Prime Minister handed it to us to examine. Written across the paper was the following line of characters:

GTACAFSSDFNODZAYCTHGYZ

'What do you make of it, Mr Holmes?'

'At present, sir, nothing. Please allow me time in which to study the letters and see if I can solve its meaning. All we can say at the present is that we are dealing with some type of code.'

With that we returned to Baker Street. As the train took us up to Euston, we debated what the alphabetical characters could mean. Suddenly I had one of those flashes of inspiration that at times come to all of us.

'I have it, Holmes! The string of characters might be, I say might be, a method of encryption using a five by five matrix. A fellow officer in India and I used to pass the time away, whilst we waited for the next attack by the hill tribes, by devising numerical puzzles and codes. If we make a five by five matrix and insert a key word to fill up the matrix starting at the top left, and then the remaining letters of the alphabet in order fill the rest of the matrix, you can encrypt a message. We could try it on this string of letters, except that without the key word we cannot get any further.'

'Is it possible then that the key is Kilmainham or Dark Pool, in the Powall letter?'

'Of the two words the latter is more likely the key because it is the shorter of the two.'

Once back in Holmes' rooms, we attacked the cryptic message.

'What we first have to do is divide the string of letters into pairs and then take each pair in turn and find its companion pair. I'll show you how.'

I explained the method I had been taught in India, although I was not too certain that my memory of the principle was very sound. I recalled that the rules were very complicated.

We set DARK POOL into the matrix and within a few minutes we had a message. It read:

SUONDGTTOUVFPVKWIYIMVW

'However we divide up the letters,' I said, 'we can't form enough meaningful words. DARK POOL is not the key. We will have to think again.'

'In these circumstances, Watson, I recommend we close our minds to the problem and concentrate on something else.'

Inwardly I groaned as he took up his violin. I admit that he was most accomplished with that instrument. However, the solo violin is not to my musical taste. I prefer it en masse as part of an orchestra. To divert my ears and mind from the sound of the violin, I decided to look up the activities of the Fenians. I noted that their campaign of 1883 included bombs at government offices in Whitehall, on the Inner Circle near Praed Street, and between Westminster and Charing Cross stations on the Metropolitan District, and explosives found on the line in the Primrose Hill tunnels of the LNWR. In February 1884 a luggage office at Victoria station was blown up. The campaign continued until January 1885 and included blowing up a Metropolitan train near Gower Street station as well as bombs at Scotland Yard, the Palace of Westminster and the Tower of London.

I turned my thoughts away from Irish activities and looked round the sitting room, and at the now-familiar pictures on the walls. As Holmes would have observed, my thoughts wandered from the picture of Gordon of Khartoum to my years in the army. As I recalled the periods of utter boredom, interrupted now and then by moments of great danger and excitement, I remembered being attached to the Dublin Fusiliers. A singular coincidence, to be thinking about that regiment and its name, when at the time Holmes and I were involved with matters concerning Ireland. At one time the regiment was in barracks at Beggar's Bush outside Dublin. With that particular remembrance, the name Dark Pool came to mind.

I looked over at my companion. 'The key, Holmes. The key. I think it could be DUBLIN. You see Dark Pool is the translation of the Gaelic word for Dublin.'

'Excellent, Watson. An inspired idea.'

We formed a matrix of twenty-five squares, five by five. DUBLI was arranged across the top line with the N on the second line. Within a few minutes we had the message. It read:

PO IN NE RR IN GF IV EW FR OM WX

It did not take us long to see the message: PO INNER RING FIVE W FROM WX.

'What are we to make of that? One clue has led to another and then onto yet another. This is going to require a great deal of careful thought. I wonder if Frances Powall was aware that what she assumed was the important document itself was only a clue to its whereabouts? All the time she has been guarding just a sheet of foolscap on which was printed a string of letters.'

'As you say, Holmes, we need to think very hard. I am sure she knew nothing of the contents of the envelope.'

'Are you sure you have worked out the message correctly? It does not seem to make much sense.'

'I agree. We need to consider it first. I suggest we start with the words "inner ring".'

We spent the afternoon trying to understand the message. By one of those fortunate chances or coincidences, I stooped to retrieve from the floor a screwed-up sheet of paper. As I was about to put it in the waste-paper basket, I saw that lying at the bottom of the basket was an uncollected underground ticket bearing the inscription 'Inner Circle'.

'Holmes, could the words "inner ring" refer to the inner circle of the Metropolitan and District?'

'Ah, yes, indeed, you may have broken into the secret message. Now if it does mean the inner circle, then can we deduce that "five W" indicates five stations west from "WX"?'

'The X may stand for cross. As in Charing Cross for example,' I responded.

'However, we have a W not a C. Ah, of course, as you explained, an X was often included to make up the twenty-five letters. So if we ignore it we are left with just W. Let us assume that Powall, as a member of parliament, had in mind the station with which he was most familiar and that is Westminster. If so, then five stations from Westminster brings us to Gloucester Road. And the letters P and O may indicate the parcels office at the station.'

'Why would he conceal the document at an underground railway station?'

'I've no idea. However, we must go to Brompton and see what we can find.'

'We can walk up to the underground station and go anti-clockwise round the inner circle to Brompton,' I suggested.

'No, a hansom will do. The atmosphere in the underground is not to my liking. I cannot understand why some people having respiratory problems choose to deliberately make a journey down below.'

'They believe the fumes will be of benefit to them. Although the locomotives used are what I understand to be of the condensing type, in which the exhaust steam is directed into the water tanks, the fumes from the fire still escape from the chimney. Yet, of course, not in the great clouds of smoke we normally see coming from an engine.'

At Brompton station we immediately discovered that the idea that the letters P and O referred to the parcels office was a false lead, because there was no such office at the station. We examined all the likely places in which Powall may have hidden the document. However, because our quest had to be kept secret, we were unable to seek the assistance of the station staff.

'There are so many cracks and crannies throughout the station,' said Holmes, 'that we would need an army of searchers working for a week before every possible hiding place had been inspected. I confess that, for the moment, I am baffled. It's back to Baker Street and some deep thinking away from the noise of trains and people.'

As we stood outside the station waiting for an empty cab to appear, I noticed a sign indicating that a post and telegraph office was close by.

'Holmes, what if P and O stands for post office?'

'Of course. The letter may have been left poste restante. However, we do not have a name which will enable us to collect the letter. Now this is where we have to take a chance. It could be Powall or, perhaps, Francis, or any of a thousand names concerned with Irish affairs. Therefore we have really only two options to start with. I will be Powall and you will be Francis.'

Francis it was.

Suffice to say we had found the document describing Lord Marsham's dangerous appreciation.

The Prime Minister arranged a most generous payment to Holmes for his success and reluctant involvement in politics. The portion that Holmes passed over to me brought a smile to the otherwise critical features of my bank manager.

'By the way, Holmes, is or was there any significance in the word Kilmainham?'

'Now you mention it, of course, it was where Powall and Parnell were imprisoned in 1881 for their activities with the Land League and for inciting violence against landlords. It also gave its name to the agreement of 1881 reached between the Liberal government and Parnell.'

Notes

Watson's army friend may have anticipated the Playfair matrix that at the end of the nineteenth century came into use with many European armies.

The 'Ascendancy' referred to the Anglo Irish who owned much of the land and held the majority of high administrative positions.

The Tiptree Typewriter

In which the aroma of preserves leads to a clue.

My notebooks, from which I construct my accounts of the numerous cases and adventures experienced by my friend Sherlock Holmes, contain many that must remain unpublished. Some because the persons involved might be caused great distress if the facts became public knowledge. Others concern Holmes' involvement with foreign governments and whose disclosure might engender a diplomatic scandal. There are even some that would betray the nation's secrets if they were published. However, the passing of time and subsequent events relating to certain cases justify them being brought to the attention of the world at large. The history I am about to recount is just such a one. It involves, unfortunately for me, devices and mechanisms the understanding of whose workings are far beyond the mental abilities of a one-time army doctor and now a general practitioner. Later, I came to understand that the events were played out against the race for naval supremacy between Britain and Germany. Sherlock Holmes became involved when the race had only just started. It was a time when the Royal Navy was making great efforts to advance from the method used to aim Nelson's cannons to one that would enable a shell to strike a ship five or more miles away, and even when that ship was moving.

Part One

The Admiralty papers

I recall that it was in the late autumn of '99 when Holmes became involved with two cases that in the end became one. We had just finished our breakfast. Holmes moved over to his favourite armchair, taking his coffee cup with him. Soon after the table had been cleared, there was the sound of the front door bell and voices in the hallway below.

'At this time of the morning it is sure to be Superintendent Lestrade,' said Holmes.

The tall figure of Scotland Yard's most redoubtable detective entered.

'Good morning, Mr Holmes. Good morning, Doctor Watson.'

He waved away Mrs Hudson's proffered cup of coffee. 'No, thank you, Mrs Hudson. I managed breakfast before I left the Yard.'

'I see from your appearance, Lestrade, that you may not have slept well,' observed Holmes.

'Mr Holmes, I've had to spend most of the past two nights struggling with trying to untangle a problem. I am charged on the highest authority to seek your help. Important plans have been removed from the Admiralty.'

'Important, you say. What sort of plans?'

'If a foreign agent were to gain sight of them the Royal Navy would lose its present command of the seas. Apparently, there is a device that would enable our ships to aim their guns with deadly precision.'

'So their lordships want me to help you recover them?'

'It is not as straightforward as that, Mr Holmes. They were removed from the Admiralty but what is so strange about the whole affair is they were eventually returned. Unfortunately, the officer responsible for their safety cannot be certain about when they were taken or exactly when they were returned.'

'The first and obvious conclusion and one which I am sure, Lestrade, you have already reached, is that they were taken so that they could be copied.'

'Indeed, Mr Holmes, that is a certainty.'

'Obviously, the Admiralty is most concerned that it is possible for secret plans and documents to be stolen. In this case they have, as we might say, been "borrowed". Not only that, it seems from what you say, no one was aware they had been taken or returned. I assume you have visited the scene of the crime?'

'Yes, I was instructed to go to the Admiralty. The naval officer responsible for them, a Lieutenant Dreyer, showed me the locked cabinet from which the secret papers and drawings had been removed from their folder. He said that a thorough search was made but they were not found. Now this is the strange part of the affair. I asked the lieutenant to open the cabinet so that I might look for some evidence as to how they had been removed. He unlocked the door and took out the folder in which the plans were kept. When he opened it he was very surprised, as I was, to find that the missing plans had been returned. He had no idea when they had been put back.'

'The obvious question, Lestrade, is how many people have a key to the cabinet?'

'Only Lieutenant Dreyer. He told me that he kept the key with him at all times.'

I accompanied Holmes and Lestrade to the Admiralty. We were shown the buff folder stamped 'Most Confidential'. It lay in the top drawer of the cabinet. Holmes closely examined both the drawer and the exterior of the cabinet. Both Lestrade and I expressed no astonishment when he lay on the polished floor and closely studied its surface. However, Lieutenant Dreyer raised a questioning eyebrow at the sight of the great detective lying prone.

Holmes got up and, turning to the lieutenant, said, 'Could anyone have made a copy of the key to the cabinet?'

'As I told the superintendent, I keep it with me at all times.'

'Now, Lieutenant, am I to understand that you have no ideas concerning when the papers were taken and when they were returned?'

'I regret, Mr Holmes, I have none. All I can tell you is that during the ten days before I found that the papers were missing I had opened the cabinet a few times in order to take out various other papers. During that time I had no occasion to take out that particular folder. Although I clearly remembered that each time I opened the cabinet I could see it lying in the top drawer.'

'Well, thank you,' said Holmes. 'I cannot recall many similar cases with which I have been involved, where valuable items have just been borrowed rather than stolen.'

The lieutenant explained that the device involved many gear wheels and ballistic cams. I had no idea what a ballistic cam was. Apparently it had been conceived by a civilian dabbling in artillery matters as a pastime, when he was not managing his very large and successful shop-fitting company. Holmes indicated that he may have deduced how the plans had been removed and returned. However, he refused to devolve his reasoning until he was absolutely sure.

On our way back to Baker Street he said, 'This may turn out to be a most interesting case.'

'No doubt, Holmes. However, I found the lieutenant's description of the device described in the plans most difficult to understand. Surely, as with our field artillery, all one has to do is to make sure the gun is pointing at the target and allow for the range?'

'Although I'm no expert on such matters, Watson, I can appreciate that when one ship is firing at another, and that both are moving, then a gun has to be pointed ahead of the target. Just as in the same way when shooting at a running animal we have to "lead" the target. In a duel between two ships, the distance between them could be constantly changing and this too has to be taken into account. Of course, what the plans are all about is not so important as finding where they have been, and who took them.'

Part Two

A Miss Smith arrives

The next day we had just finished breakfast when Mrs Hudson brought in a hand-carried letter. Holmes read it and said, 'Listen to this, Watson. It urges me to help the bearer, a Miss Smith, who is most distressed. It's signed by an acquaintance of mine from our time up at Cambridge.'

'Mrs Hudson, please show the lady in.'

Our visitor was a handsome young woman. She was neatly and not ostentatiously dressed. Her leg-of-mutton sleeves were not the exaggerated width affected by so many women. After introducing me, Holmes led her to the chair facing the window so that he could study her expressions and her dress.

With a smile he said, 'Now, Miss Smith, you have an unusual name.'

'Mr Holmes, I would rather not use my real name. Is that important?'

'Not for the moment. However, you may have to reveal it at some time. The letter from my friend suggests the matter is urgent. I can see that you are most distressed. Tell me how Doctor Watson and I may be of assistance.'

'We were kidnapped. That is, Jack Forest, my fiancé, and myself.'

'Kidnapped, you say. That is very serious. Now, Miss Smith, please let us start at the very beginning of your harrowing adventure and tell me everything that happened. Please leave nothing out. The seemingly most insignificant detail can prove in the end to be of the greatest importance. Just a moment. Before you describe what happened to you, would you mind removing your gloves?'

She looked surprised but took them off.

'I see you are accustomed to using a typewriting machine.'

'How could you know that? We have never met before.'

'It is my profession to note such things. For the moment, never mind how. Now please continue.'

'Mr Holmes, my fiancé and I were abducted from outside my home three days ago. When we were taken they separated us.'

'Then as you are here I can assume that both of you were not held for very long.'

'I was held for only about a day yet the dreadful thing, Mr Holmes, is that, even though they let me go, they still have my fiancé.'

'What have the police to say about all this?'

'Nothing, Mr Holmes. They seemed not to believe what I told them. They said they would look into the matter. I have heard nothing since. I appealed to my uncle for help and it was he who gave me your name.'

'Were either of you molested or injured?'

'No, more shocked than injured. Although I have no idea where Jack is or whether he has been harmed. A strange thing is that when they released me they offered me fifty guineas.'

'Fifty guineas, Miss, er, Smith!'

'Yes, they told me it was in payment for the work I had done for them.'

'Typewriting, no doubt,' said Holmes.

'That is so, but I refused to take their money. I questioned them about Jack but they would not tell me anything.'

Part Three

Abducted

I poured out some coffee and handed Miss Smith a cup. She took a few sips and then, slowly at first, she told us what had occurred.

'I am an orphan and live with my aged aunt in Notting Hill. Jack and I were standing on the steps of the house. It was about nine in the evening. We were saying goodbye when two men rushed upon us. One held a gun to Jack's head. The other seized my arms and said, "Don't cry out or your lover will be dead". We were bundled into a cab that had been waiting close by. It was then that a handkerchief was pressed to my face and I began to feel most peculiar. I can only recall a few things after that. I felt as if I were in a dream. I remember the sounds and smell of a large station. I was dimly aware of being in a train, of being half supported off the train at some station and then a long journey in a cab. Some time later, I have no idea how long except that it was getting light, I found I was lying on a bed in a strange room. A tall woman stood by the bed and said, "Make no noise. No shouting or your Jack will suffer".'

At that point in her account, Holmes said, 'Were you able to see anything out of the windows?'

'No, they had thick paper or cloth covering them. I could not see out.'

'Was the room large or small, and what did you do?'

'It was large and the ceiling sloped at the sides. I got off the bed and went to the door. It was not locked and I discovered that I was being confined to the upper floor of a large house. There was a bathroom, a hallway with a locked door and two large rooms, one of which was where I had been lying. The tall woman brought me food and after I had tried to eat some of it two men came in. One was carrying a typewriting machine. The other put some drawings and typewritten sheets on the table. I was instructed to sit at the machine and copy what was on the papers. Although, as you have observed, Mr Holmes, I am a typewriter, I found the typed documents were full of some very strange words. Some symbols and Greek characters had been inked in because they were not part of the usual keyboard.

'As I operated the machine one of the men stood behind me and now and then told me to stop and ignore the next paragraph I was copying. Instead, I was to typewrite what was written on a sheet of paper he placed beside me. After I had done that I had to continue copying from the pages as before. I was kept at the task for most of the morning. A severe headache caused me to work very slowly.'

I could see that she was finding the strain of retelling her adventure too much for her. I persuaded Holmes to let Mrs Hudson take care of her for a while.

When we were alone I said, 'I know you do not place much importance to coincidences. Nevertheless I think, in this case, we have a singular coincidence.'

'What do you mean, Watson?'

'The Admiralty papers that were taken, and those that Miss Smith was set to copy.'

'Of course. Most observant of you. I have been thinking entirely along the wrong lines, Watson. What made you connect the two cases?'

'As one might say, an elementary observation. Our lady typewriter told us about the strange words and the symbols that had to be inked in. The Admiralty papers that had been taken and then returned described a very complicated machine that involved abstruse mathematics and Greek characters.'

'Yes, yes. We have it, or I should say you have it. The villains, as we might say, "borrowed" the scientific papers describing the ballistics calculating machine and made Miss Smith copy them. However, that explanation is too obvious. No, this is more than just copying secret plans. If some foreign agent wanted to obtain the

Royal Navy's secret, why make a copy and then just return it?'

When Miss Smith felt able to continue her account, Holmes put questions to her that he hoped might provide an indication to where she and her fiancé had been taken.

'Miss Smith, when you were in the house could you tell from any sounds coming from outside whether you were in a large town? Could you hear any vehicles and possibly many people passing by?'

'I am sure the house was not in a large town. There was little sound from outside.'

'Could you hear what I would term country sounds? For example, the bleating of sheep or the lowing of cattle? What about the smell associated with haymaking?'

'All I could smell, Mr Holmes, and it was very strong, was that of fruit.'

'Fruit, you say. Apples, for example?'

'No, more like the smell I remember when my mother made jam.'

'Most interesting. Now let us go back to the nighttime journey to the house, wherever it was. I appreciate that you had been drugged and that your memory of the events may not be clear. Now, please, and this is very important, you are sure they took you to one of the big termini?'

'Very sure. There was a lot of noise of trains moving about and there was much smoke in the air.'

'Good, we are making some progress. My next question is a vital one. When you were forcibly placed in the cab, I presume the effects of the drug had not taken full effect?'

'That is so, Mr Holmes.'

'Then the question is, were you aware of the cab crossing any of the bridges over the river? The sounds would be distinctive. Your home is not far from the river and on this side.'

'I'm certain we did not cross a bridge.'

'Now, when you were taken on to the train, were there any very distinctive sounds?'

'I am afraid one station and its trains sound very much the same.'

Holmes turned to me. 'Watson, as a railway enthusiast, you have recently acquired a considerable interest in their minutiae. Can you suggest something that may help. A sound, for instance?'

I was flattered, I have to confess, whenever Holmes involved me directly with a case.

'Miss Smith, I am going to try and imitate a noise some locomotives make. Please listen to my amateurish effort of mimicry. Did you hear a "pish tish" noise frequently repeated?' was my first question.

'Oh, of course, yes, I do recall it. That sound seemed to be all round us as we waited for the train to start.'

'Excellent. Now during the journey did you hear anyone outside the train shouting out the name of any of the stations at which the train may have stopped?'

'I dimly recall the name "Chester" being called out. I also remember thinking how strange to be in Chester.'

'Any other names,' I asked.

'Doctor Watson, the events of that night were very confusing. I cannot be sure about anything that may have happened. Perhaps I did hear the word "Ford".'

Holmes listened to my attempts to elicit facts about Miss Smith's journey.

'Two things puzzle me, Watson. Would there have been time in which to reach Chester before dawn and what is the significance of the "pish tish" sound you made?'

I resisted the word 'elementary' and replied to his questions. 'The "pish tish" noise is the sound made by the Westinghouse air brake pumps of locomotives. Miss Smith recalls the sound and, if I am correct, she is sure she had passed through a large terminus. You can hear the sound of air brake pumps at Victoria, Fenchurch Street and Liverpool Street and at London Bridge as well, but that station is over the river. She also recalls the very smoky atmosphere and the sounds of many trains. At that time of the night Liverpool Street is still very busy and full of smoke. Therefore, I am certain Miss Smith was taken through that station.'

'Now that is interesting, Watson. She heard the name Chester. Can one get to Chester from Liverpool Street and at that time of the night? Surely it's Euston for Chester?'

I warmed to the railway aspect of the case and responded, 'And from Paddington or even from St Pancras, although you may have to break your journey.'

'Now, Miss Smith, how did you get back to your home?'

'I regret I cannot help you very much, Mr Holmes. That night I was once again taken in a closed cab for a very long journey. The woman was with me all the time, even when we stopped for refreshment. I dared not call for help because I did not want any harm to come to Jack.'

'Now this is a very important question. Can you recall how long the journey in the cab took?'

'It seemed to go on for hours. And then we took a train.'

'Watson, please will you help again?'

'Miss Smith, once again I must ask you to remember details of the train and any unusual sounds. Can you recall details of the compartment, for example?'

'I'm sorry, Doctor Watson, I cannot help you any more. Throughout the dreadful journey I was hardly aware of anything about me. I am certain they had put an opiate in the drink I was given before we left the house.'

'Can we assume that the train was going to London?'

'Well, yes. After a time my mind was clearer and I recognized King's Cross station. It was there that they hailed a cab, gave the driver some money and my address. When the cab started I ordered the driver to take me to the nearest police station. As I told you, they were not very helpful.'

Holmes listened patiently to my efforts at playing the interrogator. When I decided that it was unfair to press Miss Smith on the subject any further, he suggested that I summarize the implications of what we had been told.

'The villains, obviously, took great care to hide the location of the house. That is why they took Miss Smith through Liverpool Street and then brought her back through King's Cross. As you reminded me, Holmes, journeys have often been deliberately extended and taken devious routes in order to confuse the direction, distance and destination. I can only conclude that the house is somewhere within a triangle formed by the Cambridge line of the Great Northern and the main line of the Great Eastern.'

'Very good, Watson. You have applied very good reasoning to the case. Now if we study the railway map it may provide a lead.'

He opened out the railway gazetteer.

'If we consider the aroma of jam or, perhaps, marmalade

manufacture, there are two places that we need to consider: Elsenham and Tiptree. They are about twenty-five miles apart. Both are on the Great Eastern from Liverpool Street. Which of the two to select, I am not sure. I do not approve of gambling and I do not let chance enter into an investigation. However, there have to be exceptions. In this case the new marmalade that has been on the breakfast table recently carries the name Tiptree. Furthermore if we concentrate on the Great Eastern main line and look at the station names we find Chelmsford. There's your "Ford", Miss Smith.'

'Yes, Mr Holmes, I must have just heard part of the name Chelmsford.'

'Moving on, we come to Colchester and there's your "Chester".'

'From Colchester, you were taken in a closed cab to the house. You cannot recall in which direction or for how long. As Doctor Watson mentioned, in similar cases the villains have confused the search by taking a roundabout, time-consuming route.'

'I am sorry. I cannot remember much about the journey from the station which you say must have been Colchester.'

'What you have remembered, and in particular the smell of fruit and your recollection of your mother making jam, has led us to Tiptree in Essex. I conclude that you were held somewhere near the famous preserves producer Wilkin and Sons. Watson, please will you look through the newspapers for the day concerned and determine the direction of the wind.'

After a search I was able to answer, 'It was from the south west.'

'That places the house somewhere to the north east of Tiptree. I conjecture that the smell of preserves in large quantities could be detected for up to a mile away. We need to look for a house with two dormer windows facing approximately south and not too far away from the preserves establishment.'

'Shall I look up the times of trains to Colchester, or rather Witham, because that is closer to Tiptree?'

'Please do. However, first we must bring Superintendent Lestrade into the case. The Admiralty and the abduction case are, I am now certain, one and the same thing.'

Miss Smith gave a startled look and became pale.

'The Admiralty, Mr Holmes?'

'Are you feeling all right?' I said.

'I am surprised. You see, my Jack is a clerk at the Admiralty.'

Holmes then said, 'Has he held his position for some time?'

'About a year. Previously he was with Handel, Farmer and Triton of Victoria Street, the consulting engineers to the Admiralty.'

Holmes made a note and then stood up and took Miss Smith's hand saying, 'We have questioned you enough for today. Please go home. I can assure you that we will find your fiancé.'

Part Four

One case, not two

A telegram to Lestrade brought him round as fast as a hansom could travel from Scotland Yard.

'I received your message, Mr Holmes. You say that a case on which you are engaged may be connected to the disappearance of the Admiralty papers.'

'More than may be. Watson and I are certain they are one and the same. Can you arrange for the local constabulary to assist us if we visit Tiptree in Essex? I shall explain further once we are on our way.'

'Certainly, Mr Holmes. First I must send a message to the police at Colchester. May your boy take it round to the telegraph office?'

Lestrade composed his message and Billy took it to the telegraph office. I looked up the times of the trains and within an hour we were on our way to Witham. An inspector of the local police was there to meet us. A cab was hired and Holmes instructed the driver to take us to the east of the preserves factory. The wind was in the west and soon we could smell the aroma of fruit.

Holmes sniffed the air and said, 'If I am not mistaken they are in the process of preparing marmalade.'

Under Holmes' direction, the cabman took us along lanes that passed between fields of strawberries, rows of blackcurrant and gooseberry bushes and other fruits.

'Stop. Look, there is a house with two dormer windows facing south. See, the one standing away from the others. Let us get closer. Go on, cabbie.'

We left the cab after making certain that it could not be seen from the house. When we got closer, I pointed up at the upper windows. 'Look, they are papered over, as Miss Smith told us. This is the house. What happens now?'

'A good question, Watson. Now, Lestrade, what do you suggest we do?'

Lestrade and the inspector conferred and they agreed that the latter would knock on the door. The rest of us kept to one side, ready to rush in. The knock was answered by a tall woman. Before she could say anything we all rushed into the hallway. Halfway down the stairs was a young man. Holmes said, 'Mr Jack Forest, I believe.'

The two police officers seized him. Lestrade said, 'We believe that you may be implicated in a robbery of crown property. Who else is in the house?'

Apparently, he and the woman were alone. We found the upper floor rooms and some drawings and papers. Lestrade believed they were some of those that had been 'borrowed' from the Admiralty for a few days.

On the way back to London, I asked Holmes why he knew it was Jack Forest on the stairs of the house.

'Because up to that moment,' he replied, 'I had assumed he was a prisoner in the house. As he was obviously not under restraint I deduced instantly that he may have been involved with the crime. He must have gone to the Admiralty at the same time as the villains were taking his fiancée back to London. There he replaced the purloined pages and drawings. On realizing that an investigation had started, he returned to the house only to find that his accomplices had left.'

It was a very distraught Miss Smith when she was told of her fiancé's involvement with espionage. Apparently, they had wanted to marry the previous year but she had no dowry, and he had lost all his savings on that downfall of many men, a 'certainty' at the races.

Part Five

The end was not the end

The Admiralty congratulated Holmes and Lestrade on clearing up the affair.

We were taking the air by walking in Regent's Park.

'By the way, Holmes, how did you know when Miss Smith came to see you that she was a lady typewriter?'

'A very simple observation, Watson. Her fingernails were cut very short and there was a very faint red and blue stain on each of her thumbs and index fingers.' Suddenly he stopped, turned and said, 'Watson, we must find a telegraph office. The Admiralty case is not closed.'

The next morning we were standing in front of the cabinet with Lieutenant Dreyer. He had been surprised to find that there was more to consider.

'Lieutenant, Miss Smith, Forest's fiancée, told us that she was ordered to start copying from page three onward and therefore could not know that they were naval documents. In fact, as she said, the first two pages did not appear to be there. Please will you open the cabinet?'

The top drawer was pulled out and there lay the buff folder marked 'Most Confidential'.

'As you said, the papers may have been taken much earlier than you thought and, as there was no occasion to take the folder out, you never suspected that it was empty. That is, all except the title page and the next page. You did tell us that the secret device described had been approved, and that you were waiting for the plans to be collected by the company which was to build the device.'

'That is so, Mr Holmes.'

'Now what about Jack Forest? Had he access to the cabinet? No, of course not. You have the only key. I presume he knew about the secret?'

'He was well aware of it because he took the minutes of all the meetings when it was discussed.'

'Then he is very much implicated.'

Holmes produced the papers we had found in the house along with the rough copies that had been made of the drawings. 'These may be some of the original pages. I presume that the title sheet and the next page were concerned purely with administrative matters and therefore of no interest to a foreign power.'

'A correct assumption, Mr Holmes.'

'If I am again correct, some of the pages of the original have been replaced by others typewritten by Miss Smith. If we look closely, even though the same make of typewriting machine and the same Admiralty paper have been used, there are differences. For example, the letter "p" has a broken descender. Furthermore the ink used for the mathematical symbols and the Greek letters is not the same as on the other pages. I suggest that when the plans were returned to the cabinet, deliberate changes had been made. I advise you to bring the inventor in and ask him to go carefully over every detail, particularly the fearsome equations. They may have been altered, thereby rendering the working of the device uncertain.'

'I still do not understand, Mr Holmes. How were the papers taken out for a few days and then replaced without the cabinet door being forced?' asked the lieutenant.

'You may recall that I examined the floor in front of the cabinet. It was then that I was able to discern faint scratches. They indicated that the cabinet had been moved away from the wall. Now, gentlemen, let us pull it away.'

At the back of the cabinet and at the level of the topmost drawer a narrow slot had been cut through the back panel.

'See, that is how the drawings and papers were removed and later replaced. I suspected that that may have been the method used. When I first examined the cabinet I noticed traces of sawdust in the back of the top drawer. In all this, Lieutenant, I fail to understand how Forest was able to move so freely between here and Tiptree and cut into the cabinet without you or others noticing?'

'I regret to have to admit it, Mr Holmes, none of us was aware of the need for excessive security. I have been taught an important lesson. I now remember that it was part of Forest's duties to visit the Admiralty patents agent in Chancery Lane. When he was absent for all or part of a day I assumed that is where he was. The doorkeeper would not have been surprised to see him arrive or leave at times outside the usual office hours. He would then have been alone in the office.'

Needless to say, Forest was convicted of stealing state secrets and was sentenced to thirty years' hard labour breaking rocks in the mists of Dartmoor. The woman in the Tiptree house was sentenced to penal servitude for a number of years. As for their accomplices, they were never traced. Further investigation by the Admiralty revealed that the equations had been changed on the originals. Had the device then been made and assembled, the navy's gunnery fire control system would have contained errors that may not have been detected for many years. Eventually the navy decided to abandon the device and encourage the development of another that was far more accurate. This was the invention of Arthur Pollen, who, by coincidence, was also a civilian having an interest in complex calculating devices.

Whenever I reach for a pot of conserve and the name Tiptree catches my eye, I am reminded of Miss Smith's tragic face when she was told about her lover's crime.

Notes

Female operators of typewriters at this time were called 'typewriters'.

A railway was not constructed from the main line to Tiptree until the twentieth century.

Both Dreyer and Pollen were key figures along with Admiral Percy Scott in the development of fire control systems for the Royal Navy.

At the time of this tale there were many alternative routes available from London to the principal cities.

The Mystery of the Wires

In which a four-wheeler is taken and not a hansom.

Part One

Among the many cases of Sherlock Holmes which I have the pleasure of setting before the reader are those involving the marvels of our age. I refer, of course, to the steamship, the railways, the submarine, the breech loading guns and, most importantly, the telegraph. The last enables us to communicate virtually instantaneously over vast distances.

One day in the spring of 1900, just as we were about to finish our breakfast, the page boy brought in a letter that had been delivered by special messenger. The seal on the envelope indicated that it had come from the Foreign Office.

'What are we to make of this, Watson? Very official. Not another secret treaty stolen from under the noses of Her Majesty's government! Perhaps a minister has been caught in flagrante and I have to mitigate the situation?'

I was impatient to learn of the contents. 'Come on, Holmes. Open it.' I pushed the paper knife across the breakfast table.

'From the Foreign Minister himself and in, what I presume, is his own hand. Yes, it is. It's signed Craneford.' He read through the short letter and said, 'Watson, we are requested to be at the Foreign Office as soon as possible. English can be a very subtle language.

The tone of the letter is extremely polite. However, there is a veiled meaning that implies this is an order. I assume you will come with me?'

'Certainly. I've always wanted to see the inside of the Foreign Office.'

'My reply will request that you accompany me.'

A ministry porter was waiting for us as we alighted from a hansom. We were led up the great staircase at the top of which stood an elderly gentleman. He greeted us, saying, 'Good morning. Please come with me. His lordship received your message and agrees that your companion may accompany you. I did not greet you by name. This was deliberate because his lordship does not want your presence to be known for reasons which he will explain.'

We went along a corridor, past numerous large paintings depicting notable events in our country's history, and were shown into the room in which important decisions had been taken concerning Britain's standing in the world.

After greeting us, Lord Craneford introduced the other person in the room.

'Mr Holmes, Doctor Watson, this is Mr Harcourte-Smith, the postmaster general, who will now explain a matter of the gravest concern.'

'Good morning, gentlemen. As his lordship says, this is a very grave matter and one which not only places the government in a very difficult position, it threatens the commercial standing of the post office telegraphs, were the press to get wind of the affair.'

'Grave indeed,' responded Holmes.

'For some years,' said the postmaster general, 'we have operated telegraph lines for the exclusive use of the Foreign Office between here and two telegraph stations: one on the shore of the German Ocean and the other on the south coast. From those two points messages are carried by the commercial submarine telegraph cables to the continent.'

'The information is extremely confidential and involves matters passing between here and Her Majesty's ambassadors in many countries,' said the Foreign Minister.

'When did you become aware that your messages to ambassadors were being illegally read?' asked Holmes.

'It was about a month ago. I called in our intelligence people immediately. Unfortunately they are out of their depth when it comes to this sort of situation.'

'The delay is most unfortunate. Any clues may have been obliterated by time.' Holmes turned to the postmaster general and said, 'Please tell me more about the wires along which the messages are sent.'

'My engineers tell me that the telegraph wires between the principal London telegraph exchange and the shore end of the undersea cable are mostly on poles alongside the railway. Only between the telegraph office here in the Foreign Office and the top end of Whitehall is it possible to identify particular wires, because there are only a few. From that point onward they are carried on the same poles as the public and private lines. Somewhere between here and the top end of Whitehall we are sure the wires are being "tapped". That is, an illegal connection is being made which enables someone to read the messages.'

Holmes made some notes and then said, 'Do I understand then that someone might be able to reach the wires and, as you say, "tap" them in order to extract messages?'

'That is possible, Mr Holmes. The wires are strung on insulators mounted on poles on the tops of most buildings between here and where they join the other wires. Access to the roofs is not difficult, otherwise our linesmen would not have been able to install them in the first place.'

'You would say that in order to tap the wire or wires, someone has to have special understanding of telegraphy?'

'Indeed, Mr Holmes, I am given to understand, by those who know about such things, that just to attach a wire and a Morse apparatus would, as they say, unbalance the circuit. Specialized knowledge would be essential in order to devise an apparatus whose presence could not be detected.'

'Presumably you have searched along the wires for an illegal connection?'

'Certainly, that's the first thing my engineers and linesmen did. We suspect that the eavesdropper removed the connection when he heard our men approaching. Once they had moved on to the next roof he reconnected it.'

'Therefore we have to find a rogue wire, as it were, leading off the wire into a room or some place in one of the buildings along Whitehall. A very difficult task.' Holmes paused for a moment and then said, 'A heavy-handed search would only alert the criminals and they would flee. I shall have to have time in which to consider a number of possible methods of solving the problem. In the meantime, my lord, I recommend that you either limit your messages in number or change the cipher more frequently. Which brings me to the question, how do you convey to your ambassadors the need to change the cipher?'

'We send a message that includes a number, and that indicates which of over a dozen ciphers is to be used.'

'And that of course leads to the conclusion that whoever is "tapping" into your most secret telegrams must have acquired all the ciphers. It also means, of course, that we are looking for three criminals: one, I regret to say, is more than likely within the Foreign Office, another on a roof or in an attic and a third, the mastermind, who deciphers and makes use of the information. Having three quarries can be an advantage. It increases the chances of success. Find one and you bag the other two. Ah, wait a minute, what about your own telegraphist? We must include him as a suspect because he is, surely, aware of the nature of your very confidential messages?'

'He is obviously aware of their importance although, of course, cannot read them. They are just a string of random letters. Furthermore they are handed to him personally by my private secretary. He stays beside the telegraphist as the encrypted message is sent. When it has gone and been acknowledged, the message is brought back and filed with the others in the safe.'

'May I examine the safe?'

'Of course. It's in a room next to my office.'

The Foreign Secretary unlocked the door and led Holmes into a small windowless room.

'I see you have no electrified lighting in this room,' commented Holmes.

'The office of works people have yet to get round to providing it.'

Holmes examined the small safe and observed that the

combination lock was of a very old pattern and therefore not likely to prove too difficult to manipulate.

'What are you doing?' exclaimed Lord Craneford as Holmes lay full length on the carpet in front of the safe.

'Carpets can often hide more than just dust,' replied Holmes. He appeared to be scrutinizing closely a barely distinct mark among the elaborate pattern of the carpet. He even sniffed the mark. 'Our culprit is left-handed, my Lord. Are you aware of any, as it were, sinister members of your immediate staff?'

'No, Mr Holmes, I cannot say that it is something to which I have paid much attention. My private secretary definitely is because I have long noticed that he always stands to the left of my desk when submitting documents for approval or signature, whereas others stand to the right.'

'If you will allow, may I have the opportunity of covertly ascertaining the hand preference of your immediate staff, particularly those who know of the existence of the safe?'

'Certainly, Mr Holmes. Take any steps you consider necessary in order to find a solution.'

Later that day, six secretaries and two ministry porters were asked ostensibly to answer questions put to them by a detective from Scotland Yard investigating the disappearance of a valuable bust from the great staircase of the ministry. The bust had been deliberately removed previously and the detective was, of course, Holmes himself, suitably disguised. The interview of each suspect was brief. Nothing more than asking if they had seen anything and a request to mark off their name on the list placed in front of them.

At our next meeting with Lord Craneford, Holmes reported on three left-handed people who were possible suspects.

'The first, my Lord, is your own private secretary. As you say, you are absolutely certain of his loyalty. Not only has he been with you throughout your illustrious career he is, as you explained, privy to the cipher book and that it is kept in the safe. There is also the fact that he is your cousin. I am sure you will agree that he can be eliminated from the list. We are left then with two possible suspects. Your other private secretary, I understand, has been with the Foreign Office for over forty years. He is more than financially independent because of the death of his extremely rich father two years ago. Therefore, he is not susceptible to bribery. The other suspect is the young secretary Charles Botomoly, recently returned from your embassy in Russia. Here we find a young man on a modest salary yet his attire bespokes the very best that Savile Row can cut. I have not reached these conclusions without making a further observation. I applied a simple test, and I even included your cousin; I pretended that my pocket watch must have stopped and asked them if they could hear it ticking. Your cousin is deaf in one ear. The older of the two secretaries is very deaf in his right ear. However, Botomoly has very acute hearing.'

'Mr Holmes, I fail to understand what the ability to hear has to do with all this?'

'Elementary, my Lord. To listen to the combination lock tumblers of the safe clicking into place requires an acute ear. Therefore, Botomoly has to be a suspect. In the meantime I suggest that no move be made against him. If he is involved in a conspiracy we do not want to alert him and the other members of the conspiracy.'

'I quite understand. Thank you for taking on this very serious investigation. In the meantime, should you require anything please do not hesitate to communicate with me.'

Part Two

When I came into the sitting room the next morning I found Holmes curled in his favourite chair smoking his old clay pipe. The room was so full of tobacco smoke that Holmes appeared to me as if he were a smouldering bonfire of dead leaves.

I had to remark, 'Obviously, Holmes, from the state of this room you have not been to bed.'

'Good morning, Watson. This affair at the Foreign Office has exercised my mind for most of the night. Have you any thoughts on the matter?'

'I regret to say, very few. However it does remind me of my time in Afghanistan when Russian agents working with the tribesmen would read our heliographed signals. I must confess I am intrigued by the cunning manner in which you determined which of the three had opened the safe. You know, when you were explaining how you eliminated two of the suspects you left something out. How on earth could you know that the safe had been opened by a left-handed person in the first place?'

'The singular characteristics of a stain on the carpet in front of the safe. As we know, the room had no electric lighting, therefore a lantern had to be carried. I was able to make out on the carpet a circular stain to the left of the safe door, and detect the faint odour of the oil used in the lantern. A left-handed person would carry it in that hand. When he knelt in front of the safe he placed the lantern on the carpet to the left of the safe and applied his right ear to the combination lock and his left hand on the dial of the lock.'

'A masterful deduction, Holmes.'

'Thank you. Now we are to meet Superintendent Lestrade in Whitehall at ten. I've received a telegram to say that he has been ordered to assist us. I expect such an order may have offended his dignity. The official police often resent the activities of amateurs, such as myself, becoming involved with criminal investigations. They would rather we confined our work to searching for errant husbands, disappearing vestry funds and exposing secret assignations.'

When our cab reached Whitehall, Lestrade of the Yard was waiting for us. Holmes greeted him tactfully. 'Good morning, Lestrade. I am pleased that Scotland Yard has put you in charge of the case.'

'Good morning, gentlemen. I'm honoured to have been selected by the commissioner. I understand it involves matters of great importance to the government.'

Holmes spent a few minutes giving Lestrade an outline of the meeting with the Foreign Secretary. Diplomatically he said, 'I fail to understand why you were not brought into the affair much earlier. Never mind, you are here now. Let us study carefully the roofs of the buildings opposite.'

The crowd of people lingering, pacing or hurrying along Whitehall ignored us as we studied the skyline of the buildings lining the eastern side of the road.

'Lestrade, I suggest we pay particular attention to the telegraph poles and their wires on top of that building,' Holmes said, pointing to the one immediately opposite where we were standing. 'That is the most probable place for attaching an illegal wire. You see the shape of the roof and the attic roof with dormer windows? They are close to the wires.'

'Yes, Mr Holmes, I suppose someone could just about reach out and attach a wire.'

'Now, how are we to gain entry without disclosing our purpose? We do not want to look too much like policemen,' said Holmes.

'I have arranged for that. See, here are documents I have had prepared, that identify us as being from the town hall and that we are reassessing the rateable value of properties.'

Holmes examined the papers and said, 'You certainly have some very skilled forgers in the Yard.'

'Needs sometimes must,' he replied.

The building, into which we entered through an ornate portico, was mostly given over to the West End Turkish Bath for Gentlemen. I played my part by appearing to be taking down particulars. We made only a perfunctory inspection of the various steam rooms and then we requested to be shown the apartments that made up the upper four storeys. The establishment's commissionaire led us up the stairs and explained the purpose of the various apartments and rooms, and who occupied them. In the attic room with the dormer window we paid particular attention to the window.

'Is this set of rooms occupied?' inquired Lestrade.

'Well, yes and no. I've never been in here until now. I understands the rent is paid but, as you see, there isn't much furniture.'

'Who uses the room?'

'A young feller.'

'Tall, short, fat, thin?'

'Difficult to say. The few times I've seen him come and go he is always in a long overcoat. It's much too big for the likes of him. Mind you, he walks funny.'

When we had finished our examination we repaired to a coffee house and pondered our visit to the house of the Turkish bath. 'I saw that you examined the window, Mr Holmes,' said Lestrade. 'Did you see a wire leading out to the telegraph poles?'

'No. However, there are marks on the window ledge that suggest a metal object has been pushed across. With the commissionaire hovering around I did not want him to think we were detectives. I was only able to make a cursory inspection. However, I did find this short length of coloured wool. Somewhere in that room is the telegraphic apparatus, I'm certain. However, what is more important to us is the person using the apparatus. Did you see anything strange about the room, or notice any unusual marks on the carpet?'

'I did not find much of significance,' replied Lestrade, 'although I did notice a wire wound round a water pipe. As you saw, I tried the handle of the large cupboard but it was locked. With the commissionaire present I decided not to force the lock. I had better apply for a search warrant which may take time. Mind you, I could be back with some constables and bluff my way in.'

'My advice is to leave things undisturbed. We don't want to warn whoever they are that we are on to them.'

*

The next afternoon I was busy writing up the affair of the fairies at the bottom of the garden. Holmes had retired to his bedroom. Some time later I was aware that he had entered the room. 'Will this do, Watson?'

I turned to find a clergyman standing by the fire. Holmes rarely lost an opportunity to conduct an investigation in some form of disguise.

'Most impressive. I assume you are on your way out?'

'I intend to station myself outside the Turkish baths.'

He returned some time later. I could tell from his expression that all had gone well.

'You've found out something?'

'Indeed I did. I waited outside the baths. The time was just after five. I chose that time to be there because that was when the Foreign Office telegraph operator usually finished for the day. I assumed that the person in the top room would leave his post soon after. About fifteen minutes later a man wearing a long overcoat a few sizes too big for him came out and stood looking for a cab. A hansom driver, ever alert for a fare, pulled up and called out, "Cab, guvner?" The man waved him away and beckoned to a four-wheeler that had come along. He got in.

'I hailed the hansom and told the driver to follow the growler. I said there was a sovereign in it if he didn't lose sight of it. I'm sure that such an award put any thoughts out of the driver's mind about the propriety of a man of the cloth behaving in such a peculiar way. The trail led to a square in Islington. I paid off the hansom and sat on one of the seats in the square. My customary attention to every detail of a disguise included in this instance a Bible, which I pretended to read while keeping watch on the house into which the young man had gone. A young lady emerged and walked away. Once she had left the square, I went up to the house and rang the doorbell. It was answered by a stout woman who seemed somewhat surprised to be visited by a member of the church.

'I gave a beatific smile and said: "My dear madam, may I trouble you to help me with a—" ' She interrupted me. "Speak up, I can't hear proper. Thinks you said trouble. Is it money you're after? I puts some in the plate every Sunday. . . ." '

I smiled at Holmes' mimicry of the woman's voice.

He continued: ' "No, no, my call is not about a donation, it concerns a search for a young couple who have eloped recently. The family of the girl have asked me to intercede. You see, they are not married in the eyes of the church. The parents are distraught, worried."

'She replied: "Well, I never. Young people these days do do some wicked things. But there's no couple livin' here. There's just a young lady what pays for the top rooms. She's very quiet. The way she speaks is not like most round here. She's just gone out." '

'I asked her if the lady had any visitors.'

'Her reply was most rewarding: "Now you mentions it, there's a young man who I've seened a few times who calls of an evening. I did not mind cos he looks like her and I supposed he's her brother. If I'd thought they was, er, you know, I'd turf her out. This is a respectable neighbourhood. Mind you, cos I can't hear proper he could 'ave been up and down them stairs a dozen times a day for all I knows."

'I left her saying: "My good woman, you have been most helpful. They are certainly not the couple I am looking for. They must be somewhere else. Bless you." '

Part Three

After listening to Holmes account of his visit to Islington and his impersonation of the woman, I commented, 'My dear fellow, you should have been on the stage.'

That evening we went to the Café de l'Europe for supper.

Holmes glanced through the menu. 'I say, Watson, look, they have my favourite steamed marmalade pudding for dessert.'

'Hold on, old chap. What about what comes before?'

'Quite right, let us start at the beginning.'

I could not wait to put forward a conclusion I had reached. 'Is our quarry a woman and not a man?'

'Indeed, you may be right. Consider the singular happenings I observed outside the baths, Watson. He or rather she took the growler not the hansom. As you know, females do not usually use a hansom unless accompanied. Furthermore, when "he" prepared to enter the cab I observed that, instinctively for a woman, a hand reached down and back in order to gather her skirts up. It was an action of the hand and arm that occurred in a blink of the eye. And, of course, the piece of coloured wool that suggested knitting to pass the time. It was enough to confirm my suspicion that we are dealing with the fair sex. Also I recalled that the postmaster general mentioned that over forty per cent of telegraphists are young girls. Apparently they can learn the Morse code and operate the sending and receiving apparatus more readily than men. Yes, I am sure she is the one who taps the wires and writes down the messages. I have also spoken to one of the post office engineers and, without disclosing the reason for my questions, I learnt that the Morse apparatus is small enough to fit into a cigar box. And I also learnt that a wire needs to be attached to a water pipe. He called it an earth. You recall that Lestrade mentioned a pipe and wire. In addition, a Leclanche cell is needed, and that fact explained the damage to the carpet in the attic room, where some of the acid from the cell had escaped.'

'Splendid, Holmes. What is the next step in this case?'

'Well, we have to determine how the messages she has intercepted are passed on, and to whom.'

'I expect she uses what I have heard you refer to as a "drop".'

'More than likely, Watson. The trouble is this is a very big city with thousands, perhaps millions, of places into which the messages could be dropped to await the real villains.'

'She will be followed then?'

'Yes, Lestrade is on to it as we speak. I anticipate he will find the drop. Then we have to take up the trail again after the messages have been picked up. Somewhere, somebody awaits them.'

Lestrade came round to report that the lady telegraphist had been followed to one of the embassies. After he had left, Holmes started to prepare an account for Lord Craneford of all that had happened.

The next day we went to see the Foreign Secretary.

'You and Scotland Yard have certainly made progress with the investigation.'

'Yes, my Lord, I am pleased to say we have. It appears that every evening the young lady carries her day's work to the Transylvanian embassy. There could be someone in there who is able to decipher the messages.'

'Mr Holmes, I am anxious to avoid a diplomatic incident. For the present let us leave out the name of the country involved. What we need to find is some way of identifying the person. I trust the ambassador of that country. However, I believe that someone in the embassy is trying to mar our relations with them. Can you gain access to the embassy?'

'I believe I can, my lord.'

'I am relying on you, Mr Holmes, to find that person. You must understand that with cases of this sort, on behalf of the government, you will be on your own. Should you be caught in some devious act in an embassy which is, of course, foreign soil, you will be officially disowned. But, of course, unofficially you will have the full support of Scotland Yard and will be well rewarded.'

Back in our rooms I put the obvious questions to Holmes. 'An invidious position to be in. How will you proceed? Can I help?'

'To your first question I have no idea. To the second, my dear friend, your help may be essential. Our first move will have to be a survey of the embassy from outside. Who shall we be? Itinerant singers of ballads? You have a fine voice, Watson. Perhaps two road sweepers?'

The embassy was in an area of large mansions, each with its own grounds. At one time it had been a private residence. Few paid much attention to the two disreputable and inebriated tramps slumped among the bushes at the side of the avenue. There were few people about, even in the other two roads alongside the embassy, to notice us as we went swaying along the pathway.

'Watson, we have a problem that on first thought seems insurmountable. The embassy is surrounded by a high wall and all the windows on all floors are barred.'

'Well, as you have remarked in the past, just walk straight in through the front door.'

'Yes, that might be the answer were it not for the fact that embassies usually have members of their military on duty, who would insist on seeing a plausible invitation or being given a valid reason for entering. I have even considered the trick we employed in the case of a Scandal in Bohemia.

'Yes, I remember. You used a smoke device, and in the confusion learnt where the incriminating letters were secreted.'

'Not this time, Watson. The building is far too large and too far back from the road for hurling a smoke device through a window. Even if one were to be open. From my observations that is unlikely. And I cannot see that making smoke and shouting "Fire" will avail us this time.'

'Then we need a disguise and a reason for being in the embassy. The former is not a problem for you, Holmes. Yet I have to admit that finding a reason could be. Is there a servants' entrance?'

'It's at the back and well guarded.'

'They must have to let tradesmen in?'

'I did keep a watch on that possible means of access, Watson. The staff not only searched the butcher, the baker and the candlestick maker, I could see that they referred to what I assume was a list of acceptable deliverers of goods and victuals.'

'There you have it, Holmes. Take the place of one of the delivery men. Surely Lestrade can arrange it.'

'I have another thought, Watson. I saw that the identical mansion next to the embassy has an agent's for-sale board fixed to its wall. Let us pose as potential buyers and visit the agent. It could prove most useful.'

The agent was able to give us a copy of the floor plans. On our return to Baker Street we sat down and studied them.

'Now, Watson, if we assume that there have been no major changes to the order of the rooms, these plans indicate that a servants' passageway and staircase lead from the scullery to all the principal rooms. If I can just get into the passageway, and if I am able to change my disguise from tradesman to a household servant, I should be reasonably free to explore the house.'

'I doubt that you will have such freedom, Holmes. You are going to step into the middle of the spider's web.'

'I shall rely on the assumption that the occupants of a heavily guarded house are often so satisfied about the security of its outer walls that they are complacent about what happens inside. There is also the fact in my favour that we know the accredited entourage of the ambassador is made up of only six people. Which means, I hope, that only four are on duty at any one time, and that they are outnumbered by the servants. Therefore, I can rely on the good chance that I am not going to be encountered and challenged.'

'In all the cases with which you have been involved, Holmes, I cannot recall another where you depended so much on chance.'

'I've little choice.'

Choosing a suitable time, Holmes entered the embassy grounds. I waited anxiously outside. There was nothing for me to do. Everything depended on Holmes. When he eventually returned and we were in a cab on our way back to Baker Street, he recounted his adventure.

'As you know I was disguised as a butcher so that I could bluff my way in, using credentials and meat order documents provided by Lestrade. I did not question where the heavy side of beef slung across my shoulders came from. It was enough to ensure that I was directed to the cold storage room down a passageway off the kitchens. Fortunately, the cooks and others were so busy preparing dinner for the ambassador and his guests that none noticed that the butcher had not returned from the cold room. I was now in the clothes of a servant that I had worn under my butcher's long white coat and apron.

'In the laundry room I was able to sweep up a pile of clean linen which I then held high in front of my face. I moved quickly along the passageways and up the stairs. All the activity in the embassy was concentrated on the first-floor dining room. Only after passing a dozen or more rooms did I discern a light shining below the foot of a door. I surmised that whoever was in that room was engaged on business of far greater importance than being sociable at a formal dinner.

'There was no other course of action open for me. I knew that I had to walk boldly in on the pretence that I had mistaken the room for another. That is if the door was not locked.'

'You were certainly taking a great chance,' said I.

'The door was not locked. I entered, saying, "Oh, excuse me, sir, I thought that this was the linen room." In one glance I took in the important details. A man crouched over a pile of papers laid on a desk. No one else in the room. Then the hand reaching for the revolver lying on the table. As if lunging with a rapier, I snatched the gun away and at the same time sent the pile of laundry into the face of my opponent. The thought flashed through my mind, Am I right, or have I made a dreadful mistake? Is this the end of my career? Then my concerns were swept away by the sight of pages of messages in cipher.

'For a moment the pile of linen I hurled confused him. He fell back and I wrestled him to the floor. As I did so I hit my head on the edge of the table. At that he seized me with both hands round my throat. As the effects of the blow to my head subsided, I was able to gain the upper hand, prise his hands off and deliver a heavy blow to his jaw. Before he could recover his senses, I used some of the linen to gag him and to tie him to a chair.'

Despite his languid manner and appearing to spend much of his time sprawled in his chair or on the sofa, Holmes had muscles and sinews of steel.

'How did you manage to escape?'

'I returned the way I had come. On passing the dining room a voice behind me said, "Mind giving me a hand? This lot's too heavy for me." I turned to find a maidservant carrying four massive silver salvers she was taking back to the kitchen. "Certainly, give me a couple. Go on," I said. Being in company with one of the servants and carrying some dishes, no one took any notice of me and I eventually found my way out past the guardians of the back gate who, as I had anticipated, were not particularly interested in anyone leaving the embassy.'

His request to see Lord Craneford without delay was granted.

'My Lord, I have solved the case. It is now most imperative that you inform the ambassador concerned that you know all about the attempts to read your messages,' said Holmes.

'My thoughts exactly, Mr Holmes. I shall request that he comes to me without delay, and I shall tell him that one of his staff has indulged in espionage, without his knowledge, and has compromising material. I am sure I can convince the ambassador that Her Majesty's government, although aware of what has been going on, will, in the interests of good relationships between our two countries, make no demands. The ambassador had advised me, some months ago, that there was a secret society plotting against his country. This group was intent not only on compromising good relations between our two countries but also on destabilizing his own country and even overthrowing the monarchy. I will of course deny that anyone on my staff was involved with such an undiplomatic and despicable act as trespassing on the property of another sovereign nation. However, I am sure he will refrain from making any protest.'

'The police have arrested the young lady telegraphist, my lord,' said Holmes, 'and, as you are aware, one of your secretaries. The girl, apparently, had been employed by the post office but was dismissed for some misdemeanour. She resented losing her one-hundred-a-year position, with the result that she was easily persuaded to spend a part of each day in an attic, listening to and writing down your messages as they passed through the Morse apparatus. However, what we have yet to find out is who was the mastermind, or rather, still is the master mind, behind this ingenious scheme.'

'Well, Mr Holmes, I am extremely grateful to you for stopping this leak, as it were,' said the Foreign Secretary. 'Scotland Yard will continue to search for the mastermind. In the meantime, you deserve a well-earned rest and please address your account directly to me. I doubt that our civil servants will immediately accept such a strange bill of events. They would make you wait for your money forever and ever. Good day to you, sir.'

And that was that.

Notes

The post office telegraph system was of the 'closed' type requiring a 'local' accumulator, as opposed to the American 'open' system. Presumably, a high resistance had to be in the 'tap' line to avoid unbalancing the circuit. The female operator might have been required to listen to the faint clicks, or observed the movement of a galvanometer needle.

Morse telegraph operators at the time were comparatively well paid.

An 'earth' is called a 'ground' connection in North America.

Not Cricket

In which a change of field leads back to South Africa.

As I recall it was late August 1900. Events in South Africa filled the newspaper columns. Had I been twenty years younger and had the full use of my limbs, I would have volunteered my services as a doctor.

Holmes sat holding an orange between his long fingers. It was pressed to his nose and I could see the pleasure with which he savoured its aroma. 'That orange reminds me, Holmes, of your advice that, in the solving of a crime, as few as only two clues are all that is needed. Sometimes just one is sufficient for solving a mystery. An orange, for example.'

'That is so, Watson. Even those who write fiction involving a mystery avoid cluttering up their tales with too many clues. Wilkie Collins and your friend Tom Hardy, for example.'

'I agree Tom Hardy is a good example. Although it is some years since I read Collins' *The Woman in White*.'

A telegram arrived, as they often did at that time of the day. Holmes started to open it, saying, 'I expect this is another plea for help with untangling the cords that become twisted between man and wife, or some criminal act to be frustrated. As you are aware, I am inundated with telegrams that begin: "Sir, I beg your help, my husband is acting in a most perverse manner." This one may be yet another such. Oh, it refers me to another telegram I should have received.' He sorted through the newspapers, opened letters and telegrams that spread out on the carpet around his chair.

'Ah, this must be it. Let's see what it says: "You will receive a plea from Lady Constance Roget-Gascoigne concerning her relationship with her husband. I urge you to take on the case. I hesitated at first to remind you of your promise some time ago, that you would do anything I might ask. You will recall your unfortunate involvement with a member of the ruling house of Ruritania. This matter with Lady Constance is such a deserving case that I must impose on your promise." '

'I doubt that you can refuse to honour a debt, Holmes. You do not say who sent the telegram. Can we assume it is someone of importance?'

'Yes, it is. He writes about one of the Roget-Gascoignes. It concerns a branch of the family whose estate is in the Dorset Winterbornes. It does mean, though, that I must take up the case without delay, and we must be off to Dorset. That is, I presume you are coming, Watson?'

'Of course,' I replied. 'This sounds a very intriguing affair and most surprising that once again we have to visit Dorset. It will give us an excuse to escape the dust, noise and heat of the city.'

'I am hoping that we are not going to be away for more than one night. Do you mind telegraphing a hotel in Blandford, and determining the quickest way of reaching that remote town?'

Holmes might tolerate a quick sortie out from the Great Wen. However, to stay more than one night away was not his idea of pleasure. I was the one who usually spent nights away on a case, with Holmes making short appearances for just a day.

I realized, at the mention of Blandford, that here was an opportunity to travel on the Somerset and Dorset Joint. It would mean changing from the South Western at Templecombe. The difference in the length of the alternative journey, via Bournemouth, was not so much that it would arouse Holmes' suspicions about my motives. I decided not to burden Holmes with my acquired knowledge about railway matters. So I did not mention that, a few years earlier, to reach Bournemouth and the connection with the Somerset and Dorset required going round by 'Castleman's Corkscrew', through Ringwood and Wimborne.

We arrived at Blandford after an exhausting ten-hour journey. The railways involved had contrived on that day to allow their trains either to suffer mechanical problems with their locomotives or the wheels to come off the rails. The day continued badly. At Blandford the Crown Hotel had not received my telegram, and we were directed to the Station Hotel. It was a small building close up against the station; more a large public house than hotel. That night my bed was against the window looking directly onto the narrow station platform. The night was stiflingly hot. I was torn between suffocating or, with the window open, being deafened by the snorting of an engine moving cattle trucks in and out of a siding. When I did manage to sleep, my dreams were compounded of bleating sheep, mooing cows and the hisses and clanking noises of an engine. All seemed to be in my bed at the same time.

In the morning we were received by the worried wife. My first thought on seeing her was, Why would any man forsake such a beautiful woman for another?

Her husband was away until the next morning on some affair of business; otherwise, as she explained, we would not have been invited to the house. She had told her husband and the servants that our visit was to do with a charity, of which she was patron.

Holmes, as usual, came straight to the point. 'Lady Constance, nothing is to be gained by sparing your blushes. What of your most intimate relationship with your husband? I am sure you understand to what I refer.'

'In such matters I have to tell you that the husband that came back from South Africa is very different from the one that set out for the war.'

'I see. Now I must ask about any financial arrangements between yourself and your husband. I understand you inherited a considerable fortune. Does your husband have access to it?'

'I should explain. When we agreed to marry, Percy was most insistent that any marriage settlement would not involve the transfer of my fortune to him. He did not want people to say that he was marrying me for my money.'

'Did he have money of his own?'

'He was reasonably well off when he was a bachelor. However, since he came back from South Africa not only has his manner changed, but he has on a number of occasions asked for large sums of money. When I questioned why, he became morose and behaved in a domineering way. He even said that it was no concern of mine, that we were husband and wife, and what was mine was also his.'

'An attitude very much in conflict with the marriage settlement,' commented Holmes.

'Indeed,' she replied. 'Naturally, Mr Holmes, I attributed the changes in him to his experiences in South Africa. He was wounded and was present when his cousin Patrick died from a wound received in the same battle.' She turned to the table on which there were numerous framed photographs. 'This one is of Percy and Patrick when they were up at Oxford.'

'I see that both have the distinctive Roget-Gascoigne features. Indeed they might be twins. Don't you agree, Watson?'

'Very much so,' said I.

Throughout the meeting I observed that Holmes was applying his customary attention to the details of the room. When Holmes had completed his tactful questioning, he said, 'In the meantime we will observe your husband's movements without rousing his suspicions. Perhaps I might borrow this photograph? I realize that you are worried that he has become entangled with another woman. Unfortunately, it is the first thing that comes into a wife's head. Although I have had to deal with only one or two similar cases to yours, none has involved infidelity. A common reason is financial blackmail. Another, and I have to say this, relates to a criminal past. We are staying at the Station Hotel, Blandford should you need us.'

'The Station Hotel! The Station Hotel! Surely there is something better? In other circumstances you and Doctor Watson would have been most welcome to stay here.'

As we could not face the pewter plates and tankards, and the crude fare offered by the railway hotel, we took supper in the Crown Hotel. Afterwards we sat in the comfortable lounge and discussed the case. My first question to Holmes concerned why he wanted a photograph of Sir Percy.

'We may need to ask others to follow him,' was his reply. 'I may be on a completely false trail, but we must first try and eliminate the involvement of another woman. I understand that Roget-Gascoigne is playing cricket tomorrow afternoon. That will give us the opportunity of observing his behaviour.'

'A splendid idea. It is just the weather for cricket,' said I.

*

The beautiful countryside slumbered under the warm sun. The cries of birds were stilled and the cattle in the adjacent fields stood close and silent under the shade of the trees along the river bank.

'This is idyllic,' I remarked to Holmes as we sat on canvas chairs in the shade of a splendid oak. His only reply was a grunt. He half reclined with his long fingers touching; his body exhibiting his languid approach to life. The smoke from his charred and discoloured old clay pipe contrasted with the clean air of the countryside. I am sure it was being smoked as a gesture of protest at having been persuaded to stay in such a remote part of the kingdom. All around were the supporters of the two village cricket teams: squire and ploughman, pig man and parson, all together.

Although we avoided meeting Roget-Gascoigne, we kept close to him. We observed that his manner was brusque and he appeared not to be on good terms with other members of the team. As he went in to bat, Holmes said, 'We can relax for a while. Nudge me when he is given out and I shall be all attention again.'

'Yes, he has taken his stand at the wicket. We shall now see how good a batsman he is. Ah, wait. They are changing the field. He bats left-handed.'

'Left-handed, you say. How interesting, Watson,' was the languid reply as he stifled a yawn.

Holmes took no further interest. I knew that he had played cricket in his youth and was a formidable boxer and swordsman. However, he now viewed sporting activities as a waste of time. He told me of a cricket match played in Peking by the embassy staff, and how the Mandarins watched in silence and gave no indication that they found it of interest. After the match one of them commentated, 'We are astounded that important British officials should conduct themselves in such an undignified manner. In China we would order our servants to undertake such menial and pointless tasks.'

As we were about to leave the match, a letter was handed to Holmes.

After reading it he said, 'It is unsigned but I am sure I know who sent it. Apparently, Sir Percy is to travel up to town tomorrow on the 8.53 from Templecombe. I want to be on that train, even though I anticipate that I may have to rise at six in order to catch the connecting train from here. Make sure I am awake in time. Do you think the landlord of the Station Hotel could provide some sandwiches for the journey?'

Later the next day a telegram from Holmes just said: 'Suggest you come back to town.' I was reluctant to leave bucolic Dorset, although the thought of another night in the dreadful hotel was too much to bear.

When I returned to Baker Street, Holmes recounted the events of the previous day. 'At Templecombe, I followed Sir Percy into a first class compartment of the South Western train bound for Waterloo. As was customary with travellers, we did not converse. As I already knew who he was, the usual scrutiny of dress, accoutrements and gestures was not really necessary. I used the *Morning Post* as a screen for observing my companion, who spent most of the time intently reading *The Times* as the train ran toward London. Now and then he used his fountain pen to mark certain items. As the train approached Waterloo, the paper was flung onto the seat with the financial pages in view. Some of the items were ringed and marked in ink. He left the newspaper behind so I took it with the intention of studying those items he had marked.'

'What happened at Waterloo? It can be a very busy and confusing place, Holmes, especially if you are trying to follow someone.'

'You are right, Watson, there was a dreadful confusion of milling passengers, porters, ticket collectors, news vendors and pickpockets. Passengers trying to reach their train were impeded by those trying to find their luggage or jostling for cabs. I observed that the low roofs of this collection of disparate sheds, masquerading as one of the most important termini in the capital of a great empire, trapped the smoke and noise. It is time the South Western tore the whole station down and started again.'

I responded to his criticisms and account of his journey by saying, 'I understand they do intend to do something about it. Did you manage to follow Sir Percy when he left the station?'

'There was a press of people endeavouring to find a cab and in the confusion I lost sight of him.'

'So, then what did you do?'

'I decided to walk across Waterloo Bridge and there I leant

against the parapet and interested myself in the busy traffic on the river. Faintly, on the wind, I heard the sound of a military band. That prompted me to think about the army and in turn that led me back to thoughts of Sir Percy. As an officer he would no doubt be a member of the Army and Navy Club. You know, Watson, whenever you need a cab none is in sight. I had to walk the length of the Strand before I found one.'

'Is he a member of the Army and Navy?'

'Yes, I inquired at the club. Apparently, he frequently uses it and often takes a room for the night. On the pretence that I had hoped to meet him there, I was able to find out from the hall porter that Sir Percy had telegraphed for a room and had indicated that he would not be arriving until late that evening. I asked the porter to suggest where I might find him. He showed me a message that had been received the day before which was signed 'Athens', indicating that Sir Percy was expected at a place or meeting someone of that name in the evening. In reply to the porter's question, "Who will I say has called?" I said I was Major Strubbshaw.'

'Athens could be a restaurant or even a club,' said I.

'My thoughts exactly. I had hoped that the porter, like most of his kind, would be a depositary of the most detailed information about restaurants and clubs and would know about such a place. Unfortunately, he could not help me.'

'A Greek connection?' I opined.

'Possibly, possibly. Thank you, Watson, your suggestion prompts me to look through my commonplace books. To do so will require the assistance of some strong tobacco. I shall not feel offended, old fellow, if you now decide that you have some business that will take you out for an hour or two.'

I needed no excuse to leave. The mere thought of the throat-rasping clouds of smoke that were about to assail the sitting room was enough to make me reach for my hat and coat. For some unaccountable reason my footsteps took me to the waxworks of Madame Tussaud. Under the influence of the memory of all the cases and adventures of Holmes that I had recorded, I was drawn to the amazingly lifelike wax figures of notorious criminals. I suppose a psychologist, a profession that was not high in the estimation of my friend, could have studied their past behaviour and deduced much about their future behaviour. To my surprise, many had the most benign features. Only a few exhibited what I would term an evil look. The most interesting were, of course, those who had gone to the gallows because of the diligence of Holmes.

On my return to Baker Street, I was greeted by Mrs Hudson and told that Holmes had gone out. 'I've opened all the sitting-room windows, Doctor. Do you want me to close them now?'

One breath of the noxious atmosphere prompted my reply. 'For the time being let us leave them open.'

I did not see him again until breakfast the next day. Not wishing to be so uncouth by venturing a serious conversation at breakfast, I bided my time.

Eventually, I asked, 'What of Athens?'

'It is a place, not someone's name,' was his reply. 'Exactly where I was not sure of, though I felt it was in London, certainly. I found nothing in my books that would provide a clue. Therefore, I decided to go after Sir Percy and that the best place to start would be at the Army and Navy Club. When I arrived I found that he was not there. I decided to wait. He arrived late in the afternoon. I immediately left and waited across the road. An hour later he came out and took a cab and I followed in another. We only went as far as Grosvenor Square, where he alighted. I followed him on foot as he walked toward Piccadilly. In a narrow alleyway near Shepherd Market he went down some steps to a basement door. I stood close by to see if there was a name on the door. It was just a very plain one in need of a coat of paint. He gave a succession of knocks on the door, which was opened quickly and shut behind him just as quickly. To my surprise, who should then come along but someone I knew well. In fact a member of the Cabinet. He was just about to step down to the basement when he saw me. He became flustered and muttered something like, "Oh, it's you, Holmes, good evening." And at that he turned and retraced his steps. I thought it a very strange behaviour for a government minister. No sooner had he gone than I realized that another important person was approaching. I stepped back so that he would not see me. During the next half an hour a number of well-known gentlemen made their way through that inconspicuous door.'

'I hesitate to mention it, Holmes. Is it possible that you were standing outside a place of ill repute? There have been a number of scandals in society recently in which notable people have been accused of engaging in unusual practices.'

'I have to disabuse you on the subject of scandals in high society. You see, I managed to take a look at the contents of one of the bins that stood at the top of the steps. In order to avoid any suspicion, I contrived to fall and in doing so I tipped over the bin. Two passers-by helped me to my feet, although not before I had observed among the rubbish a broken croupier's stick and a playing card cut in half. From those two objects I deduce that your house of ill repute, Watson, is nothing more than a secret gaming club. Furthermore, it could be that Sir Percy has been losing large sums of money. You remember I mentioned that I had taken his copy of *The Times* that he had with him in the train? The ink marks he made against certain shares in the Stock Exchange report clearly indicated frustration. Many had been fiercely scored out. From that I concluded they were those in which he had lost heavily in the market.'

I responded, 'That being so, then we can tell Lady Constance that her husband is not involved with another woman. I'm sure she will be most relieved.'

'She may well be reassured of her husband's fidelity, Watson, and may come to accept his change of character. She may also accept that he is involved in what must seem to her some very unprofitable ventures including gambling and, no doubt, involving her money. However, I am not satisfied that this is the end of the affair. There is more than meets the eye with Sir Percy. You will recall an event which, at the time, appeared an insignificant happening at the village cricket match. I mean when some of the fielders moved across to take positions for a left-handed batsman. That batsman was Sir Percy. Now I recall that the photographs his wife showed us clearly indicated that he was a right-handed batsman.'

'I think I know the line of reasoning you are taking, Holmes. You suspect that Percy is not Percy. A very dangerous assumption to make should it prove to be wrong. Yet I have to admit that the left-handed stance at the wicket may be irrefutable proof.'

'I did come to that conclusion some time ago. To make absolutely certain I entered into a casual conversation with one or two of the players that afternoon. I learnt two important facts. One, Percy, that is the person they assume to be Percy, only started to play for the village team on his return from South Africa. Therefore, none would have reason to comment on his handedness with the bat. And two, his wife took little interest in the game and, as far as I could gather, had never attended a match. As we know, my dear fellow, those that study human laterality have determined that most of us have a preferred limb or hand for specific actions, such as kicking a ball, holding a gun or holding a bat. Such preference can be contrary to their left or right-handedness for, as an example, writing. "Percy" is, as I have observed, predominately right-side preferring. Only when holding a cricket bat is he left-handed. When he took a stand at the wicket he reverted from a predominately right-handed person to a left-handed batsman.'

Holmes adopted that look of his which said, 'I know I'm right'.

'I should have noticed that,' I replied.

'These letters which Lady Constance has allowed us to examine can provide additional proof. Handwriting, as you are well aware, Watson, can reveal much, not only about the writer's character but subtle changes over time. Here we have two letters written a year apart. I compared the handwriting of the letter from before the war with that written after her husband's return to this country. The former was an affectionate letter that expressed clearly his profound love for her. The latter was written in the same style yet somehow, and this is a difficult thing to explain, the tenor seemed different. At first sight the hand is the same. Only when I made a close examination of the formation of some of the letters did I discover differences even though both were written with the right hand. The signature unfortunately tells us little because Sir Percy just scrawls the single letter P.'

I did not look forward to our next meeting with the anxious lady. We were about to turn her world upside-down. For once Holmes was reluctant to come straight to the point. He even took a cucumber sandwich to have with his tea. It was some minutes before he cleared his throat and said, 'What I am about to tell you concerning your husband may come as a great surprise.'

'Who is the woman, Mr Holmes?'

'It is not another woman. It is far more complicated than a simple lack of fidelity. I regret to have to tell you that your husband, or the man you assume to be your husband, is an impostor.'

She half rose from her chair and her face took on a waxen pallor.

'An impostor! What can you mean?'

'I mean just that,' responded Holmes. 'We are reasonably certain that the man you welcomed back from South Africa so affectionately over a year ago was your husband's cousin Patrick. The unhappy fact is that you may be a widow. I know that is a dreadful thing to have to tell anyone. You have to face the truth.'

For a moment or two she just sat there trying to settle her troubled mind.

'Madam, if you will now cast your mind back over the past year I am certain that you will recall things, however trivial, that will confirm what I am saying. If you will allow, I will leave you with Doctor Watson so that I may walk on the terrace and consider some of the facts.'

I realized that Holmes deliberately wanted to leave me with the shocked widow. He expected that she would confide in me, as a medical man, concerning the more intimate aspects of her time with the impostor during the past year.

When Holmes came back into the room, she had regained her composure and listened intently while we told her about the strange financial affairs of Patrick. We learnt that he had used over ten thousand pounds of her money.

'But what of Percy, what could have happened to him?' said she. 'Why was his death not listed? Perhaps he is still alive. Surely Patrick would not have been involved?'

Holmes replied, 'The disappearance of your husband will have to be investigated. This will certainly involve the police and the military authorities. Do you want us to help? We shall make every endeavour to keep the press away. However, such a serious affair may prove very difficult to conceal.'

'Certainly, Mr Holmes, I should welcome your continued involvement with this dreadful affair. If only because I must hope that Percy may be found alive.'

Mycroft Holmes soon produced documents that indicated that a Lieutenant Patrick Mayhew Roget-Gascoigne had died from wounds. His report also mentioned that Sir Percy Marmaduke Roget-Gascoigne Bart had been in the same field hospital at the same time.

After reading the report, Holmes' first comment was, 'We can be fairly certain that Patrick took the opportunity to change places with his dead cousin. Somehow, he was able to exchange personal effects and papers before Percy was buried. It is significant that Mycroft's information mentions that, at the time, there was much confusion among the field hospital staff over the identity of wounded and those who were dead. With the two cousins so much alike, it would not have been difficult for Patrick to change places with his dead cousin.'

I nodded agreement and for a moment or two my mind was back in the army, with thoughts of the times when I had had to deal, in the confusion of a battle, with the injured and sometimes the dead. Then I said, 'Surely there must have been a motive. Patrick would not have suddenly decided on such a complicated plan and one that could expose him to severe censure were it discovered. He must have planned it before the battle, or even before leaving for the Cape?'

'Certainly, a motive has to be found. Can you reach the bound *Illustrated London News* for 1898? Its pages may provide a motive.'

Holmes spent over an hour carefully reading through every issue in the volume. 'Ah, ah, I've found it. I have found a motive.'

He pushed the volume over to me with his finger on an illustration. It was of a beautiful young woman. Underneath I read: 'The Lady Constance Langhope, third daughter of the Marquess of Forfar and Elgin, whose engagement is announced to Mr Patrick Mayhew Roget-Gascoigne of Clonmare.'

'I don't follow,' said I. 'She married Percy, surely?'

'Indeed, eventually she did. It seems that the engagement with Patrick was broken off and instead she married his cousin just before both sailed for the war. Frustration and revenge compounded by greed were the motives.'

'I suppose Patrick can only be charged with deception?'

'I believe you are right, Watson. I cannot think immediately of another specific charge related to impersonating a woman's husband, other than intent to deceive. However, as you discovered, they had an intimate relationship which could lead to a very serious charge.'

We confronted Patrick Roget-Gascoigne with his crimes. He admitted to them. In exchange for not being handed over to the police, he agreed to disappear and travel in disguise to one of the colonies, and there to take up a new life. That he should be allowed to escape the punishment he deserved was in the interests of the woman he had so cruelly deceived. Mycroft arranged the necessary documents.

As far as the world would know, Sir Percy Roget-Gascoigne Bart's body was never recovered after his small sailing boat was found drifting and abandoned. Only four people knew who was buried in a South African military cemetery beneath a metal cross inscribed 'Lieutenant Patrick M. Roget-Gascoigne'.

Note

Despite Holmes' indifference to the activities of the aristocracy and their customs, he addressed the deceived wife correctly as 'Lady Constance' and not as 'Lady Roget-Gascoine' because, although she was the wife of a baronet, she was the daughter of a marquise.